Darren Turnerhurst is an author who has dyslexia along with other learning difficulties such as dyscalculia and dyspraxia. He learned to read and write at a late age, making school life difficult. However, his mother, Carol, would read to him and buy him books, starting his love of literature. Throughout his life, he dreamt of one day getting his own stories out into the world.

The Dream Merchant

To

Mary

D Turner-hurt

Darren Turnerhurst

The Dream
Merchant

Vanguard Press

A CIP catalogue record for this title is
available from the British Library.

ISBN 978 1 80016 981 4

*Vanguard Press is an imprint of
Pegasus Elliot Mackenzie Publishers Ltd.*
www.pegasuspublishers.com

First Published in 2024

**Vanguard Press
Sheraton House Castle Park
Cambridge England**

Printed & Bound in Great Britain

Irene Hurst. Who always believed in me.

Acknowledgements

Carol Kirton, David Turner, Charlotte Turner, Anna Nurmukhametova, Daria Maesa and Liz Monument

CHAPTER 1

M any people think there is something more to the world than we see with our own eyes, but Edgar, to his dismay, knew what that was and yet he had no one to blame but himself.

There were un-played messages on his answering machine. He knew it would be his little brother Peter or perhaps his daughter Lydia. Whoever it was, he felt no desire or need to call them back. Instead, he sat on the floor facing the television in a room covered in video tapes with labels with dates written on them in blue ink. The only one who ever got to see Edgar now was his Alsatian Juno, named after the Roman goddess. Juno was lying behind him, her brown eyes closed, not fully asleep yet, as Edgar ejected another videotape. He wasn't sure how long he had been watching the tapes. At first, he watched them only to see his long since deceased daughter, Victoria. It had been nineteen years since she died, but the pain of a child's death never leaves their parents.

After such pain, many men would turn to the bottle or take therapy, which Edgar did try but decided it wasn't for him. No, Edgar wasn't like most men. Now an old man with wrinkled skin and grey hair, he felt like a shell of himself. Once, Edgar Knightley was one of the top men working at one of the world's most successful electronic companies designing the newest and latest technological advances. He was a man with a vast intellect and low social skills even before Victoria's death. Edgar saw it as nothing short of a miracle that he managed to find a woman to marry him and give him two daughters.

Happiness never did last long for him. She died when Victoria was only three years old. He tried to raise the girls as best as possible, but after Victoria's death, he let his money raise Lydia, paying for nannies while he worked and studied, all the while developing a keen interest in psychology, trying to work out how the mind works. Dreams were something he was particularly interested in. He ponders whether dreams are meaningful or just pictures in our minds. *Do they tell you anything about your nature? For instance — does one who has violent dreams have tendencies towards violence?* These questions never left his mind; even the hands of time will not release those thoughts from his mind.

Just before he pressed play on another video, Juno's eyes opened, and she started to growl, showing her sharp teeth. Edgar looked back at her. She knew it was here before he could but now, he knew it was here. He felt fear grab him as the walls around him seemed to breathe in and out like the house was alive. Looking back at the TV, he saw the old familiar grey static, but there seemed to be something different about it. It seemed as if a skinny figure stood in it. Only its silhouette could be seen. The shape slowly pointed its right hand at Edgar, or perhaps it was pointing at something behind him. He quickly looked behind him, seeing Juno standing up with her teeth showing, trying to threaten the demon. She could see it far more clearly than he could.

He stood, stepping away from the TV. The sudden sound of Juno barking made Edgar jump in fright.

"Daddy," he heard the voice of a little girl cry. He couldn't help himself. He looked up and he saw a most unusual sight: Victoria stuck in the ceiling, only her head and upper body visible while the rest of her were under the old drywall. There was a long, skinny, pale arm with a hand with abnormally long fingers that seemed to dig into the young girl's chest, drawing out little drops of blood that seemed to fall on the floor and disappear without making a mark on the carpet. "Help me, Daddy," Victoria cried out, and it was a distressing sight for him, but he had to tell himself the truth, that the little girl he could see now wasn't there.

"You're not really her," he said.

"Please help me," she cried again.

"You're not her. You're not real," he said again, as Juno continued barking.

"Daddy," she screamed as another long hand came from the drywall, grabbing hold of her throat and pulling her in, making her disappear from Edgar's view.

"Maybe it's you who isn't real, Edgar," he heard an elegant female voice say. He turned to see his eldest daughter, Lydia, in her late twenties, sitting on the sofa with Victoria lying down with her head on her lap. Lydia was stroking her brown hair with one hand while holding a glass of red wine in the other. "You never really felt real to me, Father. After all, where were you when I was growing up?"

"I'm sorry, Lydia. I did the best I could for you."

"No, you forgot about me. That's why I'm a thousand miles away, and you still ignore my calls. Why?"

"I've been busy, Lydia," he cried, falling to his knees.

"Oh, always too busy." She looked down at Victoria lying dead on her lap. "You were too busy for her too, right? Yeah, of course, you were." As she said that, a line of what he first thought was blood dripped down from her forehead until he realised it was black like tar.

Edgar knew this wasn't Lydia. The actual Lydia was in Greece, but the line of black liquid on her head still began to scare him. Was it a sign of the future that he was unable to interpret? An absurd thought, but lately, his life was absurd.

She put the glass of wine down on the floor, saying, "There's only one way to save me, Father." She pulled a knife out of her trousers and showed him the blade. "What would a father do to save his offspring?"

He knew what the demon was saying as it used his daughter's voice: kill yourself and spare Lydia from the same fate he was facing. Could the creature get to her while she was so far away from him? He doubted it, but the creature was full of surprises and who was to say there weren't more of its kind in Greece? He wasn't sure.

He looked to the small black box he put his life and soul into that was now plugged into his VCR. The small box that brought the demon into his life, or back into his life. He had pondered several times if this demon was the monster that Lydia used to see in her nightmares when she was still a child. Could it be that when a child says there are monsters under their bed or that they have an imaginary friend it could be more than a child's overactive imagination? Whatever the case, maybe he should destroy it, but something inside him stopped him from doing so, some kind of force perhaps, or perhaps it was just seeing years upon years of work being destroyed. He looked back at the sofa where the image of Lydia once sat, seeing nothing other than the knife she was holding now resting alone on the seat waiting for him.

CHAPTER 2

The back garden of Edgar's old Tudor house was somewhat overgrown and looking a little unloved, but it was still a beautiful sight in its own way. Edgar faced an old water feature that ran water from a series of small pots. Beyond the white walls of the garden stood a large hill where his girls used to play, but now two other figures stood on top of it. They were too far away for him to see anything but the dark clothes they were wearing. He couldn't even tell if they were male or female. The question that ran through his mind more than any other was there: are they real or just another trick by the demon? This constant questioning of what he saw with his own eyes was driving him into madness; it made him feel physically sick. He looked to Juno who was just lying on the floor relaxing and in that way telling him that the creature wasn't here, so who were the two figures on top of the hill. It was a warm sunny day; it was more than likely that they were just two people relaxing, having a picnic. He recalled the many times he would picnic up there with his wife and later his daughters.

***

Danny and Mark were lying on the grass, not having a picnic as the rational side of Edgar's mind said they were, watching the old man from the top of the hill.

"He just saw us," Danny said with worry in his voice; he lowered his binoculars from his blue eyes. He had dark blond hair that was cut short and a small scar on his right cheek that had faded with age and was now barely visible. Danny got the scar as an infant and hadn't got a clue how. His foster parents also didn't have any idea. Mark was a bald man with a round head and dark eyes. Danny used to call him Charlie Brown but stopped doing so after the seventh punch in the gut.

"Don't worry, the old man is as blind as a bat. He didn't see shit," Mark said as he held out his hand for the binoculars. Danny gave them to him, and he looked around the old house. "It looks like he doesn't have an alarm," Danny told him.

"Nope, he has a dog, though," Mark said, looking towards the Alsatian lying beside the old man.

"Don't worry about the dog. I have some strong sleeping tablets that will knock the dog right out, and the dog will be fine afterwards."

"I'm not worried about how the dog is gonna be feeling afterwards, Danny. I'm more worried about the bastard ripping my throat out." He gave the binoculars back to Danny before saying, "You see, that's why I'm a better thief — you have too much heart, mate."

"Sure." Danny smiled as if it was a joke.

"You can't worry about hurting dogs, men, women or children in this line of work."

"So, if you had to, you could kill the old man. Is that what you are saying?"

"Yeah, I could."

Danny looked at his friend, wondering if he was serious or not.

"I'm hungry," Mark told him. "I'm thinking Chinese?"

"Sure, I could go for some Chinese," Danny said as he got up off the ground, and then Mark followed him down the hill and through the quiet field where they were watched only by a handful of sheep dotted around the green grass. "So, what if the old man had a kid staying with him. Are you going to just kill him in front of his kid?" Danny asked him.

"I wouldn't like to do that, but if he's standing in my way, then yes."

"That's cold," he commented as they walked to a red metal gate in a stone wall. The entrance led to a quiet road where the only vehicle on it was Mark's white van.

"It's like my dad used to tell me. You never get anywhere in this world by being a nice guy," Mark told him as Danny climbed over the gate.

"Yeah, but there is a big difference between being a nice guy and being a cold-blooded psycho," Danny said, watching Mark as he climbed over the gate.

"I'm not saying be a cold-blooded psycho. What I'm saying is if it is me going into prison or him going into the ground, it's going to be him going into the ground. You know what I mean?"

"I think so."

They walked towards the van, and Mark took the set of keys out of his jacket pocket. Danny stopped at the passenger side door, waiting for Mark to let him in.

After their meal, Mark drove Danny back to his house. He parked up just outside of it, and before Danny got out of the van, he turned to Mark and asked, "Do you want to go out to the pub or something tonight?"

"No, sorry, I can't. It's mine and Monica's date night."

"Right."

"Yeah, we're having a meal at Gustosa Italia and then see what showing at the cinema."

"Sounds good," Danny said feeling hint of jealousy that he had no one to go on a date night with. Although his neighbour, Emma, had been showing some interest in him lately. "All right, see you later, mate," Danny said as he exited the door.

"Yeah, bye."

He shut the van door, and Mark drove off, leaving Danny to walk to his small, terraced house on his own. He noticed that his attractive neighbour, Emma, and her daughter were coming out of their house. She had light skin with long, jet-black hair, deep brown eyes and a cute little button nose. Danny had the feeling that someone in her gene pool must have been oriental, Chinese or Japanese perhaps. She was wearing a dark green jacket over her red T-shirt and tight blue jeans. Her seven-year-old daughter looked like a much younger version of her but only in the face. She had blonde hair that she clearly got from her father.

"Hello," he said, with a wide smile, as they walked out of her garden and closer towards him.

"Hello," Emma said with the same wide smile. "It's nice weather today, eh."

"Yeah, yeah, it is." He smiled and looked up at the blue sky and tried to think of something to say. "I heard it's going to rain tomorrow, though."

"Yeah, I heard about that too." She sighed. "Well, I have to be going."

"You off to work?"

"No, we're going to the dentist, not for me but Libby. I almost forgot." She looked to her daughter and said to her, "Don't be rude and say hi to Daniel." Libby looked away and at her feet. "She's still shy."

"It's fine," he said, with a friendly smile on his face.

"See you later," she said, walking off and just before she got past him, he reached into her jacket and pulled out her pager and quickly put it in his pocket without her even noticing. He knew from days and days of watching her leave her home where she put it. He took his keys out of his other pocket and let himself into his small, terraced home and walked to his sofa, which was underneath a poster of the 1956 movie *Mysterious World*, both of which faced his small television.

He took the pager out of his pocket and looked at the little black plastic thing with a green screen that told you if someone wanted to contact you. There was a feeling of guilt as he did and thought, *This is a bad way to get a girl to like you. if she finds out, she will hate you, and if she doesn't, you will always feel guilty that you stole from her or borrowed without asking.* He put it back in his pocket, picked up a television remote, and turned the TV onto a news report talking about the death of Princess Diana. It was showing footage of her destroyed black Mercedes-Benz in a tunnel in Paris. While watching the horrifying images of the Princess's destroyed car, he took out a cigarette. He lit it with a little golden lighter. Danny took a deep breath, inhaling the smoke before getting off the sofa and walking towards a shelf full of videotapes. Most of them were Hollywood movies of all genres.

However, he also had some American and British sitcoms and even football videos. He picked out a copy of *The Wicker Man*.

After the film ended, he debated with himself whether he should put another one on. But instead, he just stared out of his window, waiting for Emma to return; that feeling of guilt that surrounded his risky plan never stopped entering his mind. *If this works and she became my girlfriend, he told himself, I would make it up to her by being the best boyfriend. I could stop stealing altogether and get a real job.* Though he had no idea how he would do that.

A few minutes after he heard Emma getting into her house, he went and knocked on the door, hearing a yell coming from inside the house. "Just a minute." He could hear the stress in her voice as she must have been looking everywhere for the pager. There were only a few seconds of waiting, but Danny's nerves and feeling of guilt built up just before Emma opened the door and looked at him. "Hi," she said, sounding out of breath.

"Hi, I was going shopping earlier, and I found this on the pavement. Is it yours?" He took the pager out of his pocket and showed it to her.

"Yes, Thank you so much!" she said in relief before snatching it from his hand. "You're a lifesaver."

"Yeah, no worries," he said with a wide smile.

There was a short moment of awkward silence where they just stared at each other. It was soon broken by her asking him, "Do you want to come in for a cup of tea?"

"Yeah, sure, I would love one," he said, walking into her house.

"How do you take it?" she asked as she shut the door.

"Do you have coffee?"

"Yeah, it's the cheap supermarket brand stuff, but it still tastes all right, in my opinion."

"That's fine, thanks."

They walked into the living room, where he saw Libby sitting cross-legged in front of the television watching cartoons. "Libby, say hello to Daniel."

She looked over at him with no smile and no sense of warmth on her young face. "All right, kiddo?" Danny said with a wave of his hand, but she just turned back to the television, and Emma walked past them and entered the kitchen. He looked around the living room and saw a leather sofa and a leather armchair next to it and a large picture of Paris above it. He looked at the other photos, mainly of Libby as a baby and at the end of the room, he saw an old guitar resting against the wall. "Nice guitar"

"Thanks," she called back from the kitchen. "Do you play?"

"Yeah, I mean I'm no Jimi Hendrix, but I like to play now and again."

"I like Mark Knopfler myself."

"Mark Knopfler?" she said in shock and walked back into the living room, looking at him with a surprised look on her face. "You like Dire Straits?"

"I love Dire Straits. Knopfler's solo on *Sultans of Swing*. Oh, it's just perfection."

"Yeah, it is, but my favourite is *So Far Away from Me*."

He sang part of the chorus, his singing sounded nothing like the band, but more like a bag full of cats.

"That's the one," she said with a soft giggle before walking back into the kitchen.

Danny looked over to Libby, who was still watching cartoons on the television, paying no attention to Danny or her mother. "Do you like music?" Danny asked, but the only reply he got is a shrug of her shoulders. "So, what are you watching?" he then asked, not expecting to get an answer.

"*Teenage Mutant Ninja Turtles.*" She sighed.

"What's that about?"

She turns her head back towards him with a frown and sighed. "Teenage turtles."

"Right, who are also mutant and heroes, so sounds good," he said, before looking at the television.

"So, Daniel, do I call you Danny or Dan or just Daniel? I never asked," he heard Emma say from behind him. He turned around and saw her holding two mugs, one with the AC/DC logo and another that was just plain white.

"Any but most people call me Danny." He took the white mug and sat on the sofa with Emma sitting next to him.

"So, do you play?" Emma asked.

"I'm sorry?" he said, not quite hearing her.

"The guitar, do you play the guitar?"

"Oh no," he said, now wishing that he had learnt. *Playing the hell out of that thing would be a sure way of impressing her*, he thought. First, he looked at her long legs in tight jeans and then up at her breasts covered with her red T-shirt, then quickly up at her thin red lips that he so longed to kiss.

"OK, maybe I can teach you one day?"

"Yeah, I would like that."

"So, what was the last gig you went to?" she asked him, and the answer to her question was that he had never been to one, *But a little white lie won't hurt anyone, right.*

"Led Zeppelin." *Shit,* he thought to himself, *they broke up years ago*.

24

"Oh, you went to the reunion gig," she said in delight, and he thought to himself how lucky he was not to be found out as a liar. "I missed that. What were they like?" Emma asked.

"Oh, you missed one hell of a gig; they were great," he said thinking that he was now digging himself an even deeper hole.

CHAPTER 3

It was eleven p.m. the next day when Danny started making his way out of his house and towards Mark's flat. He was wearing a pair of earphones, listening to an old Walkman playing a mixtape that Emma had made for him. Danny wasn't really into music but did like her taste. He was listening to a soft rock song by a band he didn't know. He had three voices in his head: one was telling him to turn the music off and try to concentrate on the job ahead; one was telling him about the life he could have with Emma if he only could stop his life of crime and get a real job and be a good man. The other was the voice of the singer of the rock band he was listening to. He tuned out both the music and the voice telling him to think about the job and imagined himself living in a big stately house with loads of land with Emma as his wife. He would no longer live a life of crime; he would be someone.

Mark lived on the second to the top floor of a thirteen-storey tower block. He took the lift to his floor and walked on into his flat without knocking. "Honey, I'm home," he called out to Mark.

"Mark, your boyfriend is here," Monica called out. She sat on the sofa with her bare feet with pink nail varnish on a coffee table and her head in an erotic novel with a man wearing nothing but a kilt on the front cover. She had pale skin and ginger hair that was tied up in a ponytail.

"Nice to see you again, Mon."

"It's Monica," she said with a sigh, and Danny thought that looking at Monica, it was a glimpse into Libby's future — only the hair colour was different. "Mark, are you deaf? I said your boyfriend is here," she shouted at him.

"I heard you! I'm on the bloody throne. Jesus Christ, woman, can't a bloke take a shit around here," he heard him shout back from the bathroom. They heard the toilet flush, and then shortly afterwards, the bathroom door opened. "Danny," he said, walking out of the bathroom.

"Did you wash your hands?" Danny asked in disgust.

"What do you care?"

"It's just fucking disgusting not to clean your hands after a shit."

"Oh, all right, sorry, Miss Nightingale, do you want me to go back in wash them?" he said sarcastically.

"Yes."

"Fucking hell," Mark moaned, walking back into the bathroom and washing his hands. He walked back out of the bathroom, waving his hands in front of Danny. "Happy now? They all nice and clean," he said in a patronising way.

"Yeah."

"Good, so can we go now?"

"Sure."

"Let me get my stuff," Mark said, walking into his bedroom.

As Danny waited for him, he pulled out a packet of cigarettes from his jacket. He opened the box before Monica told him, "Don't even think about smoking them in here."

He sighed and put the packet back into his jacket. He couldn't think what Mark saw in Monica or what Monica saw in Mark — both of them were deeply unpleasant people to be around. He would love for the day to come when he had enough money to stop stealing and never see them again, but for right now, they were his best friends.

Mark came back out with a backpack on. "Right, mate, let's get going."

"Bring me back something good," they heard Monica shout to them as they left the flat. As soon as Mark shut the door of his flat, Danny took out his cigarette packet and took one out and placed it into his mouth.

"You're calling me disgusting, and you are smoking that shite."

"I'll quit this time next year," he said, lighting the cigarette.

"You said that last year," Mark said, walking to the lift and pressing the button to go down.

"I mean it this time."

"You also said that last year."

"Whatever. Can I ask you something?"

"Sure."

"Can you play the guitar?"

28

"No, but I used to play the flute back in school," he said, just as the lift doors opened up and they both walked in with Danny staring at him in puzzlement. Mark pushed the button for the ground floor and then looked at Danny. "What?" he moaned, hating the puzzled look Danny was giving him.

"I just can't imagine you playing the flute."

"Why not?"

"I don't know; you just don't seem like the flute playing type."

"I was a kid; what are you asking about guitars for?" he shot back at him.

"No reason, just thought it might be fun to learn a new skill."

"When have you ever been interested in music?"

"I have loads of interests."

"Mate, I have known you for a long time, and I know the only things that you find interesting are movies and tits, so who are you trying to impress?"

"Just some girl who's really into music."

"Oh, for the love of God," he moaned.

"What does that mean?"

The lift doors opened, and they walked out towards the front door. Mark pressed a buzzer that unlocked it, and they walked out of the building and into the car park where Mark's van was waiting for them. He stopped in front of it and turned to Danny. "Listen, you don't have to like the same shit as the girl. Take Monica and me — she loves ice-skating, but I fucking hate it. I like football but guess what? Monica fucking hates that. It doesn't matter. You don't have to have the same interests as long as you connect on an emotional level."

"So, what do I do to impress her?"

"You don't. She likes you, or she doesn't like you. I would say be yourself, but fucking look at you, mate. I would try being someone else."

Danny looked down at himself seeing what he meant and back up at Mark, who was now taking his keys out and unlocking the van door.

They drove out of the town and through country roads before getting to the same fence they had jumped over earlier in the day. They walked towards the hill in the dark, hardly able to see their hands in front of them. "I can barely see a thing," Danny moaned as he tried to watch his steps.

"Stop being a little bitch," Mark called back to him.

"We need night vision."

"Sure, I'll get right on that. I just have to give MI6 call first," Mark said sarcastically.

Now on top of the hill, they tried to look back at the house but could barely see it. "I can't even see the house," Danny complained.

"That's good. It means the old fart is asleep." Mark looked at him with a sly smile and said, "Come on, let's rob the bastard." They slowly made their way down the hill and through the old man's back garden. Danny got to the back door of the house and kneeled next to the bronze lock. He took out a black plastic set of metal pins and a small metal object he called a tension wrench.

He then placed the wrench into the bottom of the lock, and then as he held it in, he put a pin just under it and turned it around and before they knew it, they heard the sound of the lock releasing. He got back on his feet and pushed the door open, entering the kitchen. Mark clicked on his torch and looked around the room before he spied a vase on a dinner table designed in a Japanese style, with a picture of a resting Samurai sitting with his back against a cherry blossom tree. He carefully picked it up and put it gently into his backpack.

"It might be an antique," Mark whispered to Danny, who made no reply. Instead, he walked through the kitchen and entered the living room, clicking on his torch. The first thing he saw when the light came on was the smashed television in the corner of the room. Next to the TV, videotapes with white labels on them littered the crimson coloured carpet. Danny thought he must have watched some shit movies as he moved to the closest tape to him. He picked it up and read the label that only had a date — 2nd March 1997. He picked the next one that had another date, 17th May 1997 then looked at the TV with its smashed screen.

"He must have been watching the *Star Wars* Christmas special," Mark whispered to him, with Danny only now realising he was in the living room with him.

"Well, I guess we're not taking the telly," Danny whispered back to him as he got back up to his feet.

"Where's his dog?" Mark whispered, feeling that something wasn't quite right. If the dog were here, they would have heard from it by now — it would have woken up and would be trying to get them, but they hadn't heard from it or seen it yet. Danny then shined his torch across an oak fireplace which was full of oriental style ornaments. It had two Samurai that stood at each end of the fireplace. In the middle of it was a small picture of a six-year-old girl. The girl was wearing a red dress, smiling, with a medieval castle behind her.

"One for each of us?" Danny whispered back to Mark as he picked up the ornamental Samurai from the right-hand side of the fireplace.

"Sure, I'm just going to check upstairs," Mark told him as he ambled out of the room. He could hear Mark's footsteps moving up the stairs as his eyes went back to the smashed television. Danny found himself again wondering why someone would smash their television.

He turned around, seeing a large cabinet with glass doors and wooden shelves behind them. Inside were more ornaments. He turned and then jumped at the sudden sound of Mark screaming out loud. Danny ran out of the living room, ready for whatever was happening to Mark. He tripped on the second step as he made his way upstairs but quickly stood up. At the top of the stairs, he saw Mark standing in the bathroom doorway, his face as white as a sheet of paper.

"What's wrong?" Danny asked him. Mark looked towards the wide open door. Sauntering towards it, Danny didn't know what to expect, and there he saw the old man lying in the bath full of now cold water with one arm hanging out of it and a deep cut across his wrist. "Jesus," he cried out. In the middle of the room was a piece of paper that was folded in half. He picked it up and unfolded it, and read it to himself: 'I'm sorry, Lydia. Live the best life you can, and please you must destroy it, please do this for me.'

"What does it say?" he heard Mark ask from behind him. His mouth felt dry, and he couldn't speak, so he just gave him the note. Mark read the words aloud and then asked, "Destroy what?" before putting the message back down on the floor.

"I don't know," he whispered back.

"What?" Mark said out loud. "The man's dead — you don't have to whisper anymore."

"I said I don't know," Danny replied out loud, his body shaking. It was the first time he had seen a dead body and he did not know how to react. He turned to Mark. "What do we do now?"

"Finish what we started," Mark told him.

"But he's dead," he said in shock, not believing how cold Mark could be.

"Well, he doesn't need any of his stuff, does he?" Mark said as he walked out of the room.

Danny looked down at the man lying dead naked in his bathtub, his skin turning white. "I'm sorry. I hope you find peace in whatever comes after this," he whispered so Mark wouldn't hear him. He moved into the next room as Mark moved into the one closest to the bathroom. He pushed the door open and turned on the light. No need for the torches now. They looked around the bedroom that was in a mess — there were books, cups and packets of crisp covering the blue carpet. Wasn't much in the room beside a computer at the end of it and something small and black with a wire coming out of it resting on a pillow on his bed next to a black notebook. He picked up the notebook and saw it was instructions for the black object next to him.

He flicked through it before he noticed a drawing of it being placed on someone's head. Taking off his backpack, he placed it on the bed and put the strange object and notepad into it even though he had no idea what it was. It seemed he was only taking it out of curiosity.

On the drive back home, neither of them spoke, thinking about what they had done and the dead man they'd left there. *If the police knew we were there, we could get done for his death*, Danny thought. For the first time since he was a teenager, he feared being caught by the police.

Danny rushed back home, and with every step he took in the dark street, he looked over his shoulders, feeling that someone was following him, as multiple thoughts ran through his head. *We should have done something; we shouldn't have just left him. Will the cops think we had anything to do with his death?* He got back into his dark home and locked the door, taking a glass and bottle of whisky from the kitchen, and he threw his backpack on the floor before sitting down on his sofa. He opened the bottle and poured the whiskey into his glass as his hand shook like the last leaf on a tree. He took one sip before placing it down on the table, took out a cigarette from his pocket, and placed it in his mouth. However, he did not light it — he just stared down at his backpack, mesmerised by it.

He got back up, unzipped his bag and took out the notebook and the strange object with the wire dangling from it. He placed the black box on the table and sat back down on his sofa with the book. He grabbed the pack of cigarettes and was about to take one out before he realised that he already had one in his mouth. Throwing the packet down on the table, he lit the cigarette in his mouth and read the words on top of the front page, 'The Dream Recorder', Underneath the title was a drawing of the black machine. Throughout the night, he read through the notebook until around four o'clock in the morning when sleep finally took hold of him.

As Danny was reading the notebook, next door Libby was lying on her back in bed. She had the sensation that her bed was floating just off the ground as her body felt so very cold as if she was sleeping outside on a cold winter's night. She opened her eyes and sat up in bed, seeing a strange old man standing by her door. It wasn't the monster that haunted her nights so many times before. It was just a little old man.

"Don't be scared," the man told her. "I'm not here to hurt you."

She looked down at his hands, seeing a large scar across his wrist. *He's a ghost*, she thought to herself but wasn't afraid, which seemed odd to her somehow. She knew he was telling the truth; he wouldn't hurt her.

"You and your mum are in danger. The monster is real." And like magic, the man disappeared and soon after she heard the monster's heavy breathing.

"No," she whispered to herself as she lay back down, looking up at the ceiling where she could see a dark hole with a long skinny hand with long fingers coming out from it.

CHAPTER 4

SANTORINI, GREECE

The ring tone of the mobile phone was a sound that Lydia hated. At eight o'clock in the morning with a hangover, it was truly dreadful. She sat up, her head feeling like it had been hit by several bricks and looked at the pile of clothes on the floor. Above her, the ceiling fan rotated, but she still felt hot, and her throat felt dry. She got out of bed to a moan from the man next to her. She picked out her phone from the pocket of her combat shorts.

"Hello?"

"Hello, is this Lydia Knightley?"

"It is."

"Hello, Miss Knightley, this is Detective Andrew Williams of the Kent police service in Mayfield. Your father is Edgar Knightley — is that correct?"

"Yes, what is this about?"

"I am very sorry to tell you, Miss Knightley, but your father was found dead in his home early this morning."

She heard the regret in his voice, and then she listened to the toilet in the other room flush. Turning to the bathroom door, she saw Katya, wearing only her red underwear. She walked towards Lydia and sat down next to the sleeping man.

"Miss Knightley, are you still there?"

"Yes," she said as she held back her tears. "I'm still here. How did he die?"

"It looks like suicide, but we are not ruling anything out at the moment."

"What do you mean not ruling anything out?"

"Do you think we can meet in person? I have a few questions I would like you to answer about your father."

"Yeah, I mean, I'm in Greece at the moment, but I can take a flight back home."

Katya looked at her in shock, not believing her ears.

"Thank you, Miss Knightley, and I'm deeply sorry about your father, but please get in touch with me on this number as soon as you make it back to England."

"Okay."

"Thank you. I'll see you soon,"

Lydia put down the phone and stared at the blue painted walls and thought about her father.

"What was that about?" Katya asked her in her thick Russian accent.

She turned to her and sighed. "I have to go back to England."

"Why?"

"It's my father. He's…" She paused, not believing what she was going to say, as she felt her heart breaking and her eyes about to water. "He's dead."

Katya quickly stood up with a shocked look on her face. "I'm so sorry. How did he die?"

"Suicide maybe."

"I am truly sorry," Katya said with a voice so full of regret it was like she was the one who killed him.

"It's fine," Lydia said as she started to get dressed. "Well, it's not, but it is what it is."

"We can go to Britain with you."

"No," Lydia replied as she pulled up her shorts and knickers.

"It's fine — Ezio and I want to stay with you. In your hour of needs," she said in broken English.

Lydia walked towards her placing a kiss upon her forehead. "I love you, Kitty Kat."

"And I love you," she replied.

"But," Lydia said, and Katya's blue eyes looked up at her, "I need to do this on my own."

"But we do everything together."

"I know, but this I have to do on my own. Please try to understand."

Katya slowly nodded her head, but she hated the idea of her going anywhere without her. Lydia had changed her life. Before they met, she was a straight girl from Sochi who dreamed of seeing the world and wanted to own her own business somewhere sunny. After meeting Lydia, she became a bisexual adventurer with no fixed location. She had never been happier in her whole life. Lydia was her everything, and Ezio was just a friend with benefits, which he was perfectly fine with.

Now fully dressed, Lydia kissed Katya on the lips. "I'll be back in a few days."

"You're going now?"

"I have to."

"Well, let me wake Ezio?" she said and was about to wake him until Lydia grabbed hold of her.

"No, let him sleep and just try to explain everything the best you can when he wakes up. Okay?"

"I'll try," she said.

Lydia took a taxi to the Santorini National Airport. She loved Santorini but hated its tiny airport where she booked a connecting flight to Athens then London, from where she would take the train to Mayfield. She was annoyed when they told her that the next available flight would be in eight hours. "Oh shit," she whispered to herself before walking off towards the airport's restaurant, where she ordered herself some blueberry yoghurt pancakes along with a strong cup of hot coffee.

While eating it, she thought about Mayfield about her father, Victoria and about the old house in the country. Victoria Knightley, her little sister — was it wrong, she wondered, that she hadn't thought about her in years? She had finally escaped Mayfield, but now she was going back, and her heart bled for the death of her father as she ran her hand through her long brown hair, but she didn't know what she thought of going to that town again.

Lydia remembered the last time when she was at her father's house and made her dad and herself some dinner which they ate in front of the television. At that time,

Katya had gone back to Russia to visit her parents; Lydia recalled telling Edgar about Katya but called her just a friend. She didn't know why; Edgar wasn't homophobic, and he knew she had dated girls in the past and didn't care, but she also knew how much he wanted a grandchild. She also told him about her trip to France and Italy.

"Did you go to Florence?" Edgar asked her.

"Yeah, of course, but I only stayed there for a few hours before jumping on a train to Rome. So, I just walked around seeing some of the sights."

"You should have stayed in Florence for a few days. I love that city. You remember the holidays you, me and Vicky used to have there?" he said with a faded smile, the memories making him feel both happy and sad at the same time.

"I remember. I looked for that little gelato shop we used to love near the Piazza Della Signoria, but it's not there any more."

"That's a shame. You loved those ice-creams; you cried like a baby when you dropped one on the floor."

Lydia laughed and called out, "Hey, I was about seven. I was more or less a baby."

"You were older than seven."

"Why don't you come back to Greece with me? I'm sure you could do with a holiday."

"No, no, I don't want to cramp your style."

"You won't be."

"Well, thanks. I will think about it," he said, but she could tell from that answer that he didn't want to.

She stood up, saying, "Just need to go to the little girls' room." As she left the bathroom, she noticed his bedroom door ajar. Through the gap, she could see papers pinned up against his wall. Gently she pushed it open, seeing his walls full of notes and blueprints on the Dream Recorder. They covered almost every bit of the wall. Looking at them, she felt nervous for him and angry as he had told her not long before that he had stopped trying to create this seemingly impossible task. She walked back downstairs, seeing him sitting in front of the TV, eating his dinner, watching some documentary about the solar system.

"I thought you had given up on the Dream Recorder," Lydia said, still standing in the doorway. He looked over to her, and Lydia could see the shame in his face that he had lied to her.

"Lydia, you have no idea how close I am."

"This thing is going to eat you up, please," she said, walking closer to him. "For me, forget about it. This isn't what Vicky would have wanted."

"How do you know what she wanted?" he hissed through his teeth.

"Because she's my sister, and I miss her as much as you do."

Edgar slowly nodded, and Lydia could see a tear roll down his cheek. "I know she was, and I know you loved her. But you have to do something for me, Lydia."

"What?"

"Go to Greece or wherever you want to go and do that thing Knightleys hardly ever do, which is to have fun and enjoy life and please, I beg of you, if you love me, you will let me work on this."

As Lydia thought about it in the airport, she told herself how stupid she was just to agree to that and leave him to his madness.

CHAPTER 5

The lunchtime bell rang out in Saint James Primary School, and the children ran out of their classes, happy for their break from learning or, in some cases, pretending to learn. They headed towards the cafeteria for food that usually tasted like cardboard and the wooden benches near the football pitch or the basketball pitch. Libby walked off with her backpack over her shoulders, moving past the benches and the football pitch where a gang of boys played, shouting, "Over here!", and "Pass it!" paying Libby no attention, which suited her just fine. She walked with her head down, trying not to look at anyone walking down the school field until she reached the fence on the far side that separated school life from home life, like the prison, she often saw it. Near it were a set of bushes and a large oak tree. The faculty had often talked about cutting down the tree as they would find children climbing it. Still, for the time being, it was Libby's resting spot, a place where she could be alone when no kids were climbing it, of course.

Taking off her backpack and unzipping it, she took out her lunch box from between her schoolbooks. Opening it, she found a packet of prawn cocktail crisps, a Mars bar, a ham sandwich wrapped up in tin foil and a small bottle of orange juice. Some people had told her mother to give Libby more healthy food, but Emma always thought it was the same kind of stuff that her mother give to her, and she was perfectly healthy now and back then. Plus, Libby didn't have the happiest of childhoods anyway with her lack of friends and her constant nightmares — forcing her to eat things she didn't like wasn't something her mum wanted to do.

Libby placed the lunch box down on the grass and unwrapped the sandwich, placing it in her mouth as she took out a copy of *Through the Looking Glass*, which she had borrowed from the school library.

"Holland," she heard someone shout.

Her nerves began to shake, as she knew the voice and knew people only called her by her surname when they were angry at her. Slowly, she looked up from her book at Michelle King, a tall girl for her age with long blonde hair and a long pointy nose, making her look like a little witch. With her were three other girls all wearing the same school uniform — a dark green jumper with the school's emblem on its side and a grey skirt. Libby put her book down and put her sandwich on top of it while looking up at the four girls.

"Did you tell Miss Forrester that I cheated on the test?" Michelle asked her, and the answer was yes.

Libby hated Michelle, and it was true she saw her looking over at another pupil's paper. Libby thought there would be no way Michelle would find out that it was she who told the teacher, that surely Miss Forrester wouldn't say anything. *It's the last time I tell the teacher anything*, she thought. "I didn't tell her anything," Libby lied.

"You're such a liar and a freak," Michelle hissed as she stood on her sandwich, squashing it into the pages of the book. "Maybe this will teach you to keep your mouth shut."

Libby looked down at the black shoe moving side to side as it squashed her lunch. She felt the anger build up inside her as she heard the girls laugh. Then, suddenly, Libby jumped up and punched Michelle in the jaw. There was a shocked look on Michelle's face. Still, the punch barely made an impact, and before she could go in for another punch, two of Michelle's friends quickly moved behind Libby, grabbing hold of her arms. "Let go of me," Libby screamed out.

"You need to learn your place, freak," Michelle said before punching her hard in the stomach. The two girls let go of Libby's arms, and she fell down on the floor, holding her stomach in pain. "See you later, loser Libby," one of them said as they all walked off laughing at her misery.

She wished she could pay them back — she fantasised about going up to all four of them and beating them up, breaking their bones and cracking their skulls with the kung-fu skills that she didn't have in reality. But instead, she started to sit up with her back against the tree and saw a dark figure at the other end of the field. It looked about seven feet tall, black as night with two red glowing eyes, a wide white smile and two long skinny arms. Libby felt her heart race, and she squeezed her eyes shut and repeated in her head, *You're not real, you're not real, you're not real.* When she opened them again, the tall figure was gone without a trace.

CHAPTER 6

It was past one o'clock in the afternoon when Danny woke up, and the first thing his eyes went to as he opened them was the strange machine and the notebook on his coffee table. He got up, feeling a pain in his back before he walked into the kitchen and made himself a cup of coffee. Just as he sat back down on the sofa, he heard a knocking at the door. He sighed as the knocking continued. He put the coffee down on the table and walked to the door attempting at first to unlock it before realising that he forgot to lock the door last night. The knocking continued, and he screamed out, "Hold on," before he unlocked the door again and opened it. Emma was standing at his doorway with a smile on her face. He suddenly felt a hint of shame, thinking about how he hadn't washed, cleaned his teeth or brushed his hair.

"Hi," she said.

"Hi," he replied, feeling still half asleep.

"You had a late night last night?" she asked him with a sly smile.

"Sorry?"

"You just look a little tired."

"Oh, it was my friend's birthday, so we went out for a few drinks, and you know, few turns into many."

"Oh, I've been there," she told him and gave a little nervous giggle before saying, "Libby's dad is picking her up from school today, so I'm all alone."

"I bet you are happy for the peace and quiet."

"Oh yeah, I guess."

"I'm wondering if you may want to listen to some music or have a quick drink somewhere?"

"Yeah, uh sure. Just let me go for the three Ss, and I'll meet you in that Italian place across the road in an hour and a half. I've been there before, and the pizza is amazing. I mean, do you like pizza?"

"Everyone loves pizza, but what's the three Ss?"

"A shower, shit and shave." *Smooth, Danny, very smooth*, he thought to himself.

She slowly nodded her head. "Oh, okay then, enjoy your three Ss."

"I will and see you in a bit," he said, letting out a childish giggle.

"All right," she said before walking back to her house. He closed the door and stepped back into the living room, looking down at the black machine still resting on his table.

Danny fixed himself up pretty quickly, putting on his best shirt and some black trousers after having a shower, washing his hair and cleaning his teeth. He entered the restaurant and was greeted by a teenage girl wearing a black T-shirt with the logo on the front, a fat stereotype of an Italian chef with a big black moustache and a huge smile on his face. He was above the word 'Gustosa Italia', written in the colours of the Italian flag. "Hello, welcome to Gustosa Italia, table for one?" she said, making no effort to hide that she wished that her workday would end and she could go home.

"No, I'm meeting someone here," he told her, and she sighed and pointed to Emma, who was sitting on her own next to the window to the side of the building.

"Is that her?"

"Yeah, thank you."

"All right," she sighed again as he walked towards Emma.

"Oh, here he is," Emma said with a friendly smile.

"Here I am," he said, sitting down across from her. "Have you already ordered?"

"Nope, I was waiting for you."

"How nice of you."

"Well, I'm a nice kind of gal."

"Yeah, me too," he said without thinking, his mind still on the dead man, and she gave him a questioning look.

"I always knew it." she then said with a giggle.

"Knew what?" he asked before realising what he said, and he laughed at himself. "Oh, right yeah, that's my secret. Don't go around telling anyone."

She laughed. "Your secret is safe with me."

The waitress walked over with a pen and notepad. "Can I take your order?"

Emma picked up two menus from the table and handed one to him. "So, what are we having?"

He looked at the menu, but his mind refused to let him think of the here and now. He wanted to be with Emma, but all he could think about was the dead naked man from last night. "I'll just go for a ten-inch pepperoni pizza and a coke."

"Make that two, please," Emma told her, and the waitress walked off with the order. There was short silence apart from the sounds of the other customers talking. "Are you okay?" Emma asked, breaking the silence between them both.

"Yeah, I mean, still not feeling well from last night, that's all," he told her, and she gave him a look of disappointment.

"Well, we can cancel the order and do this another time if you want?"

"No, it's fine, really," he insisted.

"Are you sure?"

"Absolutely. I'll be fine."

"Good," she said and looked over to the waitress walking towards an old couple and taking their order. "So, what do you do?"

"I'm a repo man. I mean, please don't hate me for that. A man has to work." He gave a nervous giggle.

"True, and I'll try not to hate you for it." Emma sniffed but raise the side of her mouth in a half-smile before saying, "How did you end up in that line of work?"

"I'm not sure really — I guess my mate introduced me to it, and I kind of just got stuck with it. I guess." He was lying about being a repo man but what he said next sounded like a lie but oddly wasn't. "One day, I want to leave the repo business behind, and you know, do something to help people."

"You mean like working in a homeless shelter?"

"Something like that, yeah, maybe do some kind of volunteer work in some third world country. I like to think that my life could have some kind of meaning. That I have done some good in this world," he said, thinking about building a school in Africa or a hospital. He wondered how good it would be to actually help people instead of stealing and ripping people off.

"That's very noble."

"What about you?"

"Me. I just want my daughter to be happy, and I know it sounds mean, but to hell with everyone else. A mother's job is to take care of her child."

"True, but I meant do you work?" he asked before a waitress with long black hair and black eyeliner walked towards them with two glasses of coke and placed them on the table in front of them. They both thanked her, and she walked off without a word. "What a miserable waitress," Danny whispered to Emma. "She kind of reminds me of Wednesday Addams." Emma gave a quick and obviously fake giggle. "Anyway, you were saying, what do you do?" he said before taking a drink.

"I'm a secretary for an electoral company, and it's as boring as it sounds, believe me."

"So, it's not like in movies when the boss calls you at night to take a look at you and give you little extra hours," Danny said with a smile.

"I don't know what movies you've been watching, but no," she said with a straight face, showing no emotion. "No, not at all, and to be honest, my boss is a very respectful and professional man."

The shock of regret hit Danny like a kick in the face. "I'm sorry, I don't know why I said that." She started laughing, which made Danny smile. "You're fucking with me?"

She laughed, saying, "Yeah, I am."

"Now that's mean."

"I know, I couldn't resist. My boss is a prick, but a job is a job, right. All the same, I don't want to know what kind of movies you've been watching," she said, raising her eyebrows in an exaggerated shocked expression.

"And when you go to work, what about Libby?"

"Well, she's mostly at school when I'm at work, or if not, she stays with the other prick in my life, her father."

"Can I ask you a question about her, and please don't be offended."

"Well, I'll try my best not to get offended, but I don't know what the question is yet, so I can't say if I will be offended or I won't be until you ask it," she said, taking her drink to her lips.

"Is Libby, you know, shy or something? I have barely ever heard her say a word."

"I have no reason to get offended by that question. I guess you don't know people do you," she says with a sly smile.

"No, not really." He laughed.

"Yeah, she is shy and don't take it personally. She barely ever speaks to anyone, even to me."

"Do you know why?"

"No, not really. I've taken her to doctors, but they say it's something she would grow out of, and I really do hope so. I mean, I love her more than anything, but she worries me," she said, sounding upset about it.

"I was quite shy when I was a kid. My mum…" He stopped himself before saying too much about his mother. He just said, "I was put into foster care, and I didn't feel comfortable talking to anyone apart from this one kid Mark who I am still friends with. He wasn't in foster care, but I got to know him after being adopted."

"I'm sorry to hear that."

"No, don't be. My foster parents were really good people," he said as the waitress with long black hair walked towards them, holding two plates of pizza.

CHAPTER 7

The first thing Lydia did when she landed in Britain was to leave a message for the detective and book herself a room at a cheap but clean refurbished hotel called the Britannia near where her father Edgar once lived. The house was covered in police tape. The police told her that they weren't allowing anyone to enter the house. The day after the detective rang back telling her to meet him at the police station. She walked towards a middle-aged woman standing behind a window with a little hole in the bottom of it. "Can I help you?" the woman said in disinterest as Lydia walked up to her.

"I'm here to see Detective Andrew Williams."

"What's your name, please?"

"Lydia Knightley."

The receptionist looked through a book that was out of the view of Lydia and then looked back up at her. "Okay, Miss Knightley, please take a seat, and he will be with you shortly."

Lydia sat on one of the blue plastic seats on the other side of the room near where a bald man with a black eye and tattoo of three sixes on his head was sitting. He sat there staring at her, looking at her legs in black leggings, which she was wearing under a dark blue mini skirt. Finally, she looked over to him, and he gave a quick wink of his non-blackened eye. She quickly turned her head in disgust, prayed that the detective wouldn't be that long.

After a few minutes, her prayers were answered as an overweight man walked from a blue door that made a buzzing noise as it opened. He wore a white shirt with sweat stains under the armpits and a black tie; his short brown hair was combed to the side and full of gel to keep it down. He looked to be in his late fifties, but perhaps the long history of working for the Mayfield Police made him look older than his years.

"You must be Miss Knightley."

"Yes, that's me," she said, standing up from the chair and shaking his hand.

"Did you have a good journey back home?"

"It was okay," she said, wanting to scream at him, *How the fuck can I have a good journey after finding out that my father just killed himself?*

"You mind accompanying me to my office." He walked towards the locked door he'd arrived through, took out a key-card and held it up against a small plastic looking box at the side of the door. They heard a loud buzz, and the door unlocked. They walked through a very narrow white corridor with blue doors. He opened the door to a small room with a wooden desk with a white computer monitor on top of it. On the other side of the desk was a photo of a young woman — perhaps his wife, Lydia thought.

Behind the desk was a portable television with a VCR built into it. He sat behind his desk, and Lydia sat on a chair in front of the desk. "One minute," he said before looking through the drawers in his desk. Then, he took out a piece of paper and put it on the desk in front of her. "He wrote this for you."

She picked it up and read the note: 'I'm sorry, Lydia. Live the best life you can, and please destroy it, please for me.'

"What does he want you to destroy?" the detective asked, and she thought for a moment, remembering the time before she left him, seeing the notes on his walls about the machine to record a person's dreams. Still, indeed there was no way he could have accomplished it. "I honestly don't know," she answered.

"You don't know?" Andrew asked, not believing her.

"I don't understand this note, and I don't understand anything that is going on."

"I see. Can you tell me if your father had any enemies?"

"No, none whatsoever."

"His cleaning lady was the one who found him. She also told us that many of his possessions are missing."

"Missing? What do you mean missing?"

"Stolen, we believe, and it appears that the lock on the back door was picked."

"Do you mean lock picked?"

"Yes, but more strangely than that is that they smashed his television and near the television lying on the floor were many videotapes."

"What was on these tapes?"

"I'll show you. Because we can't really make head or tail of them, but the production values on these tapes are like you would see in a Hollywood movie." He picked up a remote control and turned on the television, showing nothing but static small white dots dancing around on a black background. "This one had the label eighteenth February nineteen-ninety-seven."

He pressed play, and the TV went black, and the static came back. Then it made a strange sound which sounded like electricity, shocking something. Then the footage went to nothing but a cloudless blue sky, and it began to move, like seeing through someone's eyes as they get up. The sky-blue screen turned to a view of a beautiful green field with one single tree with its leaves blowing in the wind. Slowly the tree came closer and closer into view, and the sound of footsteps through mud could be heard even though the grass looked dry as a bone. Now close to the branch, the footage moved up as if the person's eyes they were seeing through was now looking up and staring at the bright red apples hanging from the branches.

Lydia noticed something strange about the apples — each one of them had a human face, with its eyes and mouth closed. She looked away from the TV and at the detective who was watching her reactions.

"Daddy," Lydia heard a little girl's voice say from the TV. Her eyes suddenly went back to the television, where she saw a little girl wearing a white dress walk out from behind the tree. Lydia's jaw dropped open, her breathing became heavy, and a cold chill ran up her spine as she stared at the face of the little girl. A little girl she hadn't seen for many years. How was it possible to be seeing her now?

"I've missed you, my baby, I've missed you," she heard her father's voice say from the TV.

The little girl took a few steps back. "She's coming for me, Daddy. She's coming for me."

"Who is?" she heard her father say.

The little girl turned her head to the right; the footage moved up to the apples with the faces. Now their eyes were wide open, and mouths also wide open as if they were screaming in horror. The footage turned to where they were all looking, and in the distance, they saw a tall thin figure dressed in dirty black rags with long white hair and jet black skin, like a shadow. The grass the figure was standing on turned brown as it moved slowly closer to the camera.

The little girl yelled in a high pitched scream, "Run, Daddy, run!"

The figure dropped to all fours and ran at them like a dog, and then the detective turned the video off, and the screen went back to static. Lydia still could not take her eyes off the TV as her brain was trying to process what she had just seen.

"You know the little girl in this video, don't you?" he asked her.

Lydia nodded her head "My sister."

The detective sighed. "Your sister Victoria who passed away in nineteen-seventy-eight. So, I don't understand why she is on a video with the label of the year nineteen-ninety-seven. Well, to be honest, I don't understand any of this."

"He did it?" she said in shock.

The detective was even more confused by what she had said. "He did what?"

"You won't believe me."

"Try me."

"He became obsessed with dreams after Vicky's death. He believed he could make some kind of recorder to record his own dreams. I guess that was his way of seeing her whenever he wanted to."

"Are you telling me that the video we watched was a recording of your father's dream?"

"I know it sounds impossible, but what if it is? Did you see any strange objects that you couldn't explain the origins of?"

"No."

"The bastards must have stolen it."

"How is it possible to record someone's dreams?" he asked, the look of puzzlement clear on his face. He was getting nowhere with her, he must have thought.

"I don't know. He said something about collecting the electrical signals in the brain, but I don't know. I didn't take him seriously at the time." She sighed. "I wish I had now. If only I could turn back time."

"I'm sorry, Miss Knightley, but no technology yet has the power to record a person's dreams. It's just not possible."

"Then can you explain the video?"

"Special effects and a lookalike for your sister. It's amazing what computer effects can do nowadays. Just a few years ago, I went to the cinema and watched a film with what looked like real living dinosaurs."

"Okay, but how was my father able to use such effects and where the hell is the video filmed? My father wasn't bloody Spielberg," she said angrily.

"There are several places that look like the field in that video — perhaps it wasn't even in this country."

"Sure, perhaps" She sniffed, now thinking, *I'm getting nowhere with this guy*.

CHAPTER 8

Lydia walked through a clean street full of large homes. It had been many years since she had stepped down this street. She recalled playing with a kid who once lived here whose name had now fallen from her memory, was it Jen or Jane? Lydia stopped in front of a house with the number seven on the door and then walked towards it, banging her hand against it. It didn't take long for an old man with messy grey hair to open the door. She smiled at him, but it was a smile that failed to hide her stress and sorrow.

"Lydia, long time no see." he said.

"Hi, Uncle Peter," she said, giving him a hug. They soon let go of each other, and Peter invited her in. She walked into the living room, feeling the warmth and the familiar smell of the place that brought random childhood memories into her head. Lydia looked at Juno, who looked back up at her. "Hello, girl, you must be Juno," she said, kneeling down and stroking the top of the dog's head.

"He got her after you left," Peter said, standing behind her. "By the way, where did you go?"

"I was travelling around Europe, and the last place I was staying was a Greek island named Santorini."

"You should have stayed. He missed you. You know that, right?"

She looked back at him with her sad green eyes and said, "I know." She felt like he was blaming her. Perhaps he was — she didn't really know him all that well.

He sighed. "You want a cup of tea?"

"Oh yes, please."

He walked to the kitchen and clicked the kettle on. Lydia looked up at the television and saw that he was watching the game show *Catchphrase*. "I can't blame you for not being here for him, though," she heard him shout from the kitchen. "I wasn't there for him either. I wish I was now — maybe I could have changed things."

"I can't blame you. I blame myself, but he was never the type just to give up. Not in my wildest nightmares, did I imagine he would do such a thing."

"Yeah." She heard Peter sigh. "He must have felt like there was no other option open to him."

"When was the last time you saw him?"

"Before he passed away. He came here with Juno and told me to take care of the dog, although he didn't tell me why, and then he just left."

"And you didn't think that was strange?"

"Of course, I did, but what could I do? Drag him into the house and lock him up in the attic?" he said sarcastically.

"All right, good point."

"How do you take your tea again?"

"Strong with two sugars," she said, stroking Juno, who lay back down on the carpet. Peter walked up behind her with two cups in his hands and handed one to Lydia. "Thank you," she says, taking a sip of her drink. It was very sweet; she was sure he had put more than two spoons full of sugar, but it didn't matter — there were more important things to think about. Peter sat back on the sofa and looked at the television before back down to Lydia. "Tell me, what do you think of dreams?" Lydia asked him.

"Dreams?"

"Yeah. My dad became obsessed with them."

"Your dad had many strange obsessions. To me, dreams are meaningless, just the mind creating images. It doesn't even know what images it's creating, nor does it care," he said before taking a sip of his drink.

"You say that like the mind is an entity of its own."

He took another sip and looked at the television again, and back down to Lydia. "It is. The mind is out for itself more than for the rest of the body. Edgar is a good example of that. The body wants nothing more than to keep running; the mind, on the other hand, is much more complex. No one can truly understand it."

"Uh," she said, taking another sip of her drink. "The truth is no one really knows shit about dreams,"

"Well, I know that Edgar's obsession with dreams came after the death of your sister. Perhaps he was trying to find a way to be with her again."

"She was his favourite."

"He loved you both, but you were a rebellious kid, always getting into trouble, like me, I suppose. Vicky, she was a little angel. In any case, she was taken from us years ago, and your father was never the same after it happened."

"I know. He spent most of his time working in his study. Now I know why he became so reclusive. I should have been more supportive," she said with a heavy heart. "And you, Uncle, are right — I should have never left."

Peter sighed and rubbed his tired eyes. "It was not your fault, and I'm sorry about saying that. You're a woman who values freedom and adventure — making you stay here would be like locking up a wild lion. You take away a part of him, his soul perhaps, if there is such a thing."

"No. I thought Dad was mad, but I left him alone. It turns out that he wasn't mad, but he still needed me."

"What do you mean?"

Lydia thought for a moment, weighing up whether it was fair to bring Peter into this mess. She ended up choosing to leave him out of the loop.

"It's best that you don't know, Uncle."

"Why? The police mentioned something about a collection of tapes. Please tell me he wasn't into anything illegal like child porn or snuff movies."

She was shocked by what he said and would yell at him if she hadn't she noticed the worried look on his face.

"No, it's nothing like that. You wouldn't understand. I'm not even sure I do, to be perfectly honest."

He took a sip of his drink and rolled his eyes, giving out a big sigh. "You weren't the only person who loved him. He was my brother, remember."

"I know, and once I understand everything myself, I will explain it to you. You have my word."

He sighed again and slowly shook his head. "This darn family," he hissed.

"I'm always thinking the same thing."

She looked into Juno's brown eyes just before Juno licked her face with her big wide wet tongue. "Do you mind keeping hold of Juno for a bit longer?"

"Not at all. She's a good dog. I'll be honest with you I like her company."

"Great then. I guess she's yours now."

CHAPTER 9

D anny and Emma were walking back home when Emma noticed a beat-up red Ford Sierra with its driver side door dented and a broken wing-mirror parked next to her house.

"Oh, shit," Emma muttered.

"What's wrong?" Danny worried.

"It's nothing, just Steve."

"Who's Steve?"

"Libby's dad," she said with a moan. "Listen I had a great time, but I think it's better if I go in on my own,"

"Are you sure?" Danny said, feeling worried for her.

"Yes. It'll be fine" She kissed him on the cheek, and he felt the warmth of her lips against him. "We'll catch up later, yeah?"

"Yeah okay," he said, feeling exhilarated by the touch of her lips against his skin. That feeling soon left him as remembered who waited for her in her house. What kind of man was this Steve, and should he be worried about her? He thought about following her and meeting the man, but he concluded that it would only make things worse for her. He reluctantly left her and walked back into his house. He put his hand on the door and realised that the door was already open. He was sure that he'd locked it. He then pushed the door open and as soon as he walked on in, he heard Mark's voice saying, "Hello, Dan."

He looked in the living room, seeing Mark sitting on his sofa drinking a cup of tea. "I made myself a drink. I didn't think you would mind."

"I don't mind you making yourself a drink, but I do mind you breaking into my house," Danny fumed.

"Yeah well, I need to see you, mate. Anyway, who's the bird you were with? She's quite tasty."

"She's none of your business," he said, taking out a cigarette and lighting it before kicking off his shoes.

"Someone's in a mood today."

"Yeah well, you know, someone breaking into your house can do that to you." As soon Danny said that, another hit of guilt for the life he was leading flooded him. Then he looked at his coffee table and saw that the dream recorder was missing. Mark smiled and took the machine from behind his back. "Looking for this? A dream recorder — does it actually work?"

"I haven't tried it yet, but I highly doubt it."

"No? That's a shame," he said, standing up and looking out of his window. "You know the police are all around the old man's house?"

"And that's surprises you?" Danny asked as if he was stupid. "Are you sure our prints are nowhere to be seen?"

"How many times have we done this and how many times have we been caught?" There was a short silence as they both looked at each other. "That's an actual question."

68

"Many times, and never."

"Exactly."

"This is different. Listen, I can do time for breaking and entering but not for murder. No way I can do time for murder." Danny could now see the worry in his face, mirroring his own feelings.

"Did you kill the old man?"

"No," he said in shock.

"Then you wouldn't be done for murder because you haven't murdered anyone. His death was suicide — even this town's cops aren't dumb enough to think otherwise so stop worrying." Mark took a sip of tea and placed the cup back down on the table. "I never saw a dead body before that night. At first, it scared the shit out of me but after that, it was just like looking at a dead fly for me. Was it the same with you?"

Danny thought about it and no, it really wasn't like that for him — he hadn't been able to get the image of the dead man out of his head. "Yeah," he said, so quietly that it was almost a whisper.

"Oh well, I think I better be getting back. Monica will be wondering where I am. I was only meant to nip out for some milk," Mark said, as he stood up still holding the dream recorder in his hand. "She probably thinks I'm fucking someone else. I wish I was that lucky," he said with a laugh.

"Mark, you're having a laugh if you think you are taking that."

Mark looked down at the machine and laughed. "Right, no worries, mate, you can keep this shit," he said, dropping it to the floor before walking out of the room. "See you later, Danny boy."

"Bye," he said looking down at the machine as soon he heard the door shut and knew that Mark was gone. He picked up the machine and put it back on the table. The rest of the day he did nothing but watch television, mostly repeats of seventies' sitcoms. He put the television on mute and leaned his head against the wall, listening to the angry muttering of the voices coming from next door. Soon he heard the door slam shut and he walked to the window and watched as Steve's car drove past. He tried to look at the driver's face, but the car was moving way too fast, and he was unable to look inside. *It doesn't matter*, he thought, he could find out what he looked like another time. For now, he had to know how Emma was doing and what they were shouting about.

He walked out of the house, the door shutting behind him as he moved next door and knocked on its red painted wood. Emma opened the door, her eyes wet as if she had just been crying. "Are you okay?" he asked.

"Yes, I'm fine."

"He didn't hurt you, did he?"

"No, no, we just had a fight that's all, uh, I mean an argument, not a fight with fist or daggers sadly," she said, trying to make light out the situation.

"And Libby?" he asked out of worry. It surprised him that he did actually worry about the girl, given she only said about two words to him, but oddly enough for him he did worry about her.

"Oh, she's upstairs. Playing on her Nintendo," she said as she smiled but as quickly as the smile came on her face it fell and she said, "Listen, Danny, uh Libby is a little upset, so do you mind if we meet tomorrow night?"

"Yeah sure, that's fine."

"Great, I had a good time with you."

"Me too"

"See you later," she said closing the door on him.

"See ya," he said to the closed door before he turned around and walked back to his house.

Night fell over the town. Danny spent the night watching yet another one of his videos. This time it was the spaghetti western, *The Good, The Bad and The Ugly*, one of his all-time favourite movies. He loved the Mexican standoff at the end which for him made the movie go from great into an all-time classic. When the movie ended, he stopped and ejected the video, putting it back into its case and placed it back on the shelf. With the television now turned off and no sound coming from next door it was all quiet apart from the low hum of his fridge in the kitchen.

His eyes now feeling heavy he walked out of the room and towards the stairs but turned around and stared at the dream recorder on the table, thinking that it was a shame that he hadn't tried it. *Don't do it, Danny, it could fry your brain*, he told himself, as he picked the machine up. *Fuck it*, he told himself as he took it upstairs with him, placing it on his pillow while he cleaned his teeth and stripped off

71

to just his boxers. He lay down on the bed and put the machine on his head, putting the strap around to keep it in place. He was surprised at how light it was. Turning off the light and being the pitch black of the night, it still took him over three hours to finally fall asleep, worrying about the machine's impact on his mind and what he would see once he played back the footage, or if in fact he would actually see anything at all.

Meanwhile, Emma was sitting up in bed, her lights were still on, and she was reading a so called true story about a pagan worshipping cult in Yorkshire. She got to the end of chapter five and put a bookmark in between the pages before she put it down on the pillow next to her. It didn't take long before her mind went from the story she was reading to what she would have done with Danny if Steve hadn't shown up.

Closing her eyes the picture of Danny's face came to her in the darkness and she moved her hand slowly under her knickers, but just before she could pleasure herself, she heard the sound that she was fearing, the sound of Libby screaming. Quickly Emma jumped out of bed. Wearing only her knickers underneath her pink nightgown, she ran out of the room and into Libby's room, where her daughter sitting up covered in sweat and her eyes filled with tears.

"I saw the monster again, Mummy," she cried as Emma sat on the bed next to her and put her arms around her daughter.

"It's okay, monkey, it was just a dream, there are no

monsters, only bad dreams." But as Emma said those words, she thought she heard the sound of heavy breathing, like there was some invisible man in the room with them.

CHAPTER 10

The sun rose on another day, and a few hours later, Danny started to wake up, feeling a slight headache and the urge to vomit. It was like the worst hangover of his life, but he still had his memories and still knew that two add two is four. He took the machine off his head and looked at his pillow, almost expecting to see traces of blood on it, but there was nothing.

The first thing he did as he got downstairs was not to eat breakfast or to make a cup of coffee like he did every other morning. He turned the television on and plugged the dream recorder in the VCR, but nothing happened. He waited for a moment until he remembered that it needed a tape to record onto. He got up and looked through his collection of videos, finding one with a blue paper case and the words '240 Mega Power tape'. He picked it out and saw that it had the label stuck on its side saying 'World Cup USA final' in blue ink. Taking it out of its casing, he put it straight in the VCR and clicked record. It seemed like nothing was happening until he looked on the VCR's display and saw the numbers counting. *It is recording something*, he told himself.

Finally making himself a bowl of cornflakes and a cup of coffee, he waited for what seemed like an eternity just watching the green digital numbers changing on the black VCR. He watched as Emma and Libby walked past his house, then he went back to watching the green numbers until they finally stopped at 4.00.00.

"Four hours," he whispered to himself; that was the entire length of the tape. He couldn't believe had waited for four long hours as he clicked on play, feeling scared at what he was about to see. He looked at the television and saw nothing but static white dots dancing on a black background then he heard the sound of what could only be electricity buzzing through the screen, then the screen looked plain white and then a graveyard in the middle of a desert came into view.

He stared at the screen, his mouth open as he remembered parts of the dream about being in a graveyard. The footage moved closer and closer to a grave with a large cross with two planks of wood, one plank sticking from the ground next to the grave and another plank across it, making a shape of a crucifix. He read the name on the grave and felt a chill as he saw his name, Daniel Greenway.

"That one is for you," he heard Emma's voice say. The footage turned to reveal Emma standing in the middle of the graveyard with a sizeable scarlet dress, holding a Victorian sun umbrella over her head. Danny then heard his own voice speak on the screen, saying, "It's a lovely day for a walk. Isn't it?"

"Oh my god, it works," the real Danny then whispered to himself. "It really fucking works."

"It's always a lovely day when you're around," Emma said with a broad and bright smile. "You know I've been thinking about you, and I've been thinking about me and all the good times we can have together," she said in a voice that had a slight hint of an American accent that she never had before.

"Girl, it's funny — we are in a place with so much death, but you make me feel so alive," he heard the dream version of himself say as the dream him moved closer to Emma. Before he moved to kiss her, he saw a shadowy figure walking towards them. Danny, in the dream, stepped back, looking down at the gun holster he was wearing on his belt as he rested his hand on the gun's handle.

"Well, well," the shadowy figure said, moving closer and getting into view so Danny could see that he was dressed all in black. He had a black cowboy hat and a long black trench coat that reached down to his knees. He also had a dark and long moustache that rested under his long, pointed nose. But of course, Danny knew who this man was. Lee Van Cleef as Angel Eyes, the villain from the movie he had watched last night.

"I think you're in the wrong place, mate," Dream Danny said.

"Mate?" Angel Eyes said as he started laughing in a deep demonic voice. "Son, I don't think you know where you are, do ya? Because you ain't in Mayfield any more,"

Angel Eyes said as he reached for his gun, but he couldn't draw it as Danny fired his one shot, and he fell to the ground. The dust rose from the ground as Angel Eyes hit it with a loud thump. "Don't mess with the best, son," Danny said in the video.

"Bullets won't keep him down for long," Emma told him, and he looked back at Angel Eyes, who was floating back up like Dracula rising from his grave.

The real Danny started laughing, enjoying every minute of his recorded dream. "This is mental," he said, laughing, hardly believing his own eyes. Sitting on his sofa, he watched every minute of the four-hour video. Most of it was just like watching a strange western that was perhaps the most non-historically accurate movie ever made.

Just a few minutes before the video went off, Dream Danny and Emma found themselves running towards a cabin in the middle of the desert. He opened the door and ran on into the cabin. The place looked familiar to him, but he couldn't put his finger on where he knew it from. Perhaps it was a childhood memory that was buried somewhere in his subconscious. The cabin had an old black and white TV on the floor that was unplugged but still showing static, and also a big roaring fire at the end of the cabin that looked to have no place within the building. He slammed the door shut and locked it with a large iron padlock. "He wouldn't get through this," the dream Danny said, and the real Danny thought, *The door is just made of wood, it's not hard to break through it*. The dream Danny then moved to the fire and put his hands out in front of it while the real Danny thought, *What am I doing that for, shouldn't be cold, it's in a bloody desert.* He heard the sound of the padlock being unlocked and dream Danny turned to see that Emma had been replaced with a tall skinny woman with thick black glasses and wearing a white T-shirt and baggy grey trousers. Her skin was pale, and he could see blue veins in her arms. "Mum?" both Dannys said in surprise.

"Danny, my silly little boy. Do you really think a girl like Emma could like you?" she said as she sauntered towards him. "Girls like Emma will never like scumbags and thieves like you," she hissed as she stepped ever closer and closer to him. "No, no, no, what girl will ever like you." She grabbed his throat with her skinny arms, and the screen when to black, and when it came back, he found himself in Edgar's bathtub in Edgar's bathroom. He sat up and saw the pale and naked Edgar standing in front of the bathroom door. Water was dripping from his wrinkled body.

"You don't know what you have taken from me, you fool. You—" Then, before Edgar could finish what he was saying, the video cut off, and static came on the screen, leaving Danny staring at it, thinking about what he had just seen.

"What the fuck," he said out loud to himself as he grabbed a cigarette from his pocket.

CHAPTER 11

Lydia took a taxi to her father's house, noticing straight away the police tape around the door. She paid the taxi driver and got out of the car, closing the door after her. The driver didn't wait around; he drove off soon as the door was closed. The house brought back many memories for Lydia, but it wasn't that long since she had seen the building, as she always came back for Christmas and Edgar's birthday. Moving slowly to the front door, she felt her hand shake as she pulled the police tape away from the door and unlocked it with the key that her father gave her so many years ago. She opened the door and walked into the living room, noting the smashed television in the corner of the room. Looking at the brown sofa that faced the smashed TV, she had a vision of her father sitting there watching *Tomorrow's World* with a cup of tea in his hand. She remembered the way he liked it with loads of milk and only one spoonful of sugar. Her attention then turned to the fireplace, where she noticed the two little Samurai she had bought him for his birthday were now gone. She turned back to the television.

Did you smash the telly, Dad, or was it them? she thought to herself. Then she made her way out of the living room and up to the bathroom where she knew his body was found, seeing the now dried brownish bloodstain still on the white tiled floor near the bathtub. As she looked at it, she felt her heart beat faster, and a rush of melancholy surrounded her.

Why did he do it? What did he see in those videos? she asked herself, moving out of the bathroom and across the hall to her old bedroom. That hadn't changed since she left. Still, she could see her drawings of castles, islands with palm trees and a picture pinned on the wall of actress Lea Thompson dressed in her 1950s' clothing leaning on a car from the same era. The photo was to advertise the movie *Back to the Future*. She smiled, remembering cutting the picture out of a magazine. It was one of her favourite films with her first ever female celebrity crush. Although 1985 definitely wasn't the first time she realised her homosexual tendencies; many girls in her school caught her eye.

She was about to sit on the bed until she noticed a brown teddy sitting on the floor. Smiling to herself, she picked it up and held it close to her, closing her eyes and feeling the warm tears fall down her cheeks. When she opened them, she noticed her old brown curtains, and not knowing why, she decided to open them and looked out to the large hill behind the house. Taking one last look at the teddy's black plastic eyes, she ever so gently placed it back down on the bed as if she was scared of hurting it and looked back out of the window.

"The thieving bastards could have been watching the house from that hill," she said quietly to herself.

She walked out through the back door and through the rear garden, climbing over the small wall that surrounded it, walking up the steep hill, and then turned around. She looked back down at the house, remembering the country road that lay beyond it. She knew now where the thieves came from, but what was the point — there were no cameras around there, and no one had seen them.

She sat down on the grass and lay back, looking at the clouds in the sky, wondering how on earth she was ever going to find that damn machine. She should forget about it and go back to Katya and enjoy her travels with her. Plan their life together and say to hell with the machine and to hell with the thieves. She didn't want any of this. She just wanted to live a happy life with the woman she loved. No, she could not just forget about it; she owed it to her father to find the bastards who stole it from him and to destroy the machine that he had asked her to destroy.

Lydia and Katya had decided to phone each other at around nine p.m. for Lydia and ten p.m. for Katya. Lydia was the one who had to pick up the phone and make the call, but Katya would wait by the phone until she rang her. Lydia punched in her number, and it rang twice before she heard the Russian accent down the other end of the line. "Geiá," she said, the Greek word for hello.

"Hello, Kat, it's me."

"Lydia!" She said her name in delight. "Are you okay? How's everything going over there?"

"Well, I think I may be here in England for a little longer than I thought."

"Did you talk to the policeman?"

"I did, yeah, and things are more complicated than I first thought."

"How so?"

"It's hard to explain, but it seems like someone stole from dad before or after his death."

"That's awful."

"Yeah, one of those things that were taken was very important to our family, so I need to find a way to get it back, and I don't know where to look or, well, anything really."

"Will the police not help you find it?"

"The police are treating Dad's death as a suicide, and I guess cops in this town don't give two shits about a robbery. They looked for other fingerprints but came up with nothing. So whoever the thieves were, they were professionals." She sighed and then said, "And I cannot think of any way to find them."

"Wouldn't it be dangerous to look for them?" Katya said, and Lydia thought, *Of course, finding the thieves is both close to impossible and yes, finding them could be dangerous.* She had no idea who these people were.

"No, they're thieves, not murderers or rapists," she said, just to stop Katya from worrying, but she would be lying to herself if she said it didn't concern her.

"You don't know that."

"Please, Kat, don't worry about me. I'll be fine. I always am."

"Okay," she said, sounding worried.

"How's Ezio?"

"Gone." Her voice went from sounding worried to angry.

"What do you mean, gone?"

"As soon as he knew you left, that mudak disappeared," she said, her anger now being clearly heard through the phone. Even if her tone of voice didn't come through, she still would have known she was angry. Katya only used Russian words when she was angry or speaking to another Russian. Although once she did say, "O bozhe," in bed, and that was something Lydia soon looked up afterwards. "He only wanted you. Maybe I'm too ugly for him."

"No, my love, you are as far from ugly as any girl I've ever met. The scumbag just wanted two girls to sleep with him. He's a greedy fuckwit. It would be the same if you left instead of me. Best just to forget about him."

"Maybe, but in any case, I'm all alone now in this strange country."

"Oh, Kat, there are worse countries in the world to be in than Greece."

"Can I not be with you in Britain?"

Lydia let out a quiet sigh before answering. "Listen, my Kitty Kat. This is something I need to do on my own." She loved Katya, and not seeing her every day was not pleasant for her, but she was scared of something

83

happening to her. What if the thieves were also murderers or rapists? Like Katya said. If something happened to her Kitty Kat, she would never forgive herself.

"I know, I won't get in your way. I promise," Katya begged.

"I don't know." Lydia sighed again.

"Please?"

"Okay, okay. But remember, I'm trying to find these guys on my own."

"Great, I'll book the tickets for the next available flight."

"Okay, have you got a pen? I'll tell you the address."

"Hold on," she said before Lydia heard a thud as she dropped the phone down somewhere.

***

Danny felt excited as a child at Christmas, waiting for Mark to come by to show him his new toy. He was going over and over what he was going to say in his head. Half an hour later, Mark entered the house without knocking, just like Danny did with his flat. He saw Danny sitting on his sofa drinking a cup of coffee, looking at him with a giddy excitement written all over his smiling face. "So, what are you banging on about?" Mark asked him as he got a phone call earlier in the day to come on over.

"I'll show you." He put his coffee down and got up off his sofa before kneeling next to his VCR. He pressed the play button, and the static came onto the television with the sound of electricity.

"What is this?" he asked Danny, finding the sound the TV was making oddly creepy.

"Just keep watching," Danny said without looking at him, and then the screen turned from static to the view of a graveyard in a desert. The footage moved closer and closer to two wooden planks in the ground.

"What film is this?"

"My film that I created all in my head." Danny now turned to him with a smile, and he looked from Danny to the television screen. Now he saw Danny's name carved in the plank of wood.

"This is your dream, right?" Mark questioned, not being able to believe his own eyes. "That one is for you," he heard a woman's voice say from the television. The footage turned to reveal Emma standing in the middle of the graveyard wearing an oversized dress and holding a Victorian sun umbrella over her head. "Is that the girl you like?"

"Well, kind of," Danny said, embarrassed.

"It's a lovely day for a walk," he heard Danny's voice say from the television and Mark laughed.

Danny stopped the video and looked at Mark. "Why are you laughing?"

"You found a grave with your name on it, and the only thing you can say is it's a lovely day. What the hell?"

"It's a dream. They hardly ever make sense."

"All right, all right. So, it actually records your dreams. That's amazing," Mark said in shock, almost speechless. "I, I mean, how does it work?"

"You just put it on your head while asleep," he said, not wanting to tell him too much in case he decided to steal it. Mark was his best friend but trusting him was something only a fool would do.

"No, I mean, how does it work?"

"Oh, I don't know. The old man's notebook doesn't go into that much detail."

"Press play; let's see the rest of it."

"No, you've seen enough."

"I'm interested in knowing what's going to happen next."

"A man's dream is his own business."

"Ah fuck off, just press play," Mark moaned.

"No. I just wanted to show you that the machine works and ask for your help."

"With what?"

"We can sell people's dreams back to them. People are always trying to remember their dreams. You see them writing them down in little diaries. What if they didn't have to, if they could just watch them like they watch a movie? Think about what people would pay to see their dreams on video. To have a collection of their favourite dreams. They want to relive a dream of them fucking that hot co-worker — they can do that; they want to relive a dream of them flying like superman. Well, they can sure as hell do that."

"If you start that kind of business, it won't take the police long to learn that we were in the old man's house," Mark said.

"Yes, I know we can't go completely public with it just yet, but I know you have friends in dark places, which I don't. Friends who know how to keep their mouths shut. We don't sell them to everyone, just the right kind of people for now."

Mark couldn't believe what he was hearing. "What if my friends can't keep their mouths shut? What if the cops come sniffing? What if they ask us how we got this strange machine?"

"Before that happens, we will have enough money to get out of the country."

"Yeah. We could start a dream recording business. Maybe in America."

Danny shrugged his shoulders. "I would prefer Canada or New Zealand, but sure, the States, why not." He wondered if he could get Emma and Libby to join them in their new country. Perhaps it was a little too soon to ask them, but Danny was sure he would find a way to still be with her.

"I guess I could put the word out."

"Good, and just wait there a moment. I want to show you something else."

Mark waited as Danny ran out of the room and upstairs to his bedroom. He opened a large wooden wardrobe and took out an oversized brown trench coat and a black fedora hat. He got them for a New Year's Eve party back in 1992, which he hated like he hates all parties. Still, he attended to make his then girlfriend Kate happy. It had a theme of the rolling twenties, so the outfit was meant to make him look like Dick Tracy, although he had got the colours wrong and didn't know that Dick Tracy was 1930s not the 1920s. He walked back into the living room to Mark's laughter which made him feel ashamed and stupid, but he tried his best to ignore the laughter.

"What you think?" he asked Mark.

"You look like a shit Noir detective. Why are you dressed like that?"

"It's like an alter ego, you know? Like Bruce Wayne and Batman."

"More like Twat-man. Anyway, why the fuck do you need an alter ego?" Mark queried.

"The machine that records dreams were taken from a dead man, remember?"

"But you said we shouldn't worry about that because we didn't kill him. Don't you remember saying that?"

"I did say that, yeah, but they're still going be looking for us for questioning more than anything. So when you look at me now, what do you see?"

"A twat in a hat."

"Exactly, people will be too focused on the hat and the coat to notice the details of my face. It's like psychological, you know? To them, I will just be a hat and a coat."

"If you don't want people seeing your face, then wear a mask."

"No, bad idea. Masks scare people. We don't want to be scaring our customers away."

"All right, Mr Wayne, what's your alter ego's name?" Mark said with a slight giggle.

"Signor Crow," he replied in a bad Spanish accent.

"Signor Crow?" Mark laughed. "Why Signor? You're not Spanish."

"You think Mister Crow sounds better than?"

"I think bloody Twat-man sounds better."

"What is it with you and that word today?" Danny said, sounding annoyed.

"It's just the best word to describe you, mate," he said with a shrug of his shoulders.

CHAPTER 12

When Mark left, Danny sat back down on his sofa and re-watched the dream he had recorded. He watched the entire four hours while smoking another cigarette and eating a plate of chips. After the video had finished, Danny got up with a bit of dizziness, and his vision was slightly blurred, and his legs felt weak. It was like he was still in a dream. After another cigarette, he knew that he needed to see the other addiction in his life, Emma. As the feeling of dizziness left him, he went out of the house and went straight next door to Emma.

Standing in front of her door, he rubbed his tired eyes and tried to forget the dream. However, the images from the video were still imprinted onto his mind and refused to leave. He knocked on the door, and she greeted him with a kiss before dragging him into the house, slamming the door shut behind her. Pinning him against the wall, she leaned her whole body weight against him as she kissed the bottom of his neck.

He hadn't expected this type of greeting from her, but he liked it. Danny could feel himself getting hard as he felt her soft body against his. He closed his eyes and kissed her. Touching the tip of his tongue against hers as he felt the curves of Emma's body, his hand reached down to her buttocks which were covered in tight blue jeans.

Hearing the footsteps upstairs, he opened his eyes and looked upstairs to see Libby standing at the top of them, staring back down at him. It was him she was looking at, not her mother, and that somehow worried him. Quickly moving his hand away from Emma's behind, he tapped her on the shoulder to stop. Feeling this, Emma pulled herself back and looked into his eyes with a look of confusion.

"We're being watched," he whispered to her.

She looks upstairs at Libby with a smile. "Hey, monkey, how long have you been there?" she asked her but received no reply as Libby just walked back to her room. Emma looked back at him with an exaggerated look of guilt. "Oops," she said with a bit of a giggle that Danny found quite cute.

"I don't think she likes me," Danny told her.

"I told, you don't take it personally. She's anti-social to everyone," she said, stepping away from him. "Do you want a drink or anything?"

"Sure, coffee," he said as they walked into the living room. Danny's member was still rigid, as though it was trying to point him towards her if only his pants and underwear would allow it. He sat down on the sofa while she switched her radio on, playing Dire Straits' *Sultans of Swing*. "I love this one," she yelled from the kitchen.

"Me too, perhaps their most famous song," he said, sitting on the sofa before jumping up and walking to the kitchen where he saw her standing next to the kettle with two mugs next to it. She looked at him with a smile on her face. What a fantastic smile it was, Danny thought.

"Hey there," she said to him.

"Hey there," he said back as he started to dance and dance badly. He didn't have a clue what he was doing, but he knew he wanted to see her smile and laugh as he moved his hips to the music.

"What the hell are you doing?"

"Dancing."

"Oh, is that what you call that," she said, laughing as he danced towards her, grabbing her around the waist. "I thought you wanted a drink?" she said as he gently kissed the bottom of her neck just like she had done to him earlier. It made her breathe heavily, and she put her arms around him.

"Fuck the drink," he whispered to her before lifting her onto the kitchen counter. She wrapped her legs around his waist as she kissed him. When she jumped down off the counter, they went upstairs into Emma's room and made love. Danny stayed for the rest of the day, and at night they made love again.

That night he lay in bed looking at the ceiling, wishing that he'd brought the dream recorder with him. What was Emma dreaming of? Was she dreaming of him? If he had the recorder, he could find out. It would be wrong, an invasion of her most profound privacy. *Just go to sleep and try not to think about the dream recorder*, he wanted to tell himself, but the question of what was she dreaming about kept coming into his mind. *Do other men think of this kind of stuff — surely not?* Suddenly he lost his thoughts at the horrifying sound of Libby's screaming coming from the next room. Emma woke up and quickly jumped out of bed without saying a word, just wearing her pink nightdress. He sat up and listened to the noise coming from the room next door.

"It's here; the monster's here!" Libby screamed.

"It's just a dream. My love, it's only a dream. Remember it's not real, it can't hurt you." He heard Emma comforting her daughter.

"I'm scared, Mummy, and I hate it, I hate it!" Libby yelled out.

"It's not real, it's not real," Emma said. "He is in your head, and you can defeat him because he's nothing, okay, honey." There was a short pause before he heard Emma say, "Don't just nod your head, say it."

"He is in my head, and I can defeat him because he's nothing," Libby quoted.

"All right, monkey, you know I'm just in the other room, so if you need me. You know where I am."

"He's in there, though," Danny heard Libby say and felt, at that moment, very unwelcome.

"Libby. He's my friend, and he wants to be your friend too."

"I don't like him."

Emma let out a loud sigh. "Listen, I love you, but mummies need a kind of love that their daughters can't give them."

"I know what type of love you mean."

Emma giggled. "Okay, we will talk about this tomorrow, just try and get some sleep, please." Danny then heard Emma walking back into the room, and quickly he lay back down, closing his eyes, so it looked like he wasn't listening to them.

"I know you're still awake," she said, getting back into bed. "I'm sorry about that."

"Perhaps I should go back home," Danny said.

"No, it's fine. Libby just has nightmares," Emma said, laying her head on his bare chest and listening to his heartbeat. "Remember when you found my pager and I told you that I was taking Libby to the dentist?"

"Yeah?" he said, looking down at her dark hair while gently running his fingers through it.

"I lied. I was taking her to a therapist, but she hasn't been able to help," Emma whispered.

"Do you know what she dreams about?" he whispered to her.

"A monster or a witch — I don't know what to call it, and neither does she." She sighed.

"Would you want to see what it is?" he asked her, thinking that perhaps he could actually do some good with the recorder.

"Well, she draws me pictures — is that what you mean?"

"No, I mean actually see what the thing that is scaring her is. I have a way of showing you"

She looked up at him as if he had just gone mad. "How?"

"Get dressed, and I'll show you." Emma sat and stared at him in confusion. "I can't just leave Libby on her own."

"Oh yeah, sorry. Then wait for me while I'll get something from my house."

"Okay," Emma whispered as he jumped out of bed and got dressed. Emma got up and passed him the keys she took from her pocket from her jeans. "Hurry back," she told him.

"I will," he whispered, moving out of the room and out of her house and quickly towards his own. He picked up the dream recorder and ejected the video of his dream. He stared down at the video, knowing that it had Emma in it. How would she take seeing herself in someone else's dream, but how could he convince her if he didn't show her the video? He should have recorded another before he told her about it. Still, there was a high likelihood that Emma would turn up in another dream. Then his eyes went to the recorder, wondering if it was as safe as he thought it was. He felt fine. He had a slight headache and felt a bit sick when he woke up but now, he felt as healthy as a horse.

It's worth a try, he told himself. *She's only going to use it once — it will be fine*, so he picked up the machine and videotape and quickly went out of the house to Emma's place. Emma waited in her living room wearing just her pink nightgown with her black leather coat over her to keep her warm. Danny opened the front door, and Emma stood up and watched him walk into the room.

"What is this all about?" she asked him.

"Listen, I'm going to show you a strange video, and it may confuse you a great deal and maybe even scare you a little," he said, putting the tape into the VCR.

"This isn't one of those disgusting top of the shelf movies, is it?" she joked, and Danny looked at her wondering, what she was talking about. What on earth had she been watching in the past?

He gave a simple answer, "No," just before he turned the television on and pressed play on the VCR. Then he sat on the floor and stared at the TV. Static and then the sound of electricity came on the television, just before the footage of the desert graveyard. He slowly turned his eyes towards her, looking for her reaction. She looked back at him and then back at the screen. He felt his heart race as he knew what was coming, and then he saw a look of confusion and shock on her face.

"What the hell," she whispered, moving closer to the television. "This is, this is me, I, I, I mean, is it?" she stuttered.

"It is," he confessed.

She turned to him, her eyes wide, and mouth slightly dropped open. "How, why, I am on the telly?"

"It a recording of a dream I had," he told her, pressing stop. She looked back at the TV just before it went to black, and he ejected the video and placed it down on the floor.

"But I don't understand how; how is that possible?"

"By this," he said, taking the dream recorder from his pocket. "You place it on a person as they sleep, and it records whatever it is they are dreaming about."

"How does it work?" she said, her eyes glued to the machine.

He shrugged his shoulders. "I don't know. I mean, I wish I did, but I don't."

"How did you get it?"

Shit, — it was the question he should have known she was going to ask. He needed to think and think quickly — he didn't want her to see him as the type of man he really was.

"I found it in a skip. I don't know why I took it, but I guess I was just curious."

"So, you found a machine in the bins that you put on your body to record your dreams, and you tried it out, now you want to use it on my daughter?" Emma queried, staring at the recorder, trying to figure out how something like that could record someone's dream.

"With this device, you can find out what is haunting Libby's dreams."

"Yeah, sure, and I can fry her brain," she grumbled. "Let's not forget you found it in a skip, a skip, Danny, meaning someone threw it away."

"I have used it, and I feel fine. So I guess it's just like getting an x-ray, you, you see inside of yourself."

"Yes, with an x-ray, you see your bones, not your bloody mind — it's completely different. But again, you found it in a bin," Emma stressed. "If I found an x-ray machine in the dump, I'm not going to be saying, oh look at this, I'm going to x-ray myself. What a laugh that would be. No offence, Danny, but that's mental."

He wondered what he could say to her to prove that it was the right thing to do. "How many doctors have you taken Libby to? How many times have you heard her waking up screaming? Tell me, have you ever wanted to know what is in those dreams of hers?" He'd made her think; he could see that by the way she looked down and bit her bottom lip, the way she looked away at him and stared at nothing. He started to ask himself a question — why was he really trying to convince her to record her daughter's nightmares? Sure, he didn't want any harm to come to the little girl, and he really didn't think any could come with using the device. So why was he feeling like he was doing something wrong? Was it because of the invasion of Libby's privacy, or was he doing this out of his own selfish reasons, was it just because he wanted to see her dreams?

"Fine," Emma told him. He looked at her, feeling shocked that she would actually agree. "But we will only do it once and not tonight. Tonight, I want her to get her sleep without us bothering her."

CHAPTER 13

It had been two days since Katya had entered Mayfield. She had always wanted to see the UK although it was London and Edinburgh that she wanted to see, not a little town she had never heard of, she was sure there would be time for that after all the UK was only a small country. Lydia showed her around the town visiting the park and some of the main places that were nostalgic to Lydia. The town was a little dull, but she liked having this little inside to Lydia's history, who even spoke more about her sister Vicky something Lydia didn't really like to do. They had just returned from another walk in the park and were now both lying on the bed together, watching a romantic comedy that both of them didn't know the name of. A loud knock on the door took them out of the film, and they looked at each other.

"Are you expecting someone?" Katya asked her.

"No," Lydia told her.

The knocking continued, and Lydia got out of bed and walked towards the door while Katya turned the volume down on the tv just encase it was someone wanting to complain. But when Lydia opened the door, she found an old man standing before it.

"Oh, it's you," said Lydia stepping out of the way of the door and letting the old man through.

"Sorry to bother you," he said and looked at Katya, who stared back at him. "Who's this?"

"This is Katya." Lydia told him and then told Katya, "This is my Uncle Peter."

"Hello," said Katya.

"Hello." Peter said back with a smile, then whispered in Lydia's ear, "What nationality is she?"

"Russian," Lydia whispered back.

"Are you sure it's okay having a Russian here?"

"The cold war is over; the new millennium is coming. I think it's okay."

"You do know I can hear you?" Katya told them.

Embarrassed, Peter smiled at Katya and said, "Sorry, love, I meant nothing by it."

"It's nice to see you as always, Uncle," Lydia said, sitting back down on the bed. "But what brings you here?"

"Right, yeah. I won't be staying. I just want to say the police have had a little chat with me about Edgar. They're releasing the body."

"You what?" Lydia said in shock.

"Well, there are no signs of foul play. The knife he used to, you know, was in the bathtub with him with no fingerprints other than his own."

"So, they're just giving up?"

"No, I won't say that. They're still looking for the cunts that broke into his home, although they have no evidence that they were responsible for his death."

"No, evidence? Surely the fact that they broke into his home is evidence enough, and plus, why did they contact you and not me?" She said, getting annoyed.

"I'm classed as his next of kin. I guess he picked me because you travel a lot. Anyway, I want to tell you that I'm planning the funeral and when I come up with a date. You'll be the first to know."

Lydia sighs and shakes her head to herself. "Okay, thank you. Peter."

"No worries." he looks at Katya and says, "It's a pleasure meeting you, love."

"And you too," Katya replied as Peter left the room.

Lydia sighs again. "The fucking police in this town are useless. They couldn't catch a fish in a mug, never mind a criminal".

"You think the thieves were responsible for the death?" asks Katya.

"I don't know, but what I do know is I can't just sit around watching TV hoping for the police to do their jobs."

***

Mark had told Danny to wait at the alleyway next to a garage for their first client but told him nothing about who the client was. So, dressed in his long dark coat and dark fedora hat, Danny waited and smoked a cigarette and thought what he would see in this client's dreams. More importantly, what he would see in Libby's dream when the time came for it. Just as the cigarette came to an end, Danny noticed a small grey-haired man walking towards him. He was well dressed in navy blue trousers and had a white shirt with a dark jacket. Danny looked at him, walking towards him, and threw his cigarette on the floor. "Take it you're Mr Crow," the man said in a thick Dublin accent. "My good friend Markus told me that you have something quite special to show me."

"He's just Mark, not Markus."

"Yeah, he is, but I prefer Markus. It just sounds better, don't you think?"

"Uh, sure, I guess so," Danny said, finding the small man to be bizarre. Then he remembered Mark mentioning a man only known as the Irishman helping him out throughout many of his illegal undertakings. For some reason, Danny actually didn't think the man would be Irish, but the name coming from perhaps him having red hair or an Irish name. Yet thinking about it, he had no idea why he would believe that the Irishman was anything but Irish. Danny smiled at him. "So you must be the Irishman. It a pleasure to meet you at last," Danny said, holding his hand out to him.

The Irishman shook his hand as he said: "Let's just see if the pleasure could be all mine, Daniel," before he wiped his hand on his jacket like he was wiping off the germs he caught from Danny's hand.

"You know my real name?" Danny asked, feeling a slight bit of frustration towards Mark for giving it out if it was indeed Mark who told him.

"Aye, of course, I do, Daniel. I know a lot of things apart from the reason why I am really here."

"Then let me show you," Danny said, opening the metal door to the side of him. "Step into my office, please," he told the Irishman who walked past him, entering the garage that was full of wooden crates where Mark and Danny would store the stolen items. Some of them had been there for years while others could be sold on to the right or wrong, depending on one's point of view second-hand shops. Irishman had seen the garage before and the crates, but what wasn't there before was a bed in the corner and a mobile metal desk by its side. On that desk was a TV with VCR built into it.

"A small bed with a television next to it," the Irishman commented before turning back to him, looking into his eyes. "I don't see a camera, but still, should I be worried?"

"Not at all, but I have to say I am curious what Mark told you to get you here."

"He told me you have something amazing to show me. Is he right?"

"Well, he's not right about much, but he is right about that."

"So, go on then, show me," the Irishman said, and with that, Danny smiled and pulled the dream recorder out of his pocket.

"This is why you are here."

"And what is that?"

"Let me answer that question with a question. Have you ever had a dream that you desperately wanted to remember or one that you want to see over, over and over again? What if you can relive that dream whenever you wanted. What if you can play it back as you do with your favourite movies." The Irishman's eyes remained solely on the dream recorder and the wire that hung down from it. "This, mate, is called a dream recorder." Danny smiled. "There are no prizes on guessing what it does."

"So, what you are telling me is that little black box can record a person's dream, right?" the Irishman said, feeling downright dubious about it. Stepping closer to Danny, he stared down at the machine in his hand. "You expect me to believe you?"

"I don't expect anything."

"Oh, but you do. You expect me to give you, how much was it you were asking for again?"

"Fifty pounds."

The Irishman shook his head and sighed. "Fifty pounds?"

"Yeah, so do you want to see what this thing can do or not?"

"Against my better judgement, sure."

"Great, then can you please sit on the bed," Danny said, pointing towards it. The Irishman could now see how nervous he looked, but yet he did as Danny asked. Danny then moved off towards another crate where a red mug was resting on top of it. He picked up the cup and walked back to the Irishman. "Drink this, mate," Danny told him.

"What's in it?"

"Water."

"And?"

"Promethazine."

"And what the hell is that?"

"I thought the famous Irishman knew everything."

The Irishman smiled at him and took the mug from him, looking down into the water where the remnants of the tablet were dissolving inside it. "You know I have many powerful and dangerous friends, Daniel Greenway."

"It's just a sleeping tablet."

"Aye, but after my kip, where am I going to wake up?"

"Here," Danny told him, not expecting such a question. The Irishman then took the mug and drank from it before lying down on the bed. Danny could see how nervous he looked. Nevertheless, he believed him when he said he had powerful friends. This may be why he was willing to take the risk, but it made him wonder how he would convince other new customers.

***

The Irishman woke up with a headache, but he felt a great relief that he didn't wake up in a coffin or tied to a chair but in the bed where he had rested his head. "Welcome back, Kevin," Danny said with a cocky smile, and the Irishman was shocked that he knew his Christian name. He had spent years trying to build up a mystique about himself, and the key to that was no one knew his name.

Danny loved the fact that he had drawn a look of confusion on the face of the Irishman. "I'm guessing you want to know how I know your name, right?"

The Irishman gave no reply as Danny pressed play on the television. They watched as the television showed the point of view of the Irishman walking around on the deck of a large man-o-war ship that was completely empty apart from a woman with long white hair standing by the ship's helm. Danny's eyes turned from the TV to the Irishman, seeing his jaw drop open as he watched the footage.

"Hello, Kevin," the girl in the video said as the ship sailed on the open sea.

"I missed you, Jenny," the Irishman heard himself say on the television.

"We need to sail out of here, Kevin. Sail to a new land where we can be free," Jenny said while the Irishman took hold of the wheel. Then he looked down at the deck, seeing that it had become full of white spiders that were the size of human hands. They were crawling over each other, over the barrels and over the ropes that lay on the deck. Jenny rested her hand on his arm. "Our freedom, our lives of peace are the only things that matter. No one else, just us."

The Irishman closed his eyes and said to Danny, "Turn it off."

"All right." Danny did as he asked and pressed stop on the VCR.

"How was that possible?"

"I wish I knew this machine," Danny said, picking up the dream recorder.

"You will make a fortune with that thing."

"Yeah, the problem is I can't make it public yet."

"I see you got this device from felonious sources."

"You could say that."

"So, it's a fifty for the video, is that correct?" the Irishman said, taking out his wallet from his jacket's inner pocket, and taking out the money, handing it to Danny.

Danny counted it out before ejecting the video and handing it over to the Irishman. "It's a pleasure doing business with you," he told him.

"Can I give you some advice, Mr Crow?"

"Yeah, sure."

"You made an alias of Mr Crow. Use it. Don't be Daniel and don't use the word mate. It makes you sound common."

"I am common."

"No, Daniel is common. You are Mr Crow. Make yourself into a mystery, and your name will go much further, believe me. Also, you will have problems convincing people to hand over their cash for something that sounds like a fairy tale. Do as drug dealers do, give them a taste and get them hooked."

"Okay, thanks for the advice."

"Sure, thing and here's another for ya."

"Go on."

"Don't tell anyone about my advice nor my real name, and definitely don't go telling anyone about Jenny. If you do, you'll find yourself with a bag over your head and a blowtorch to your old meat and cherries." The Irishman then slowly got up off the bed. "I'll be seeing you around, Mr Crow."

CHAPTER 14

E dgar's funeral came on a cloudy, grey and miserable day. Lydia had been thinking about finding a job and settling down after all this mess had blown over. Not the same town, but she felt they could live somewhere in the country, perhaps in Cornwall — she had told Katya about her great memories of that county.

They were both wearing black dresses almost identical to each other as they stood facing an open grave. Standing nearby was an old, grey haired priest dressed in white robes who looked down at the black wooden coffin in the grave with a little golden cross on the lid. Katya and Lydia stood side by side, with Peter next to Lydia. Seeing the tears fall from Lydia's eyes, Katya held her cold hand as Lydia's other hand held onto a white rose. Soon Katya noticed the disapproving look of an old woman on the other side of the grave.

The priest's voice sounded soft and sympathetic as the words came out. "Lord our God, You are the source of life, in You we live and move and have our being, keep us in life and death in Your love, and by Your grace, lead us to Your kingdom, Through Your Son, Jesus Christ, our Lord." After the priest said the last part, they all said amen— even Katya, who hated religion, said the words as if she was under some kind of spell. She felt Lydia grab hold of her hand as tightly as she could. Katya also saw the lines of mascara running down her face. It was the first time she had ever seen her cry, and her heart broke for the woman that she loved and admired. Now the Russian began to think of her own parents living back in Sochi. So far away from her, and how she missed them. They disapproved of her carefree lifestyle, and they had no idea that she was dating a woman. *But perhaps I should call them*, she thought. Best to leave out the whole being bisexual part — her parents weren't the most open-minded people.

"Before we commit the body of Edgar Francis Knightley to the peace of the grave, his daughter, Lydia would like to say a few words," the priest said.

Lydia pulled her hand away from Katya, wiped the tears and mascara from her face before standing next to the priest. She looked at the small number of people who had gathered in black around the grave. She had met them all before, and there were only two of them whose names she couldn't recall. "Hello, and thank you for being here, although my father would have hated this. As you know, he wasn't that big on social gatherings, something I share in common with him. In fact, we had much in common. We both like adventure and love to seek out knowledge. The adventure part did diminish when my sister Victoria died. That was something that broke him as it broke me, but he never gave up on her even after her death. He would work in his study day after day, trying to find a way to see her again. We all thought he was crazy, but perhaps he was just too tenacious for his own good."

She sighed and closed her eyes, listening to the sounds of the birds singing in the trees nearby. When she opened them again, she looked at the coffin before saying, "My father loved inventing things. He loved technology and nature, but most of all, he loved his family and his friends. I cannot understand why he did what he did, but I understand that he must have thought in some strange way that there was a good reason for it. He was never a man to just give up but today, let's not think of how he died but let's think about how he lived." Her voice broke as she tried to keep her emotions together. "Love you, Dad," she said, as she dropped the rose on the dark coffin, the last resting place of Edgar Francis Knightley.

They all moved off to a sizeable local pub called The Anvil. It had a swinging wooden sign outside the building with a picture of a medieval blacksmith sitting down with a newly made sword. Inside, the place had a warm and friendly feeling to it with dark red wallpaper and pictures of the town throughout the years. A young man in his early twenties with shoulder length ginger hair stood behind the bar, and that was the first place Lydia and Katya went to.

"Hi, what would you like?"

"Whisky, neat," Lydia said.

"And for you?" he said, looking at Katya

"A cola, please."

Lydia looked and tilted her head like dogs do when listening to their owner but not fully understanding their words. "A cola?"

"I don't want to get drunk."

"That's not very Russian of you."

"Well, you capitalist pigs don't know what good vodka is," Katya joked, but Lydia didn't respond. She usually found it funny when Katya joked about her country's stereotypes. But today Katya found out she was in no mood for jokes. The bartender passed them the two glasses.

"Thanks," Lydia said to the bartender and raised her glass to Katya. "Ura."

Katya didn't think that she meant to use the Russian word for hurray at her father's funeral but didn't have the heart to tell her about her mistake so she just replied with, "Cheers." They then clicked the glasses together and drank. Lydia looked to the rest of the room and saw an old fat woman with a pearl necklace with long grey hair walking towards them.

"Oh, shit," Lydia whispered just before the old woman got to them.

"Lydia, I'm so sorry about your father — he was a lovely man. I have known him many, many years," the old woman said with a sympathetic tone to her voice.

"Thank you, Rosie, for coming. It would mean a lot to my father."

"Yes. Well, I got you a trifle because I remember you used to love them, didn't you?" Rosie said as she touched

Lydia lightly on the arm. "I don't recall if it was strawberries or oranges that you liked. So I made you the strawberry one because I always think strawberries are much better in trifles than oranges."

"I do love them, and I do agree with you, strawberry is better. Thank you very much." Lydia's head moved from Rosie to another middle-aged woman sitting at a table with a beer. "So, who's your friend?" Rosie asked as she looked at Katya.

"Oh, that's Katya — she's my lover." Katya couldn't help but smile as she saw the shocked look on the old woman's face. "Can you please excuse me for a minute," Lydia politely said before walking away from the two women.

Rosie looked at Katya and smiled. "So, how long have you and Lydia been uh…" She couldn't bring herself to say the word and just left it hanging in the air like a bad smell.

"Two years," Katya told her, which brought another surprised look to Rosie's face as she heard her accent.

"Oh, you sound like you're from the Soviet Union."

Katya gave her a friendly smile. "It's just Russia now."

Lydia moved towards the woman sitting on her own. She had barely known the woman, but she did remember her as her father's housekeeper. The housekeeper looked up at Lydia, who now stood in front of the table.

"May I?" Lydia said, pointing at the chair in front of her.

"Yes, of course."

Lydia sat down in front of the housekeeper. She tried to remember her name before deciding that it wasn't necessary. "I'm sorry about your father — he was a good man."

"Thank you. You were the one who found him, right?"

"Yes. It's just awful, so awful," the housekeeper said, sounding like she was about to cry.

"I know, and I'm sorry that you saw what you saw, but you know some things from his house was stolen."

"The police have already searched my house. It wasn't me," she cried out, sounding all defensive.

"I know, I know. I'm not accusing you of anything. I just wanted to ask if you'd seen anything strange before his passing."

"Yes, several things — actually all things I have told the police about."

"Like what?" Lydia asked.

"He was acting very strangely. He hardly slept; sometimes, he would be covered in bruises from unknown origins. He was also reading and researching strange things. At first, he was only interested in dreams and nightmares, then he got many books about legends and demons."

"Legends and demons?" She found the thought of her father being interested in such stuff quite hard to believe.

"Yes, the floor would sometimes be full of videotapes. He told me never to watch them, but I have to confess I stole a tape." She stopped herself and took a deep breath. "I mean, I borrowed one of them. I needed to know if it was — please forgive me — if was child porn or movies with real killing in them. It wasn't, of course. It was some strange movie which I couldn't even begin to understand."

"Where's the video now?"

"I gave it to the police."

"All right, it doesn't matter. I think I know what would have been on it anyway."

"Do you know of the dark woman?"

"No," she answered in confusion.

"He said he was being haunted by her."

Lydia thought about the creepy dark figure from the videotape the detective shown her. The housekeeper must be on about the same thing. "Haunted? You mean haunted in his dreams?"

"No. Sometimes he could see it when he was wide awake," the housekeeper told her.

Lydia's mind drew her back to memories of a boogieman who lived under Victoria's bed. It was only after months of therapy that she stopped seeing and hearing from it.

"Did he ever say what she was?"

"No, never. He never found out himself, I don't believe." "How long was he getting these visions?"

"I don't know to be honest."

Lydia found herself getting annoyed by the evasive answer. Still, she hid her annoyance well as she said, "Please, I need you to really think about it."

The housekeeper thought for a moment. "Oh, I don't know, about a month maybe two. I think."

"All right, I understand." She took the last gulp of her whiskey, pulling a face of disgust as it burnt her throat and then sat there staring at the empty glass. "Nothing is making sense," she whispered to herself, feeling the weight of the situation and the mystery she found herself in.

"Sorry, what?" the housekeeper said, thinking that she was talking to her.

"Nothing, sorry, I was talking to myself."

"Oh." The housekeeper gave her a worried look before saying, "Are you okay?"

"Yes, I'm sure I'll be fine." She got up from the table and said, "I think I need another drink. Thank you for being here and for answering my questions; my father would have appreciated it; he was very fond of you." Then she walked off back towards the bar. On her way to the bar, she saw Katya sat at a table on her own with her glass half empty. She ordered another whiskey. Once the bartender gave her the drink, she moved to the table where Katya was sitting and sat on the chair across from her.

"What was that about?" Katya asks.

"I just had to ask my dad's old housekeeper some questions."

"Did you get any answers?"

"Some, although I don't know how useful they are," she said before she took another drink of her whiskey.

"Another family member is coming," Katya told her as she looked past Lydia.

Lydia turned her head, seeing a middle-aged grey-haired man walking towards her. "That's not a family member — he used to work with my father."

"Hi, George," Lydia said to the man with a fake smile on her face.

"Hello, Lydia. I am so sorry about what happened. Who could have believed Eddy would do something like that. He was such an intelligent man. What a sad waste of a great man and a good friend."

What do you know, you haven't seen him for years? she wanted to yell at him but realised how hypocritical that would be of her.

"I just want you to know that we are here for you," he said, touching her shoulder.

"Thank you," she said, and he walked off to the bar, leaving Lydia and Katya alone again. They sat together, Lydia not wanting anyone else to speak to her. Once one drink was finished, she went to the bar and bought one after another. Her vision started to blur, and she even found herself singing the song *Mr Sandman* by The Chordattes, and she moved her arms around to the lyrics like a conductor in an orchestra.

"Think I should take you back to the hotel?" Katya told her.

"What, no, this is my father's wake, and I'm my father's daughter," she yelled back at her. Soon after, Lydia looked at the bartender, who was handing another drink to another middle-aged man in a black suit. "Hey, Kitty Kat?"

"What?" Katya said, rolling her eyes.

"Should we show the bartender a good time?" Lydia said, raising her eyebrows and smiling.

"No."

"Why not?" Lydia moaned, pulling a face like a child not getting her own way.

"Because I don't want to."

Lydia took another sip of her drink. Katya could now see how sickly her partner's face looked before she ran towards the pub's exit. She ran straight past a woman who said hello to her and flung the door open, and threw up on the pavement, just missing her black shoes.

"I think you should go home, Lydia," she heard a disproving voice say from behind her. She turned around, seeing her Uncle Peter smoking next to the wall and Katya standing by the door.

"I don't have a home. But you know that, my good Uncle Petey" she said, smiling with one eye half-closed.

"Do you think this is how my brother would want to see his daughter at his wake? Have some respect, girl," he moaned at her.

"He can't see anything. Dead people don't see shit because there no ghosts or zombies in the real world," she said before burping.

"Your uncle is right. I will get us a taxi," Katya said, her face showing her worry about her friend and partner.

"No, this is my dad's funeral, my dad who is dead, Gone, dead, is no more, is an ex-daddy. Who are you anyway?" She pointed to Katya. "No one, he didn't even know you."

"I'm your girlfriend. The woman who loves you."

"You're a mail-order fucking bride. You're only with me because you want a life in the west, so fuck you!" She then looked at Peter. "And you too," she said before running off.

Katya stared at her, feeling hurt and angry. In the whole time she had known her, she had never spoken to her like that. She was about to chase after her, but she was so filled with anger that she just spat on the floor and watched her run off before looking at Peter.

Lydia slowed down and started to stagger down the dark and quiet streets. Coming to an alleyway, a memory from her youth returned to her. She recalled that there was a nightclub just down that alleyway and across the street. *I wonder if it's still there*, Lydia thought to herself. Walking down the alleyway, her head was spinning, and she felt like she was about to throw up again. Her legs started to feel weak. She moved to a wall, close to where a metal green skip was. Feeling like she was about to fall, Lydia sat on the floor next to it, smelling rotting food inside it. She looked over to a woman dressed in a red mini skirt and saw a man in a grey suit walking towards her.

"Hey, baby," she said, turning to him.

"How much?" the man asked her.

"Eighty for an hour," she told him, and he took out a handful of cash from his pocket before they heard someone shouting out of view of Lydia.

"Hey, hey, what's going on here."

"Shit," the girl hissed before running off.

"Hey, he's not the police," the man called back after the girl. The man shouting passed the wall blocking her view of him, and Lydia could now see the bald man walking towards the well-dressed one. "Thanks a lot," the man in the suit said, turning to him in anger.

"Hey, did you a favour. I bet that girl was swimming with little sexy viruses. By the way, how's your wife?" the bald man said with a smug smile.

The man gave him a guilty look, showing him that question was a painful one. "What are you doing here, Mark?"

"I'm here to see you."

"How did you know I would be here?"

"You are always here at this time. If only the trains were as punctual, or is it predictable?"

"I already paid you for that computer."

"Yeah, I know I'm not here for that, mate. I'm here to tell you about this bloke named..." Mark paused and sighed, "Mr Crow. He can show you your deepest desires. All the crazy fucked up shit that goes on in that brain of yours, he can show it to you. Like someone would show you a film."

"What are you talking about?"

"Dreams, mate, meet him down the alleyway at Kirkless Street near Al's Garage," Mark said.

Lydia now gave them her full attention, as much attention as she could in her drunken state.

"You get to see all of your twisted and fucked up dreams in all their messed up glory."

"It's him," Lydia whispered to herself angrily.

"I still don't understand."

"You will. Remember, Kirkless Street near Al's Garage," Mark said before walking off, leaving the man in the suit on his own.

Lydia stood and shouted, "Hey you." The man in the suit looked at her and ran off in fear. She moved out of the alleyway and looked both ways down the street for Mark, but she could not see him, but she did hear her name being shouted and turned around. Then in the distance, she saw Katya walking into the street.

"Katya," she yelled out.

Katya turned to her with a look of relief on her face before she ran towards her. "There you are!" she yelled at her. "What you been doing?"

"Listening and learning."

"What?"

"I need to find Mr Crow."

"Who's Mr Crow?"

"Mr Crow knows," Lydia said, laughing out loud. "He's also near Al's Garage, that's in Kirkless Street."

Thinking that Lydia was just rambling, Katya just said, "Okay, let's just get you a taxi and a drink of water."

"Katy Kat."

"Yes?"

"I'm sorry. I love you, you know that?"

"Yes, I know, and I love you too."

"Are there many cats in Russia?" Lydia asked, sounding half-asleep.

Katya sighed. "No, we just have bears and wolves. Come on," she said, putting her arm around her and walking her down the street.

"I like wolves," Lydia said before howling to the moon, and after three howls, she looked at Katya. "Kitty Kat, remember Al's Garage. It's important," she said before belching.

"Okay, Al's Garage."

CHAPTER 15

When Lydia woke up, her head felt heavy, and she felt like she was about to throw up, but nothing would come out. As soon as she woke, she realised she was in her uncle's house and that Juno was sitting near her and staring at her with her big brown eyes. Lydia slowly sat up on the sofa, feeling like her head would just drop off as she did so. She looked at the television and saw that it was showing an old Hollywood black and white movie where the characters sounded like they were speaking in fast motion. She let out a loud moan as she felt the worst headache had felt since the morning after a wild night in Milan and just a few days before she met Katya for the first time in Rome.

"Oh, now she wakes up," Katya said, walking into the living room with a cup of coffee in her hand.

"Why am I at my uncle's house?" Lydia moaned, feeling like her head was about to explode.

"Because he offered us a place to stay. Maybe because he was scared that you would be kicked out of our hotel," Katya grumbled, clearly feeling incredibly angry at her.

"Where is he now?" she said, with her throat feeling sore and dry.

"Upstairs in his room."

"I'm going to have a drink, and I will have to have a chat with him."

"Okay, and what about me?" Katya asked as she folded her arms, staring at her.

Lydia looked back at her in confusion. "What about you?"

"What about my apology for the way you treated me last night. Not just for leaving me in a place full of people I did not know — some of whom still believe the Cold War is still going on."

"Oh, Katya," Lydia wheezed. "I'm sorry, I was drunk."

"You called me a mail order bride and embarrassed me in front of your family."

"I am so deeply sorry, Kitty Kat. I am a mean drunk. I didn't mean anything I said," she apologised and meant it. She loved Katya, and hurting her was something she didn't want to do, but she was like a Pandora's Box of emotions when she had too many drinks.

"No? You also said you love me — do you mean that?"

"No, no, I meant that one."

"Sure, you did," Katya said, walking towards the chair on another side of the room.

"Oh, my head is killing me," Lydia complained. "Do you think you could make me a drink?"

"Make your own fucking drink." Katya moaned at her.

"All right, all right," Lydia wheezed as she got up off the couch and walked into the kitchen, noticing that she wasn't wearing the black dress any more but her grey jogging trousers and a white T-shirt. Katya must have changed her clothes while Lydia was sleeping. *That mustn't have been easy*, she thought. "Listen. I can't begin to express how sorry I am to you."

Katya rolled her eyes and picked up the remote control, turning the TV up.

"But there is something." Lydia stopped, sighed, and spoke louder as she realised that Katya wasn't listening. "There is something important that I do remember from last night. Something about a man named Mr Crow?"

"You told me about him," Katya called out to her.

"Yeah, I did." Lydia was only now remembering that she found Katya after the two men had left. "What did I say about him?"

"I don't remember."

Lydia walked back into the room and looked at Katya, who just stared at the television with the cup of coffee in both of her hands. "Please try to remember," she said, standing in front of the TV.

"I don't remember."

Lydia kneeled in front of her. "Please, Katya, this is important — I need to know."

"I don't remember much, just you telling me about a man named Mr Crow who got your father's machine and something about a bald man."

"Those are the bastards who stole from my father!"

125

"Great, then now you can tell the police."

"No, I need to find the machine he built. Unfortunately, I can't have the police helping me on this."

"Why not?"

"My father wanted the machine destroyed, meaning he perhaps didn't want people to know about it." She then remembered she'd actually mentioned it to Williams.

"These men are criminals and may be highly dangerous. How do you think you will be able to get the machine off them?"

"With a little help from my uncle," Lydia said with a smile before she stood back up and walked out of the room, leaving Katya wondering what on Earth was going on. She walked upstairs and towards the shut door that led into Peter's bedroom.

"Pete, are you awake?" she called out through the door.

"Of course, I'm awake. It's twelve-thirty," he called back.

"Can I come in?"

"Sure," he said before letting out a loud sigh.

She walked into his room and saw him sitting up in bed reading a book on King Alfred the Great entitled *Alfred of Wessex*. The cover showed a picture of the king with his long brown beard and a golden crown upon his head. He put the book down and looked at her.

"You were an embarrassment yesterday. You know that, right?" he told her with his disapproving stare.

"I know, and I'm sorry."

"It's not me you should be saying sorry to. It's that poor girl downstairs. She thinks the world of you. Do you even know that?"

"Yes, of course I do."

"I don't know her that well, and my old man told me that Russians are the toughest bastards in the world, but they're still human, and your Kat seems like a good girl. So, don't go messing around with her heart."

"I won't." She found herself getting as annoyed as he was at her. She felt like screaming out, 'I'm not a child any more!' but she didn't. "I love her as much as she loves me."

"Yeah, whatever." He sighed. "Anyway, what do you want?"

"I remember once you showing me and Vicky that gun that granddad got from the war."

"So?" he replied.

"I need to borrow it."

"You need to borrow a gun — why the hell would you want to borrow that?"

"I know who stole from my father."

"You are having a laugh if you think I'm going to give you a gun to chase down these thieves? So, Dirty Harriet, what are you going to do when you get to these thieves, pop a clip in their arse?"

"It's pop a cap, not a clip, and no, just scare them into giving me his stuff back."

"You know how you sound right now? Go and get your girlfriend and go back to the Continent and forget about all this," he ordered her.

"How can you tell me to do such a thing?" she said in shock and anger.

"I don't really know what Ed was working on, but I know it drove him into madness and something that can do such a thing I don't want anywhere near me or you for that matter. Let these scum have whatever that thing is and go and have a life with your woman."

"I can't just leave everything. That machine was important to him."

Peter threw his book on the floor in anger. "Really, that's funny because you left him when he needed you the most."

"He was the one who told me to leave, that I would be helping him if I did."

"And you were stupid enough to believe him."

"I never thought he would ever…" She couldn't bring herself to say the dreaded words.

"You don't think, Lydia, and that's the problem with you. So no, you can't borrow my father's fucking gun. So, I think you should go back to your hotel, pack your bags and leave this town." Hearing her uncle saying such a thing broke her heart, but she tried her best to hide it from him. "You're an embarrassment to this family. You always have been."

"I guess the wrong sister died back in the seventies," she muttered.

"I guess so," Peter agreed; with that, she turned around and walked out of the room, straight downstairs and into the living room.

"Where are my shoes?" she asked Katya.

"Under the couch. Why, where are you going?"

She looked under the couch, took out her black shoes, sat on the sofa, put them on, and got back up.

"Where are you going?" Katya asked once again.

"I'm just getting some air," she moaned back at her. "If that's okay with you?"

"What's wrong?"

"Nothing, nothing is wrong. Well, apart from the fact that my lovely uncle has just said I should have died instead of my sister, that my dad's dead and oh yeah, I have a fucking awful hangover. So, if you don't mind, I would like to be alone just for a few bloody minutes," she ranted at Katya before storming out of the house.

She walked through the town. Seeing all the familiar buildings from the old now closed down factory next to the canal, the bowling alley where she had her first-ever date with a boy named Joe Walker. Joe, she hadn't thought of him for perhaps a decade. More memories of the town came back to her as she went into an off-licence to buy a packet of painkillers and a bottle of water. She took two pills and washed them down with the water before she kept walking on down the familiar streets. She walked and walked until finally, she made it out of the town on the small country roads. Her destination was her father's old house, although she hadn't realised it on the way.

There she spied something that she didn't expect to see — a white BMW parked up next to her father's white garage door. Lydia looked at the car in confusion. Whose was it, she asked herself — she didn't know anyone who drove a white BMW. Surely it wouldn't be the thieves unless they were stupid enough to come back to the scene of the crime. The front door opened, and Lydia froze, staring at it as Detective Williams walked out of the house looking like he hadn't slept for days. He had bags under his eyes, and his hair was wild and out of control, sticking up here and there. His complexion was paler than she remembered. He looked like he hadn't just seen a ghost, but he was living with them.

"Lydia?" he said in surprise as soon as his tired eyes caught the sight of her.

"Detective?" she replied.

"What are you doing here?" he said, looking shocked to see her.

"This used to be my home — more to the question, what are you doing here? Did you miss something with some key evidence last time you are here?"

"Just looking over the place again."

"Did you find anything?"

"No, nothing. Have you been here before?" Then, he questioned her, "You do know this is a crime scene?"

"Is it? Because I remember you people telling me that it was fine to go back into the house. Do you think that my father's suicide and the robbery is not just a mere chance?"

"I can't rule anything out just yet. At first, I thought the break-in led to your father's death, but it seems he died before the break-in. I think…" He stopped himself from talking and stared into her eyes. "I'm not meant to be telling you that."

"You're not telling me anything I didn't already know," Lydia told him as she walked towards him. "If you don't mind me saying, you look exhausted."

He smiled a nervous smile. "I am getting a bit of insomnia. It comes with the job." He was about to walk back to his car when Lydia stopped him.

"Wait."

He turned around with a hand still on the door handle.

"How many of those weird tapes did my father have?"

He sighed. "That's classified."

"Did you watch them all?"

"I did."

"What was on them?"

"That's also classified, though even if it wasn't, I wouldn't be able to explain it."

"In these dreams, was there that dark monster thing in all of them?" she asked

"You still believe they are recordings of your father's dreams?"

She nodded her head. "I know that sounds crazy."

"It does but crazy is all I have to go on at this moment. What do you know about the thing that recorded them?"

"Nothing, other than the fact he had been trying to create it for over fifteen years with no success. My father was nothing if he wasn't highly tenacious."

"How many people knew about him wanting to create this device?"

"Not many, and those who did thought he was crazy, including me."

"But why did you ask about the dark figure — is there something about this case you are not telling me?"

"No, I'm just going off the video you showed me." She wondered to herself, *Why, oh why did I lie to him*. He could help, but perhaps he would take it for himself. Edgar wanted the machine destroyed — maybe it had some kind of hold over people who watch the videos it recorded. Pretty similar to the ring from her favourite fantasy novel, *The Lord of the Rings*, she thought. Had the detective become an addict to her father's creation?

"Right," he said, but Lydia thought, *He still didn't believe me*. "Oh," he soon said as he had just remembered something or was he doing Colombo's old act? She couldn't tell. "Did your father have any notebooks or anything that you believe can help the case?"

"I don't know, you're the one who searched the house."

"Indeed," he said before saying, "Goodbye, Miss Knightley."

"I'll see you soon."

"Yeah." He sighed, sounding fed up as if the job was getting way too much for him to cope with. He unlocked

132

the car and got in before starting the engine and driving away. Lydia watched him with suspicion. She had only met Andrew Williams briefly, but the man she met then wasn't the man she had just seen. Something had changed him, broken him, transformed him into the baggy-eyed man she had just encountered.

Lydia entered the house the second time since her father's death, and still, without her father, her old home didn't feel like home. So, she moved upstairs, passing the bedroom and into the study. It was the room where he used to keep all his books and some *Doctor Who* and *Star Trek* videos on a large wooden shelf and some old photos of Lydia and Victoria. She went back to the videos, thinking that one or some of those videos could be his or someone else's dreams. She took out every VHS case, opening them up, and seeing that every one of them was the exact video advertised on the case. So, she then went to the books. She looked through each of the books' spines, finally seeing one with the title *Myths and Legends in the British Isles.* She took the book from the shelf and noticed a piece of paper falling from it. She kneeled and picked it up, seeing that it was a newspaper article from 1962. It talked about an eleven-year-old boy named Henry Winters who murdered his father and mother.

Most people in Mayfield knew about Henry. Lydia thought, *Why on earth would dad have this?* until she noticed a statement by Henry saying that a demon made him kill his family.

CHAPTER 16

It had been weeks since Danny had met the Irishman, and in that time, he had recorded the dreams of five other people, each one of them paying fifty pounds to see their dreams on film. Danny and Mark had wondered if fifty pounds would be too much, but it seemed that people were willing to pay it, and the idea of raising the price came into both of their minds. But for the moment, Danny's mind wasn't on the dream recorder or even the money but the guitar in his hands as he sat on the edge of Emma's bed with her sitting behind him. Her legs around his hips as she tried to teach him to play. It had been a long time since Emma played the guitar, but it was like riding a bike to her. You never really lose it.

"All right, put, I mean place," she corrected herself, "your index finger on the third string at the second fret."

"What's a fret?"

She smiled as she said, "The little metal lines on the neck, the long bit," moving her fingers along the top of the neck of the guitar. He placed his index finger on that third string. "Okay, good boy," she said, rewarding him with licking the back of his ear, making Danny exhale with the pleasure of it. "Now put your middle finger on the first string at the second fret and your ring finger on the second string at the third fret," Emma told him, looking over his shoulder at his fingers on the guitar strings.

"Like this?" Danny said, moving his fingers to the places she told him to.

"Yeah, well done, now leave the fourth string open and strum the bottom of the strings."

He did as she tells him, and the guitar played out the first note.

"That was a D-cord."

She then continued to teach him all the cords before he asked, "Do you ever teach Libby how to play?"

"Sure, she knows how to play *Smoke on the Water*, *Three Little Birds* and some others that I can't recall, but she's more into video games — I have never seen the point in them myself."

"Well, I used to be a master at Space Invaders. I used to show those little pixel bastards who's boss."

"I played on Libby's last game machine thingy, but I don't know, just couldn't get into it."

"And has she had any more nightmares?"

Emma closed her eyes and sighed. "Yeah, do you really think that machine of yours will help her?"

"Yeah, I do."

"I guess I will find out tomorrow night, right?"

"Right," he confirmed, "Do you want to play?" he said, nodding down to the guitar.

She hadn't played since she was in her old band. She grabbed hold of the guitar, taking it off Danny and dropped it on the floor. "Maybe later, for now, I want to play something else," she whispered in his ear before wrapping her legs around his waist and dragging him down onto the bed. Danny was now lying on top of her. He gave her one kiss before staring into her brown eyes as she looked into his, transfixed by each other.

"I think I love you," he finally whispered to her.

"You only think?" she said, smiling and raising one eyebrow, "because I want a surety. Maybe I'll go out with my other next-door neighbour, although he is in his eighties."

Danny laughs and told her, "I'm serious."

"I know, and the feeling is mutual," she said just before Danny went down and kissed her again.

Then, as things were about to get really fun for them, Danny instantly remembered he was meant to meet Mark. So he quickly moved back up, saying, "Shit, what time is it?"

Emma looked over to her alarm clock, which read 13:28. "Almost half one."

"Crap. I told my friend I would meet up with him at half one," he said, getting off Emma and off the bed.

"Oh, okay," she said in disappointment.

"I'm sorry."

"No, it's fine. Have a good time with your friend," she said with a fake smile.

***

Mark and Monica both waited for Danny at The Anvil pub. Unknown to them, it was the same pub that had hosted Edgar's wake the night before. They both sat next to one another, with Mark having a pint of beer and steak with potatoes, peas and two sausages, all covered in onion gravy. Monica had a glass of coke with a similar meal, but she had the chicken. Danny rushed towards them and sat on the table across from them. "I'm sorry I'm late."

"Late? We told you half one. It's now almost two," Monica moaned.

"Yeah, I tried phoning you," Mark said, not hiding how annoyed he was.

"You know I broke my mobile."

"Yeah, but I rang your landline too but still nothing. Where were you?"

"Just out," he told them, not wanting them to know too much about Emma.

"Out? You mean with that bird that lives next door to you, right?"

He shrugged his shoulders. There was no point in trying to deny it; they could read him like a book. Monica shook her head in disapproval.

"Well, to be fair, she better looking than your last girlfriend. She had the same shape as a bowling pin," Mark said, smiling at his own wit.

"How can someone be the same shape as a bowling pin?" Monica said in confusion.

"She didn't look like a bowling pin," Danny told her.

"She did, anyway, let's forget about pin girl and new girl, you," he said, pointing at Danny. "Get something to eat, and let's get down to business."

"All right then," he said, getting up, and he looked at Monica and told her, "She didn't look like a bowling pin."

"I really don't care," she replied.

He moved off to the carvery and came back to the table with pretty much the same thing as Monica had, but he also picked a beer like Mark. He ate one potato and sausage before he told them, "I had three clients last night." He handed Mark an envelope with his cut of the money. Mark opened it and counted the money before putting it in his pocket.

"Two of them weren't sure at first, and I'm not sure if I can convince everyone that comes in."

"Ah, don't worry about it."

"What do you mean?"

"What do you mean? What do I mean?"

"I mean, how can I not worry about it if people are scared of the machine being used on them, then they're not going to pay us to use it on them."

"People like the excitement of it, the danger of it. It brings them out of their dull existence."

"I wouldn't let you use it on me," Monica said as she bit down on a sausage.

"See," Danny said.

"Yeah, but she's a wimp," Mark said.

"Hey, I'm not a wimp," Monica moaned in anger.

"Anyway," Danny said, changing the subject, "I want tomorrow night off."

"Why?" Monica asked him.

"Because my mum has a birthday party which she wants me to go to," he lied.

"I thought you didn't have a mum."

"My foster mother."

"Yeah, fine, just give me the recorder, and I will do the recording," Mark said.

That was the worst outcome. He needed the machine with him.

"No," Danny spat out.

"Why not?"

"Because…" Danny needed to think of something and something quick. Then he came to, "Because Mr Crow is to be seen as mystical as Merlin, you know like he is the only one that can use the machine. Merlin is the wizard from—"

Mark stopped him by saying, "I know who bloody Merlin is. Give me some credit."

"What a load of shit," Monica said.

"Listen, one day off isn't killing us."

"You were just crying about people being too scared to use the machine," Monica shot back at him.

"Oh yeah, it makes them even more scared if I have one day off," Danny said sarcastically.

"Fine. Have your day off," Mark said.

"But you two are not making all that much for this machine, anyway. Can you afford a day off?" Monica asked.

"Of course, Almost every business has a rocky start. As soon as word of mouth reaches the right type of people, then we will be into the real money," Danny told her, sounding hopeful, and he was.

CHAPTER 17

The night of recording Libby's dream came. It had taken a long time for Emma to finally agree to it. Maybe it was trust in Danny or the fact she was sick of her daughter's suffering. Even Emma herself couldn't know for sure and Danny found himself wondering, *What if the monster she's dreaming of is me. How on earth can I help then? How on earth can I help now?* Emma and Danny waited in bed. There was no lovemaking that night as their minds were only on Libby and what was in her head. Emma put Libby to bed around ten p.m., and they were mostly just sat in silence, just whispering and playing with a deck of cards until the clock read 11:30.

"Will she be asleep now?" Danny whispered to Emma.

"Yeah, I think so," Emma whispered back.

Danny got up off the bed, picked the dream recorder up from the top of a set of drawers where it was lying next to a photo of Libby as a toddler with a white teddy in her hands.

"Are you sure it's safe?" she whispered to him.

He looked back at her and smiled. "I wouldn't do this if I wasn't a hundred per cent sure."

"But are you sure it will help her?"

"I'm not a hundred per cent about that, but I know it won't hurt her."

"All right, all right, let's do it." She sighed, and they sneaked ever so quietly out of the bedroom into Libby's room. It was the first time Danny had been in there. The walls were painted in lime green, and it had five posters all in a row — each one of them had a picture of one of the Spice Girls with their names above them, Ginger, Baby, Posh, Scary and Sporty. On the other side of the room were her television and Nintendo 64 with Mario Kart 64 cartridge still in the console with a drawing of Mario and Luigi pinned up against the wall above them. On the other side of the room Libby was lying in bed under her pink covers. He slowly walked towards her, seeing her blonde hair covering her forehead

"Emma," he whispered, and she moved closer to him, "I need you to move her hair out of the way." Emma gently pushed her hair out of the way. Danny slowly and slightly lifted her head, gently placed the dream recorder onto it, and tied the strap around her before putting her head down on the pillow.

"Now what?" Emma asked him.

"Now we wait," he told her. "The video only records up to four hours, but I don't need to record that much anyway. I mean, we don't want the thing still on her if she wakes up, do we?"

"So, we just wait?" she said, not believing what she was hearing.

"Yeah." He looked at the Nintendo. "We could play Mario Kart?" he said, shrugging his shoulders. By the angry look on Emma's face, he could tell that she didn't really like that idea of playing video games as they recorded her daughter's nightmares. "Or not," he said.

They waited downstairs. The worried look in Emma's eyes made Danny think about the things that could go wrong. Finally, after only an hour, Emma told Danny that he should take the recorder off Libby. He agreed and took the machine off her head as Emma helped. They both thanked God that she hadn't woken up with the machine on her. They had no idea how they would have explained what they were doing if she had. Danny didn't think anyone could make a child understand why putting a strange small plastic box on their person was for their own good.

He knelt down in front of the television, plugged the machine into Emma's VCR, inserted the video, and pressed record. Emma just stared at him, not knowing what to expect. "You can't just play the dream?" Emma asked him.

"No, you have to record it onto a video."

"I still don't understand how you got this machine," she said to him, showing how confused all of this was making her.

He stared at his reflection on the television and thought how Emma saw another man when she looked at him. Poor Emma had no idea of the real Daniel and all the bad things he had done. *You have to be honest with her, tell her what you are*, he thought to himself, but the words of his awful truth were trapped in his throat, trapped by his fear. "I told you, I found it."

"Right," she said doubtfully.

An hour had passed, both of them drank cups of strong coffee that Emma had made, and the video was finally ready to view. It was an hour long, the same length he would record for his clients. He stepped back and sat on the sofa with her, holding her hand and looking into her brown eyes. "Are you ready?"

"Yeah," she told him, and he got up off the sofa and pressed play. The television went to static and then it was followed by the sounds of electricity. He sat back down on the couch with Emma holding his hand, scared about what they were about to see. Static and sounds of electricity stopped, and the footage went to Libby's bedroom, but everything was missing. There was no television, nor posters of video game characters or pop stars. No set of drawers or wardrobe, just the four walls and Libby and the bed she was lying on. The footage then seemed to zoom out and show Libby lying on her bed.

"I thought this showed us her dreams?"

"It does."

"Then why are we not looking through her eyes, like we did with yours?"

"Some people see themselves in the third person. Making it more like watching a movie. In fact, I have had dreams where I can see myself too. I don't think it's that unusual."

144

Libby walked to her door and put her hand on the handle, but it refused to turn, keeping her locked in the room. She pulled and kicked at the door but still, it refused to open. She was trapped in her own bedroom with no way out. She turned around. She looked at the window and saw that it now had rusty iron bars over it. Her head moved and looked to the corner of the room, and she let out a terrifying scream. The footage panned out, and now Emma finally saw what had been terrorising her child. It was a tall figure all in black, crawling on her ceiling like a spider. Its fingers on its sickly green hands were long with sharp nails, and it had bright yellow eyes and a bald head.

"Stay away," Libby screamed out, just before the wall behind her started moving forward, forcing her closer to the creature. "No!" she yelled in a high-pitched scream.

The creature opened its mouth with a bit of yellowish-green drool dripping down from it. Then Libby got closer and closer and the words, "Come to Daddy," in a croaky female voice came out of the creature's drooling mouth.

Emma tightened her grip on Danny's hand, but her eyes were glued to the television.

Libby's eyes looked at the floor as it started to dissolve under her feet, leaving a long dark tunnel that she fell into with a horrifying scream. Libby fell and fell down the dark tunnel, and as she got closer to the bottom, she started to see a bright light. Then with a bang, she hit the brown floor of what looked to be a hallway of an apartment building. The long hallway was full of identical brown wooden doors with white walls. There was also a white ceiling that couldn't have been there before. Every one of them had three golden numbers on the door with each number being zero.

"Steve lives in an apartment building that's pretty similar to this," Emma told Danny.

"Similar or the same?"

"Similar, the doors and walls are different colours, I think," she said.

They could hear the loud footsteps coming from the television as Libby walked down the long hallway. She then walked to one of the doors that looked no different to the rest of them. Like the others, it had the three golden zeroes nailed on it and a golden door handle which she turned ever so slowly. The door swung open, and there they saw a woman sitting on a wooden chair in front of a wooden desk writing something with a silver pen. The woman was bald and thin, wearing a white shirt and a dark blue pencil skirt. Danny thought it was his mother for a short moment, but when the woman turned around to greet Libby, it was a face he didn't recognise.

"Hi, Lydia," Libby said to the woman.

"Who's Lydia?" Danny asked Emma.

Emma was even more confused than him. "I have no idea." She had never met a woman named Lydia, and she didn't recognise the face. "Perhaps it's the mother of a child she knows at school."

"Hello, Libby," the woman said before turning back to her writing. Libby looked down at the paper to see what she was writing. The paper, to her surprise, was completely blank, and the pen that Lydia held in her hand wasn't even making a mark on it. Lydia then dropped the pen and stood up from the desk. "It's time for me to go now," she told Libby.

"Where are you going?"

"Sometimes, you need to just go on a journey without a destination," she said without looking back at her. She walked out of the door, slamming it shut after her. Libby chased after her, opening the door again, seeing nothing but a blue sky as if she was in some kind of aircraft above the clouds.

From behind, she heard the horrifying croaky voice again. "I see you, little girl."

Libby turned around and saw the tall figure dressed all in black with its sickly pale green skin and its arms that look too long for its body hanging by its side, ambling towards her. Libby moved back and fell through the door, letting out a horrifying scream as she fell through the clouds. Then she landed in a dark alleyway on a skip full of cardboard boxes.

"I'll find you," the croaky voice told her.

"I can't watch any more," Emma said, picking up the remote control and turning the television off. She let out a long sigh and bit her bottom lip. "I mean, what the fuck was that thing. The boogieman or something."

"Or boogie-woman," Danny said, and Emma stared at him. She looked angry, and Danny wondered if he had done the right thing in showing her the dream recorder.

Sure, Emma knows what the monster looks like now, but will it make that much difference?

"What?" Emma asked.

"The creature's voice was very croaky, but it sounded female."

"That sounded female to you?"

"Well yeah," Danny said with some doubt.

"If that's what you think women sound like to you, I really worry about meeting any of your exes."

"Do you think there is meaning to this dream?"

"I don't know, but I am wondering if this Lydia is a real person, though. They do say the human mind can't create faces it hasn't seen before."

"Who says that?"

"You know they, the 'they', the eggheads, you know," Emma moaned, getting annoyed with Danny's ignorance.

"Oh, I see."

"And that hallway just looks like the one in the tower block where Steve lives," she told him, wondering if it was just a coincidence or if there was something more to it.

CHAPTER 18

Danny went back to his own house to finally fall asleep. Emma, on the other hand, had no desire for sleep. Sure, she needed it, but she also needed to speak to Libby. What was she going to say to her, though? "Hi, Libby, we watched your dream, so what the hell was all that about?" No, that wouldn't work — Emma had to pick her words. She sat downstairs with a cup of black coffee. She drank only a little bit of it and looked to her guitar and wondered when the last time she had played it was. Putting the coffee down on the floor, she walked to the guitar, picking it up and then walked back to the sofa. She held it close to her body. One hand was on the spine, and the other had a green plastic pick that ever so slightly touched the strings as the wooden instrument rested on her leg. She recalled the last time she played for an audience, at some American style bar in Canterbury she had now forgotten the name of. She was with her old all-female band, Devil Kats, at the time, with cats being spelt with a K because her friend Shelly, also the drummer, said it sounded cooler. Emma smiled to herself, remembering how she said Mortal Kombat must have stolen her idea of spelling words being with C with a K.

She started to play *The Man who Sold the World* but kept messing it up and hitting the wrong chords. "Damn," she whispered to herself. She used to know that song like she knew the back of her hand, but now it was like a foreign language from a strange culture she had never even heard of. She sat there, holding the guitar, and wondered if the other members of Devil Kats had forgotten how to play their favourite songs. She hadn't seen them since Libby was born, apart from Shelly, but she had moved to Australia just two years ago with an Australian man she fell in love with and married. *Perhaps I can try to find them and start the band up again. It used to be good fun. Scary but fun. Of course, we would have to replace Shelly unless she moves back to Britain*, she thought to herself and then found herself thinking, *If Libby hadn't been born, perhaps Devil Kats could be as big as Nirvana or even The Beatles now. I could have been a rock star. No, don't even think like that — Libby was the best thing that ever happened to you.*

She heard Libby upstairs moving around. Emma quickly got up and put the guitar away, as though she was ashamed of it and didn't know why, and quickly got back on the sofa just before Libby made her way downstairs. She looked at her mother with suspicion as she saw her tired eyes and the black coffee she held in her hand.

"Good morning," Emma said to her with a fake cheerful expression.

"Good morning," Libby replied. "Are you okay?"

"Yeah, I'm good. I didn't get much sleep, that's all."

"Okay," Libby said, turning on the television, turning the channels over until she got to CITV, which was showing an advert for a doll.

"Libby, turn the TV off for a minute."

"Why?" she said without looking at her.

Emma picked up the remote from the end of the sofa and turned the TV off before saying, "Because I want to talk to you."

Libby turned to her mother.

Okay, Emma, you've got her attention but should have thought about what you are going say before you got it, she thought to herself. "Uh," was the only thing she managed to say before just asking a pointless question. "How are you?"

"Fine. Can I watch cartoons now?"

"No, not yet. First, tell me, who is Lydia?"

"Lydia?" Libby said as if she had never heard the name before.

"You said that name in your sleep," Emma lied. She didn't like lying to her daughter, but she couldn't really tell her the truth. God, if she told anyone else the truth, she would perhaps end up locked in a padded room. "Do you know who she is?"

"No."

"Think, honey, she was a lady with a bald head."

Libby was now truly lost. "How do you know she had a bald head?"

"You mentioned something about her bald head when you were talking in your sleep."

"I remember dreaming about a lady with no hair, but I don't remember much about it."

Emma sighed and rubbed her tired eyes. She had got nowhere in understanding what was going on in her daughter's dream and thought about the long hallway. Was it the same hallway that led to Steve's flat? But what if it was? It didn't prove anything, really, but it was a start.

"Sorry, Mummy," Libby moaned.

"No, no, baby, don't be sorry. Mummy is just tired, that's all," she said with a fake smile. She wet her dry lips before she asked her one more question. "Do you like Dad?"

"Yes."

"Has he ever done anything that has made you feel uncomfortable?"

"Like what?"

"Uh…" She didn't know what to say with children. You had to pick your words carefully. She didn't know anything about being careful. Hell, if she'd been careful, she wouldn't even have Libby, although Emma was happy to be a mother. "Uh, has he ever touched you in places you don't want to be touched?"

Libby shook her head no and with it brought on more doubts in Emma's mind — was Libby lying now? Emma couldn't tell. *What kind of mother am I? I can't tell if my own daughter is lying to me*, she thought to herself, saying to Libby, "Think carefully, honey, and don't worry, you're not in trouble."

"No, he hasn't done anything like that."

"All right," Emma said, picking up her coffee and wondering if she was lying or not. Maybe lying to protect her dad or lying out of shame. She couldn't tell.

"Can I watch cartoons now?"

"Yeah, go ahead," Emma said, giving her the remote control.

***

Walter's Park was the central park in the town, the Richmond Park of Mayfield, although nowhere near as grand or as large. It wasn't too far from Britannia Hotel, and Lydia, there in the middle of it, sat on a wooden bench. Her eyes moved from the pages of *Myths and Legends in the British Isles* to the bronze statue of W.S. Walters, Mayfield's most beloved mayor, who died in 1902. He was found hanging in his office. No one knew the reason why and Lydia wondered why her eyes were fixed on his statue before she looked back to the book, flipping through the pages, reading the names of myths that were in thick bold black letters.

The book was in categories of areas of the UK and Ireland. Lydia went through almost every page that belonged to England, coming to a chapter called *Deamhan Dorcha*. It showed a drawing under it of a tall, dark figure looking down at a woman sleeping on a white bed. Under it, it read, 'Every culture around the world has their own version of the Deamhan Dorcha whose name is Scots Gaelic for dark demon. The creature is known to haunt the nightmares of children, and in some cases, adults. It is said that the creature enjoys seeing the fear of its victims. The legend goes that most people have had the Deamhan Dorcha visiting them in their nightmares, but many forget it, but for some, it has the ability to cause the victim to suffer such mental illnesses such as schizophrenia and multiple personality disorder and even has been known to have given them suicidal or homicidal tendencies. The most notable case is nine-year-old Henry Winters from Kent, who stabbed his mother and father to death in 1962 as they slept. When asked why, he told them that the Deamhan Dorcha made him commit this awful act.'

She moved her eyes away from the book again as she heard Katya walking towards her with two ice-creams in her hands. "I got you an ice cream," she told Lydia, handing it to her.

"Thanks, can you hold onto it for a minute. I would like to show you this," she said, showing the page she was reading as the wind tried its best to turn the page.

Katya looked at the page, reading the name of the creature. "You think that is the monster that you said your father was dreaming about?"

"Yeah," she said before closing the book and putting it in her backpack, which lay by her feet. "It is also linked to Henry Winters," she told her as she took the ice cream, giving it her first lick. It was not as good as what the Italians and Greeks make, but it was ice cream all the same, and she had always had a sweet tooth for it.

154

"Who's that?" Katya said in confusion while sitting down next to her.

"He was a little boy in the sixties who stabbed his mother and father to death. What if my dad killed himself to stop the monster from making him do the same?" Lydia told her and quickly licked her ice cream as she felt it melting on her fingers.

"It's just a story, Lydia. The book is title legends, and that's what a legend is, just a story."

"Every legend has a hint of truth to it."

"In Russia, we have a myth of a demon that looks very much like the one you have shown me. It is called a chort."

"And what does a chort do?"

"I don't really remember, but they are little devils. They're evil, but no Russian really believes they exist. They're just stories to scare children."

"Did they ever scare you?"

"No, because I never believed in them, but I thought I saw a ghost once when I was very young."

"You never told me about that."

"You never asked. It was just a figure of an old woman I saw in my grandfather's house once at the time. I believed it could have been my grandmother."

"And what do you believe now?"

"It was my imagination playing tricks with me."

CHAPTER 19

Danny woke up with the dream recorder strapped to his head. The sickly feeling he felt when he woke up the first night he used it was gone now. It was like he was waking up without ever using the machine. His morning ritual of making a coffee now had to be done after plugging the dream recorder into his VCR. On the floor under his living room window was a shopping bag full of blank VHS tapes with the logo of Bob's Videos, which had a blue logo of an old fashion movie camera with the two wheels on top of it and the words 'Bob's Videos' written in dark blue writing underneath. Bob himself was an overweight man with long black hair that he tied in a ponytail. Danny was sure Bob would be wondering why a man required so many blank tapes, but he was also sure that Bob didn't really care.

He plugged the dream recorder into the VCR and put the blank VHS into the machine. He pressed record on the VCR, and as he waited for it to record, he finally made his coffee and put two slices of bread in the toaster. As he stood next to his toaster watching the warm yellowish glow like a death-trap in a bad sci-fi movie burning the trapped bread, he thought about Emma and Libby. Had the dream recorder done anything to help? Although the dream brought up many unanswered questions, Danny did feel glad that he didn't turn up in it as some kind of monster.

He jumped at the sound of the toaster popping up his toast. He ate his toast, and drank his coffee, did some push-ups in the living room before having a shower. Once an hour and a half had passed, he walked into the living room again, knelt down, and pressed play on his VCR, seeing the old familiar static footage and hearing the familiar sound of electricity. When the sounds of electricity stopped along with the white snow-like static, and after the screen went to black and came on, he found himself on the screen in a large garden full of red roses, lilies, orchids and tulips. In the middle of the garden was a giant marble statue of a naked woman raising one arm in the air as her other hand held her left breast. It very much in the style of those great works of art from the renaissance era. It also stood around nine feet tall.

Along with the different location, this dream was different from his last. In this one, he could see himself like he was a character in a film. Just like Libby's dream, he remembered. He walked through the garden, staring up at the marble statue which seemed to look back at him. He moved from it towards a small lake at the end of the garden where he could see an oversized bonsai tree standing with its red leaves blowing in the wind. Danny expected to see Emma there, but hers wasn't the figure he saw sitting with their back against the tree. He moved closer and began to notice that it was an old man smoking an oak pipe. When the man turned to look at Danny, he then saw that it was the old man, Edgar, who he found dead in a bathtub, the man who created the dream recorder.

"Hello, Daniel," Edgar said in a joyful tone as if he was happy to see him.

"You?" he said in surprise.

"Yes, me. Please sit down and enjoy the garden," Edgar told him with a smile, and Danny did as he was told and sat crossed legged in front of him, facing him and the tree. Edgar smoked his pipe, and Danny watched the smoke rise and disappear into the sky. At that moment, he kind of reminded him of an early twentieth century professor.

"Where am I?" Danny asked the man

"I'm sure that you already know that. You are dreaming, my friend, and later you will be watching this on your television. Thanks to the machine that I built."

"That I stole," Danny said with a hint of guilt in his voice.

"Yes, that you stole," Edgar said under his breath

"I'm sorry about that. I really am."

"No, you're not. You're sorry because I'm dead — if I was still alive, you wouldn't be sorry at all. Would you? Which is quite ironic, if one is to stop and think about it."

"How did you create the machine?"

The old man slowly shook his head. "You won't be able to understand."

"Try me."

"No. I'm not here in your head to tell you about how my machine was built, only to give you a warning."

"A warning?" Danny asked, sounding like he was actually worried, although Danny, who was watching the dream through the TV, had no worries about the monster in Libby's nightmare apart from the well-being of the girl.

"Libby's boogieman is with you now."

"What are you talking about?" Danny said in confusion.

"Just look," the old man said, pointing to the statue in the middle of the garden. He looked at the statue and saw that the statue was now looking at him. As if it was watching his conversation with the old man. The flowers slowly start to die before his eyes, and behind the statue, he could see a tall, dark figure standing there. Its long arms rested by its side as it watched them.

"What is that thing?" Danny asked him.

"I wish I could tell you, Daniel, but all I know is it won't ever leave you," he told him with a smile as if it was funny to see him being haunted by the creature.

Danny looked back at it and saw it moving slowly towards him. It reached its hand out and touched the marble statue. Where the creature's fingers were, he started to see cracks growing on the marble. As soon as the statue was full of cracks in the shape of lightning bolts, it removed its hand, and the whole statue crumbled and fell at the side of the tall creature, which kept its yellow eyes on Danny. After the statue was gone, the creature started to slowly walk closer to him. Danny looked back to the old man in a panic. "What do I do?"

"Nothing can be done."

"How do I get away from it?"

Edgar raised his hand, showing Danny the deep cut through his wrist. "Don't ask questions you already know the answer to."

Danny got up and ran away from the old man and the creature. Now in the garden, all the flowers were dead, the green grass turned to brown, and the blue sky was now dark red. He came to a large brick wall that seemed to come out of nowhere and felt every brick with his hands as if he would find a hidden passage.

"Behind you," he heard the croaky voice of the creature say.

Danny turned around and saw the tall figure dressed all in black with its dark green skin looking over him. Its dark eyes seemed to change colour every time he saw them, and they stared down at him as it smiled its sinister smile. Its teeth looked rotten and dark as it grabbed hold of Danny's neck and pinned him against the wall. Danny, who was watching it at home, started to feel the creature's hand around his throat, finding it hard to breathe. He was being choked by an invisible force. He fell to the floor on all fours, trying to catch his breath. Finally, as if the invisible hand was now released from his throat, he caught his breath and looked back up at the TV, shocked to see the black screen, the dark mirror that it had become. In this dark mirror, he saw himself on all fours like a dog but also behind him, he saw a dark figure.

He turned around quickly but saw nothing at all. Just the back window that looked into his overgrown and messy garden. "What the fuck," he quavered. He sat back up, still breathing heavily.

"Daniel." He then heard the croaky voice coming from nowhere. Danny looked around in horror, seeing nothing. Just an empty house.

"Where are you?" he asked, feeling fear grabbing hold of him. "Where are you?" he shouted, but he got no answer.

CHAPTER 20

D anny as Mr Crow, dressed in his long coat and hat, stood in a narrow alleyway that had a metal door to the right-hand side of it. It led to an old garage which Mark used to store his van and the stuff they stole but had not yet sold. He walked back and forth from wall to wall, waiting and waiting. The thoughts of the creature he had seen last night stuck in his mind as the feeling of its invisible hand around his throat kept coming back to him, but it wasn't himself that he was worried about. It was Emma. Both of them had seen the same video of that creature. He had called around for Emma and asked how she was, but she seemed to be okay and gave no knowable hints of distress, but Danny wondered would he be able to pick up on them if she did? Perhaps he thought he should have told her what happened. He then noticed a skinny man wearing a raincoat with a hood over his head walking towards him.

"Are you Mr Crow?" he asked Danny as he got close enough to him for Danny to see the man's long and square face, and Danny realized he looked a bit like Boris Karloff in the Frankenstein movies.

"Perhaps," Danny told him.

"Mark told me about you."

"Did he now, and what did he tell you?"

"That you have something to show me."

"What's your name?"

"Owen."

"Owen, I can show you dreams. Your dreams, to be more precise, my friend."

"I have no idea what you are talking about."

"Of course, you don't. That's why I'm going to show you. If you would like to follow me into my office," Danny said, opening the metal door which led into the old garage with Mark's van parked in the middle of it and a small bed in the corner, and a metal table next to the bed. The rest of the garage was full of wooden crates full of things Mark and Danny had stolen but couldn't sell on. One of the crates had two mugs on top of it, one of which was just black, and the other had the red Arsenal logo on it. The first thing that caught Owen's eye was the small black dream recorder resting on top of the metal table. Owen walked towards the table and was about touch the dream recorder until Danny yelled, "Hey, keep your hands off!"

"Sorry, but what is it?"

"It's art, mate," Danny said and then thought, *Darn it, I should have said my friend — it sounds better, more mysterious.* "That is the thing that records dreams." He could see the confusion on Owen's face. He clearly had no idea what the hell was going on. "All right, I see you're not getting what I am getting at."

"I haven't a clue what you're talking about," Owen said in confusion.

"All right, I just need you to sit on the bed," Danny said politely, and Owen looked over to the bed and back at Danny with a worried look on his face before asking,

"Why?"

"Listen, you have no reason to worry. You are a business partner of Mark Long's, right?"

"Yeah."

"And he is the man who told you to come to me. Mark is a prick. We both know this, but he's a man of business, so he's not going to want any harm to come to his partners unless you've fucked him over. Have you?"

"No."

"Then you have no reason to worry."

"I guess you're right."

Danny smiled at him before walking to the mugs that were resting on one of the crates. He picked up the black one and walked back to Owen, then held it out to him. "Drink this, my friend."

"What is it?" Owen said as he looked into the cup — it seemed to have some kind of pill dissolving in it.

"It's Promethazine. It's a sleeping pill."

"You expect me to go to sleep here?" Owen said in shock.

"Didn't you hear me before? I said that machine," Danny said, pointing to the dream recorder, "records dreams. Now how can I record your dream if you are not dreaming?"

Owen looked back down at the cup. "Are you sure I will be fine afterwards?"

"I swear on my mother's life. You will wake up as right as rain," Danny told him, of course, Owen didn't know that Danny's mum was already dead. Owen took the cup to his lips and drank it before laying down on the bed.

He woke up on the bed with a TV that wasn't there before next to him on top of a metal desk with little plastic wheels at the bottom of it. He felt like he had been hit over the head by a baseball bat and felt like last night's dinner would make a reappearance. He definitely didn't feel as right as rain like Mr Crow promised. He looked at Mr Crow sitting on one of the wooden crates smoking a cigarette, staring at him with a disgusted look upon his face.

"You know, you've got a messed up mind."

Once again, Owen had no idea what he was talking about. "I feel sick," he told him.

"Yeah, so do I, so do I," Mr Crow sneered. Owen just gave him another look of confusion as Mr Crow jumped off the crate and walked over to the television without ever taking his eyes off Owen. Mr Crow pressed the play button and took a few steps back, not looking at the TV, just at Owen. He now saw the static and heard the sound of electricity. Owen then stared up at Mr Crow.

"Don't look at me. Look at the telly," he told him as he walked back to the crate. Owen did as he was told and moved his eyes to the television screen, seeing nothing but static. The image on TV then cut to footage of Owen lying in the middle of the woods as the sun shone down on him and in the background, he could hear the sounds of a child's laughter. Owen got up from the ground and followed the sound while the real Owen sat up, shocked by what he was seeing. How was this possible? he thought. Owen, in the dream, moved through the woods until he found a little girl, with light blonde hair tied into pigtails and wearing a pink dress. She was playing with a stick pretending it was a sword. He exhaled in shock before looking to Mr Crow, who was staring back at him with his face full of hatred.

"How did you do this?" Owen asked him.

Mr Crow just gave him one quick, simple answer: "Magic."

Owen turned back to the television, seeing himself dancing with the little girl, both of them holding hands and spinning around in circles like it was a ballroom.

***

While Mr Crow and Owen walked out of the old garage, Lydia watched them from afar as another man walked past Owen and towards Mr Crow. She was using the zoom of the camera she had taken with her from Greece to get a good look at them. So, she knew now what this Mr Crow looked like, but she couldn't hear what they were talking about or how many of them there were through that door. If she could make it through that door, she could be greeted by a gang of armed thugs. She didn't have the gun.

166

Somehow, she had to make Peter give her the gun. There was no other way. Mr Crow indeed wouldn't be intimidated by her without it. She lowered the camera and let it hang from her neck on the black strap that came with it. "What to do," she asked herself while biting her bottom lip.

CHAPTER 21

A ndrew ejected another one of Edgar's dream videos. Each time he watched one, the feeling of claustrophobia came to him like the walls of his office were closing in on him. Yet he couldn't stop watching. *Perhaps this is what it is like to be a drug addict*, he thought. He took notes about the mad genius who had found a way to record his dreams, but he did not really believe that. Why would Lydia Knightley lie about it, but how could it be true.

He read the report of Edgar Knightley. He was born in 1929. The middle child with two brothers, the elder one Benjamin, had died in France near the end of the second world war. His wife, who was the mother of his two daughters, died of cancer shortly after the birth of his second daughter Victoria who died at a young age. Whoa, this man had enough tragedy in his life to drive any man to take the express route to the exit.

He sat back, staring at the 3D multicolour pipes screensaver on his computer, trying his best to keep his eyes open. It had been so long since he had got any sleep. Just close your eyes, he told himself, just for a few minutes. As soon as he closed them, he started to hear heavy breathing all around him. Opening his eyes, he saw the walls around him breathing in and out. The monitor of his computer showed the colourful pipes with blood slowly dripping from them. He stood up quickly, rushed out of the office and headed toward the toilets and towards the sinks, where he ran the cold water splashing it against his face.

"Get a grip, Andrew," he whispered to himself. "Get a grip, Andrew," he said more loudly now. "You just need more sleep, that's all. Everything will be fine. Everything is fine."

The cubicle door behind him opened, and another detective, DCI John Gallaway, came out, looking at him. "Are you talking to yourself, Andy? You should be careful. They say that's the first sign of madness."

Andrew had always hated Gallaway. Maybe it was because he wanted to be the chief inspector, and the fact Andrew believed he was accepting bribes off one of Mayfield's more notorious criminals, Kevin 'Irishman' McKell, although Andrew didn't have enough proof to convict him. Even if he did it wouldn't matter. Gallaway had his fingers in a lot of pies he was even good friends with the mayor. He now stood next to Andrew, washing his hands.

"I'm fine. Just one of those days, you know."

"By the sounds of things, you have been having many of those days," he said, turning the tap off and drying his hands with a paper towel.

"As I said, I'm fine."

"You want to know what I think. I think you can't cut it in this line of work anymore. Perhaps you are better doing some other type of job. What kind of jobs are there for fat fucks anyway?" he said with a cocky smile, a smile that Andrew so longed to knock off his face.

Andrew stared right into his eyes, squaring off against him. "You've got a problem with me?"

"Don't go squaring off with me, mate. I'm higher in the food chain than you." He crumpled the paper towel into a ball and threw it in Andrew's face. "I'll see you later, mate. I have some real police work to do."

Andrew looked at his reflection as he envisioned himself smashing the mirror, taking the shard of glass that would fall from it and driving it into Gallaway's throat. He knew he would never do such a thing, no matter if it was scum like Gallaway.

At night he sat at home in his dark bedroom, his heart filled with anxiety. The only light was that glowing from his television screen. The digital clock next to his bed read 2:35 a.m. He had work in the morning, but there was something about those tapes he had taken from work.

He couldn't stop watching them, even if each one of them was four hours long. How many had he seen today? Clearly too many — he hadn't done anything but watch the videos all day. His mind wandered to the case of Henry Winters. "I need to find out where he now lives and interview him. That's if I could make any sense from a loony like him. It is not a coincidence that Edgar used the newspaper about Winters as a bookmark," he whispered to himself and looked down at his bare, hairy and large belly over his black belt. Now turning off the television, he told himself, "I'd better try to get some sleep," as he lay down on his bed, wishing that he was still with Paula. He missed having someone to hold and whisper to before falling asleep. He missed the warmth of her body, but there was no way he could stay married to a woman who would sleep with his best friend behind his back. Even though he wished he had someone just to make him stop watching the videos. It was clearly affecting his mind.

Right on cue, he heard a quiet tapping coming from outside the bedroom door that was followed by the all familiar cold chill that went down his body. "It's here," he said so quietly it was barely a whisper or even a sound. *Close your eyes, Andrew and go to sleep. It's like Roosevelt said, the only fear is fear itself. Ignore the fear. You're a grown man, a detective for the police — sure, the police in a small town but still the police, so man up*, he told himself.

Then the cold wind hit the room, and it felt as though his bed had lifted off the ground and was floating in mid-air. He quickly opened his eyes and saw nothing, only the glow of the digital clock reading 3:10 a.m. He moved his bare feet down off the bed and felt the carpet below him. The bed wasn't floating — it was just his mind playing tricks on him. Nothing was happening at all. It was a fat man in a dark room — nothing at all. He closed his eyes again, hearing the dripping of a tap coming from the bathroom. Drip it went as each drop fell from the tap and hit the sink below it. Drip, drip, drip. He tried to ignore the dripping. Just water dripping from the tap, it doesn't matter. Drip, drip, drip.

He got up and walked out of bed towards the bathroom, seeing the dripping tap and drops of water hitting the sink. He turned the tap, and the dripping stopped. He looked at his reflection in the mirror and saw the dark bags under his eyes, his wild hair that looked to have a mind of its own. Turning around and started to walk out of the bathroom, he heard it again just before he got to the door. Drip, drip, drip. He turned around, and there it was, the dripping tap. He rolled off a bit of toilet paper and put it under the tap to lessen the dripping sound.

Again, he turned around and was about to walk out of the room until he heard not the dripping but the rushing of water. He quickly turned around and saw the tap fully on. The steam that was coming from the sink showed him that it was the hot water that was running. He felt a rush of fear wash over him again and felt his body shake as he walked back to the sink and turned the tap back off.

There must be something wrong with them, he told himself. He turned around and saw a tall and skinny figure with pale skin and long white hair, wearing a black tunic, standing in his doorway. It had a long and pointy nose, and it smiled a wide and unnatural smile, showing its dark yellow rotten teeth.

"I see you, big boy," the creature said. It had a strange way of speaking as though an old vinyl record was being played backwards, like the reversed messages that were once popular on them.

He ran downstairs to grab his coat, quickly putting it on and taking the keys out of the pocket, unlocking the door and running to his car that was parked in front of the house. He started the engine, zipped up his coat and looked at the house with the top floor window lighting up in the darkness. He stared at the window but could only see his bedroom wall through it. He took a deep breath, feeling the warm tears rolling down his eyes, and his body shaking like a leaf on a dying tree. *What the hell is it*, he questioned himself. Tomorrow he would try getting more information from Lydia, but it seemed like she didn't know either. He knew one thing — he couldn't sleep while that thing was in his house.

He turned on the lights and then the radio, switched on his CD player and played his collection of sixties rock 'n' roll songs. He drove off listening to Jefferson Airplane singing *White Rabbit*. His bare feet felt strange against the car's pedals. He drove at about thirty miles an hour down country roads that had the national speed limit, for he wasn't going to any destination. He was just going. The lights lit up nothing but trees and signs telling him when the next turning would be.

His eyes felt heavy, and it felt like it was hard to breathe. It had been a long time since he had a good night sleep, a very long time. The weight of his insomnia was upon him now. He'd find somewhere safe to park and go to sleep in the car. He felt the seatbelt pushing into his stomach and chest, so put his hand down the side of his seat and pressed on the red button that unclipped the seatbelt, and then he felt as if he could breathe again. His eyes just stared out at the dark road in front of him, feeling like his heart was racing, sweat building upon his forehead, and he felt the feeling of someone or something in the car with him.

It was here in the car with him. He knew it. He could feel its presence though he could not see it. Without even thinking, he switched the CD player off, listening to nothing but the sound of the engine and the wheels moving along the tarmac road. He felt every shame and heartache of his life. He felt the feeling he felt when his true love, Paula, left him for another man. Andrew felt the shame he felt when he wet himself in the first year of junior school. He felt the fear he felt when he first saw the creature.

"Drive faster," he heard the creature whisper in his ear, but still, he could not see it, just feel it. He pressed down on the accelerator. The car engine roared in anger as it went from thirty to forty to fifty. The bright lights of an oncoming car were now coming his way. Sixty, seventy. He couldn't slow down. He wouldn't slow down. *Have to go faster, have to go faster*. The other car beeped its horn at him as it drove past. The driver of that car was warning him to slow down. He knew it.

Pay him no mind and keep driving, must go faster and faster. Eighty miles an hour now. *Must go faster*. He saw a sign, the sign telling him to slow down, tight turn ahead. *Ignore it, must go faster, faster, faster*. Ninety miles an hour and then a hundred miles an hour. He then saw out in front of him the road turning to the right and the metal guard rail with large oak trees behind it. He came to his senses, but it was too late as he put his foot hard on the brakes. The wheels screamed and smoked. It was too late — he was going too fast, and the car couldn't stop in time. He knew for a few seconds before the car hit the guard rail with a terrifying bang and smash that his life was coming to an end. The airbag released, and Andrew's body flew forward into it, but the front of the car crumpled, crushing Andrew's neck.

CHAPTER 22

Lydia walked back to the hotel with bags of shopping in her hands. She had just gone to the local Tesco to pick a bottle of milk and microwave curries for her and Katya. They were cheap curries, but Lydia was looking forward to having something to eat — her stomach cried out for it. Katya would have loved to go to restaurants every day, but Lydia was different — she wanted to be alone with just herself and Katya. She put the key into the door and opened it, and saw Katya sitting on the white bed in the middle of the room. She was watching the television with a worried look on her face.

"Right, I got us some of these microwave tikka masalas, they're not that great, but they're quick." Lydia then looked at the microwave they had bought a few days ago. It was a cheap white thing with little plastic buttons on the side of it. "I also got some milk — speaking of which, do you want a drink?" she said, holding up the bottle of milk to show her.

"I think we should go back home," Katya said, ignoring her question.

"Oh, Kitty Kat, I am home. I mean, I will be once we move back into my father's house."

"I want to forget about the machine your father made."

"You what?" Lydia asked her, feeling annoyed by her before she put the milk bottle on top of the microwave.

"Have you heard the news?"

"What news?"

Katya leaned over the bed, picked up a local newspaper from off the floor, and showed her the front page. "Andrew Williams was the detective you saw, right?"

"Yeah."

Lydia walked up to her and took the newspaper from her hand. The headline read 'Local detective Andrew Williams Dies in Car Crash'. She then read on:

'SIO Andrew Williams, 48, a well-known and well-liked detective working in the Kent Police Force for twenty-seven years. He had seen a lot and encountered many gruesome cases. Sadly, he became a case himself after he lost control of his 1994 BMW 3-Series Sport after driving head-on into a tree on Rose Hill Road near the small town of Mayfield. Mannering factory worker Barbara Edwards, 62, witnessed the white BMW travelling over ninety miles an hour at 4:12 a.m. Mrs Edwards returned to the scene to find that Detective Williams was dead in his car.'

Lydia didn't read the rest before throwing the paper down on the bed. She remembered the way he had looked and acted the last time she saw him. Something had disturbed him. Lydia thought perhaps this was just an accident, but what if it wasn't? She recalled his worried look and the dark bags under his eyes. Something had happened to him before his death, and Lydia believed it had something to do with the videos of her father's dreams. She was scared, but also, she felt an uncontrollable and perhaps deadly desire to see all of the videos. She looked at the worried look on Katya's face and worried about her. *I should have told her to stay in Greece*, she thought to herself. She hated to think of any harm coming to her. She even thought maybe Katya was right. *Maybe this is way too much for me, maybe*. She thought about how they could buy a nice house in Cornwall. Try to get Katya her British citizenship and live in a little Cornish village. Now that Lydia's wild days were over, she would be more than happy to stay in a new house and have a beautiful garden, and Katya — well, Katya just loved Lydia. She only cared about being with her.

"Well," Katya said, bringing Lydia out of her thoughts.

"Well, what?"

"What do you mean well what?" Katya cried out. "Did you not see the newspaper? The policeman died."

"Yes, and I feel very sorry for him, but it was an accident, that's all. He was speeding. It happens." She knew as soon those words came out of her mouth that she wasn't going to just forget about the thieves or her father's machine.

"Maybe you're right, and it was just an accident, but I'm worried, Lydia. I feel like there is something not right about this whole situation," Katya said and Lydia let out a quiet sigh as she moved on the bed next to her.

"Come here," she told her, and Katya lay her head on her shoulder as Lydia put her arms around her, feeling her soft hair touching the side of her face. "Everything will be okay. I will find this fucking thing my crazy dad made, and then when I destroy it, we can look for a home together."

"A home? You mean no more travelling?" Katya questioned.

"Well, we still can travel every now and again, but we will have a place of our own. With a dog, perhaps. You like dogs, right?"

"I love them," she commented.

"Well, in that case, we can have two dogs." There was a short pause as Lydia listened to the sounds of Katya's breathing. "And perhaps a baby."

Katya moved back and stared into her eyes and gave her a questioning look. "A baby?"

Lydia nodded her head slowly. "Yeah, I know you'll be a great mother, and I think I can be one too."

Katya smiled. "You know that neither of us has the right things for making children together," she said, her own statement bringing an amused smile on her face.

"The right equipment, I know," said Lydia with a laugh. "But there are always ways around that."

"I would love to spend my life with you, Lydia, but you have to make me a promise."

"Okay?"

"No threesomes, no more random men or women. You will be mine, and I will be yours, and that's all."

"I thought you liked them?"

"I did, but that was before I fell in love. Now I just want you for myself."

"All right. No more." Lydia said, and Katya leaned in to kiss her, but Lydia put her finger to Katya's mouth.

"But first, I have to fulfil my father's dying wish. It pains me that I wasn't there for him. You have to understand that."

"I understand family is important to you. It is for me too. So, I won't get in your way, but you have to be careful. Don't put yourself at risk, or I'm leaving this country and you, and I won't come back."

Lydia put her hand on the back of Katya's neck and moved her head close to hers, and kissed her lips as they embraced each other.

CHAPTER 23

The early afternoon was the most boring of times for Danny when he would just watch TV. Maybe if he was feeling particularly energetic, he would do some push-ups and sit-ups. Today he didn't feel energetic, but he still didn't feel like watching a film, his go-to lazy day activity. So instead, he just sat on the sofa listening to the mixtape that Emma had made him. The phone started to ring, and Danny knew who was ringing him and knew Mark would be unhappy hearing that he didn't charge Owen for his dream recording. Taking his money would feel dirty. He would have to wash his hands over and over again after touching it, but Mark wouldn't care about that. He couldn't put it off. He had to answer the phone, or Mark would never stop ringing. Standing up, he walked to the phone and picked it up.

"Hi, Mark."

"Danny, did you see Owen?"

"Yeah, well—"

"Well, what?"

"Well yeah, I recorded his dream, but I haven't taken any money off him yet."

"I'm sorry, I think I'm going a little funny in the head here because I thought you said you didn't make any money off him."

Danny sighed and rubbed his head. "Mark, how do you sell a man something he doesn't believe in?"

"This was your idea, your idea to sell people videos of their dreams. Sell being the bloody operative word in this. Please, tell me you got money off the others," Mark screamed down the phone.

"Well, you didn't get me the greatest client, did you? And yes, of course, I made money from the others," Danny argued back.

"Money is money, who gives a flying blue fuck-a-do where it comes from."

"Do you know what was in his dream?" Danny asked.

"No, I don't, and I don't want to know. Mate, I couldn't give a crap. I don't, really don't. He could be dreaming about bringing back Nazi Germany for all I care. We are in this for business. That means profit, money. You know those paper things with the picture of the queen on them? And another thing, it's his dream. People don't pick their dreams, you idiot."

"Well, don't worry, he'll be back, and so will his money."

"He fucking better be," Danny heard Mark shout before he slammed the phone down. Danny also hung up before hearing a child's laughter coming from upstairs. It was the same voice he heard from Owen's dream. He shut his eyes and whispered to himself, "It's not real," and when he opened them, he saw his mother laughing at him as she stood in the hallway in front of the open door with a syringe sticking out of the blue vein in the joint of her arm.

***

Mark slammed the phone down in a rage, screaming out at the top of his voice, "That fucking moron!"

"I take it you are referring to Daniel," Monica said from the doorway that led into the living room, where she also wore a smug look on her face.

"No, I'm referring to the damn Virgin Mary," he yelled at her, his face red with rage.

She laughed and then said, "Well, what did I tell you. This whole selling people their own dream is just foolhardy. You just keep doing what you've been doing all along, and by the way, baby, I have a great job for you."

"You didn't see that dream recorder work as I did," he said, pushing her out the way and walking towards the couch. He sat down, resting his head against the back of it.

"Well, if this machine is so amazing, why are you letting Daniel keep it?"

He stared at her as she stood in the doorway like a statue. "What are you talking about?" Mark asked her.

"We're thieves, are we not? We should just take the machine from him, leave the country and try to make money out of it in America, as you mentioned before."

"I don't steal off my mates," he told her, reaching for the TV remote control and turned the TV onto a Gun N' Roses music video.

"But do you really need him anymore. You're a good enough thief to be working alone," she tried to convince him.

He didn't want to tell her that he feared that he wasn't good enough to rob people's homes without Danny's lock-picking skills. It was like the man was born to be a thief. But the idea of taking the dream recorder for himself had crossed his mind from time to time. Monica was right about one thing — they would have to move country to get any money from it. If anyone knew about the machine, they would realise that he and Danny were in the old man's house the day he died. He wasn't too sure about his chances of getting away with the machine and his freedom. There was also the chance that in their new country, be that the US or any other country, the British could come and force them back to the UK for questioning. He didn't know enough about international law, but he was sure that the government could do something like that. It was a risk, but the inordinate potential of the machine was too much for him to resist.

Still, he had to think things through — it wouldn't be the easy money Monica would like to think. For one, how could he explain how the machine worked or how he came by it?

"Anyway," Monica said, sitting down next to him. "Let's just put a pin in that for the time being because I have a job for you."

"Oh yeah, and what job would that be," he asked.

"You know my friend Lucy, right?"

"Yeah, the black girl," he said, remembering the overweight black woman in the green dress who he met during Monica's thirtieth birthday party. For reasons unknown to him, she had her nails painted in bright orange.

"No, that's Judy. Lucy is the skinny blonde one."

"Oh yeah, I remember, the bird with a chest like an ironing board," he said, now remembering her.

"Typical male pig," said Monica under her breath while rolling her eyes.

"What, she has," he said in defence.

"I don't care. You shouldn't identify a woman by her tits. It's sexist," she moaned at him.

"I remember you saying something similar once about her or some other girl. I don't recall who."

"Yeah, but I'm a woman. I'm allowed."

"All right, all right. What's the job?" he said, just wanting to end the argument.

"Lucy has just found out her boyfriend Tony has been cheating on her. So naturally, she's dumped the dickhead, but she wants him to suffer just a little bit more."

"You want me to torture him?" he said like it was the most normal thing to think, like asking if she wanted milk in her tea.

"No, nothing like that. Just shut up and listen, okay. He's a drug dealer, so naturally, he doesn't want to keep his money in the bank. He has some of it in an unknown location and ten thousand pounds resting in his home. So, what if he was too, I don't know, to lose that ten thousand pounds. What a crying shame that would be." she said, giving him a sinister smile which Mark thought made her look so sexy.

CHAPTER 24

Emma saw the white hallway with brown doors every time she closed her eyes. It was there, a vision in her mind's eye. She tried asking Libby about it but got nothing but confused looks from her. She even asked about Lydia, and still, Libby had no idea what she was talking about. The creature was the only thing she could remember from her dreams. Emma walked with Libby to her school and watched as Libby walked through the gates. She watched the other kids around her laughing, chatting and playing football, none of whom was taking any notice of Libby at all. She took a look around at the other parents, most of them making their way back home apart from one, a skinny pale man who stood across the street.

He was wearing a hood over his head, so Emma couldn't get a look at his face, but it looked as if he was watching not just one kid but all of them. He soon noticed her looking at him, and he quickly walked away. Emma thought of chasing the man down and asking him what he was doing there but then thought that he could be making sure his son or daughter safely made it to school. *Forget it. It's more than likely nothing at all*, she told herself as she walked away from the school. Walking through the busy Monday morning streets with her head down and her hands in her jacket pockets, she had her head lost in her thoughts of Libby, the dream, Danny, and his machine. Where did he get it from? She didn't for a minute believe that he'd found it in a skip, and he wasn't smart enough to have created something like that. He was lying to her, but why? What secrets was he hiding? There was no time to think about him — now more important things were on her mind at that moment. Libby came first, and then she would deal with the enigma that was Daniel Greenway. She took a bus over to the most eastern part of the town, which was also the most rundown part of the town.

Old, abandoned factories filled the area with their dark orange bricks, smashed windows, and long chimneys used to pump out dark smoke into the air. Now those buildings were just a home for the homeless and for those looking to explore creepy abandoned places, but once the site had been the town's financial centre. Not far from the old factories were three large grey and ugly tower blocks with a small playground in front of them. Three teenagers were wearing dark hoodies with the names of new metal bands on them and baggy jeans sat chatting and smoking. Looking at them, she recalled the days when she used to do the same with Steve, Shelly and some of her other friends who have now gone from her life. *Did I, at their age, see myself as a mother with a job and debts?* she asks herself. *No, I was going to be a rock-star, of course.*

The front door to the middle tower block, which was the way to Steve's apartment, was locked. At the side of the door was a metal keypad with an intercom. Emma punched in the number 407 and heard ringing from the intercom before a tired voice answered, "Yeah, who is it?"

"Emma."

"Emma? Is Libby with you?" he said, sounding surprised to hear from her.

"No, of course not. She's at school."

"Oh yeah, right, right," he said, realising now what time it was. "So, what you want?"

"I want to chat to you about Libby."

"All right, come in," he said before she heard a buzz and the door unlocking. Pushing open the door and walking to the lobby, Emma called down the lift and then took it to the fourth floor. The metal doors of the lift slid open, and she stepped out into a white hallway with blue doors, not brown like the ones she had seen in Libby's dream. Each door in the hallway did have the same three golden numbers nailed upon it. Was it the same hallway in her dreams, she asked herself. Perhaps her mind, for whatever reason, changed the colour of the doors — but why? *It was a dream. Do dreams ever make sense?*

She banged on the door with her hand made into a fist, and Steve opened it after the third bang. He had short blond hair with light eyebrows that could barely be seen, and he had on a Kiss T-shirt and grey jogging trousers.

"All right?" he said to Emma as he let her into the flat. The place looked a mess, with cans of beer, two crisp packets on the floor and a dirty ashtray on top of the TV. The only picture on his wall was that of Libby at age two playing in a sandpit. "Do you want a drink or anything?" Steve asked as she stood in the middle of the living room.

"No, I won't be here that long."

"So, what brings you here then?"

"I'm here because we need to talk about Libby."

"All right."

"This place looks like World War Three," she told him as she kicked a can of empty beer out of her way. "I'm not even sure if it's safe to have a child in here."

"Oh god, Emma, I will clean up before Libby gets here. I always do."

"Fair enough," she said under her breath. Steve sat down on his sofa, and then he picked up a packet of cigarettes from a small wooden table next to him. "So go on, Emma, why are you here?" he said, putting a cigarette in his mouth and lighting it with a green plastic lighter.

"Libby has been having nightmares lately."

"Yeah, I know," he sighed, breathing out the smoke.

"Did you know she dreamt about the hallway of this building?"

"No. Did she tell you that?"

"No, not really, and it could have been another building, but it looked like this one."

He gave her a perplexed look before asking the obvious. "Then how do you know she dreamt of this building?"

"I told her to draw me a picture of the nightmares she's been having, and she drew a picture of the hallway just outside that door there," she lied while pointing at the front door behind her. She realised that telling the truth would be foolish, and Steve would just think of her as mad.

"All right, so what?"

"Why would she have a nightmare about this building?" she asked him, but he shrugged his shoulders.

"Not a clue."

"How has she been acting with you?"

"Fine. You know she's a quiet girl but well behaved as always. She has told me about you dating some new bloke. Someone named Dan or Danny, I believe," he stated while he stared at her. He was jealous, and she knew it — his love life was now DOA. He hated that Emma could find another man while he couldn't find another woman.

"Yes, Danny, so what?"

"Well," he said, taking a puff of his cigarette, "it's just funny, isn't it. that you didn't tell me about him,"

"Why would I tell you? The only reason I still see you is because of Libby."

"That's cold. You know that is very cold. We were in love once."

"Yeah, that's before you stuck your dick in the dumbest tart in town who ended up dumping you anyway," she said with a grim expression on her face.

"I made mistakes; I hold my hands up to that. But I'm a different person now. I know what is important to me now. I love you, and I love Libby, and I want to be a family again."

She rolled her eyes and shook her head slowly. "I don't want to hear this."

"You may not want to hear it but it is true. We are better off together, and deep down, you know it. Libby needs her father and mother together." He leaned over and put the cigarette in the ashtray. "So, what do you say? How about we try to get things back together?"

"You're barking up the wrong tree. I have a new boyfriend. Why would I go back to a man that would cheat on me the first chance he gets?"

"I told you, I am a changed man?"

"I don't care. I'm not here to talk about you and me. I'm just here to talk about Libby and how you treat her."

"What does that mean?" he said in shock.

"How often do you shout at her?"

"What?" he said, not quite believing what she was asking.

"Just answer the question please, how often do you shout at her?"

"Hardly ever. In fact, I don't even remember the last time I raised my voice to her."

"Have you ever touched her?" She wondered if she was just jumping to conclusions.

"Have you lost your bloody mind?" he said, standing up, his body tense with rage.

"I need to know."

"You are really asking me if I touch my own daughter. You're sick in the head, you know that."

"Why else would she be having nightmares of your building?"

"I don't know. It's a fucking dream, Emma. I had a dream once that I was in space — that doesn't mean I'm a fucking astronaut, does it," he screamed at her. "Emma, you can say what you want about me. Call me a pig, bastard, every bad name under the sun. I don't care, but don't ever accuse me of doing any harm to my daughter." As he yelled at her, his face turning red with rage, she found her questioning herself. "I love that girl more than anything. I would die for her, and you accuse me of doing things I can't even begin to think about." He walked toward the window and ran his hand through his hair. Through the window, he looked at the grey neighbouring tower block. "I know I upset you, but that is not the type of question you can pull out of nowhere."

"I didn't pull it out of nowhere. There is something wrong with my little girl, and I need to know what it is."

He turned to her with his face full of disgust. "There is nothing wrong with her. You were a wild and outgoing kid, so you think Libby, as she is your daughter, will be just a little version of you, but it doesn't work like that. She's shy. Introvert, I think that's the word."

"She's not just shy. There's something more to it."

"Listen, Emma, kids have nightmares. Some kids believe there is a monster under their beds. It's scary, but it's something they grow out of." He was now speaking more calmly.

"You haven't seen what I have seen," she said, touching her head and feeling the pain of the memory of the video.

"What, a bunch of drawings?"

She let out a long sigh before saying, "It's not just that."

"Did I ever tell you about my brother Adam?"

"Yeah, he died in the Falklands."

"Well, before that. When he was just a kid. He would have nightmares all the time and would see monsters under his bed and in all other kinds of places. My mum and dad took him to doctors, but nothing worked until he just grew out of it one day. The same thing is happening to Libby, and yeah, it's awful, but it is something that happens to some children, and they just grow out of it." He sounded more empathetic now.

"What did your brother's monster look like?"

"I don't know. It was such a long time ago."

"Think."

There was a short pause while he went back to the sofa sitting back down. He then remembered. "Oh, a tall skinny man with jet black skin. Like a shadow."

Emma felt cold — it was the same creature. "How did he get rid of it?"

"He just outgrew it. Like I said."

CHAPTER 25

Danny sat on a crate recording the dream of one of his clients. A cold chill filled the garage, and Danny knew it was back again, along with the sound of a little girl's laughter. He slowly turned his head, seeing the little girl in the pink dress standing in the corner of the room. No longer dancing, just staring at him with a large cut on the top of her head with a red line of blood dripping down the side of her face. Quickly he looked away at the sleeping man on the table and found his mother standing in front of him staring at him like the little girl.

"It has hold of you now. My little Danny boy," she whispered to him before he heard the ceiling cracking right above his head. He slowly looked up, seeing the creature pushing itself through a dark hole and smiling its wide yellowish smile. Danny jumped off the crate quickly, knocking it over, and waited for the creature to drop down, but it never did. Looking up, he saw the dull grey ceiling with no holes in it and there was no sign of his mother or the little girl.

Danny then looked at his watch, realising that it was time to wake his client up. The client paid for the dream. Danny went back out into the alleyway to wait for the next one. However, still, he felt his body shake with the fear that any of the three entities could show themselves again at any moment. His eyes went straight to a homeless woman sitting down across the road with an old and ripped blanket over her. He felt the money in his pocket and recalled all the times he wished he would change his ways. He walked over to the woman who asked, "You've got some change, love?" in a cockney accent.

"Sure," he said, taking out his cut of the money his last client gave him and handing it over to her.

Her eyes widened in shock as she saw the notes. "Thank you, God bless you," she said in delight.

"I hope he does," Danny said before walking back to the alleyway.

It was early in the morning when Lydia woke up from a nightmare that she couldn't quite remember. Only that the deamhan dorcha was chasing some little blonde-haired girl through a narrow alleyway, but everything else had gone from her memory. Lydia wondered would she use the dream recorder if she had it to try and find out what happened to that little girl, not that the girl was real in the first place. Still, it could be fascinating, if not too horrifying, to discover the outcome that her mind had created or what the deamhan dorcha created. What a ridiculous thought. She told herself the deamhan dorcha was nothing but a psychological effect. Her mind clearly formed the creature because she had been reading about it. It's like people who said they had seen a ghost in an old house or Bloody Mary when saying it three times in the mirror.

She turned her head and looked at Katya, who was still sleeping at her side. The digital clock at the side of their bed read 5:23 a.m. Katya would often only wake up around nine o'clock. Ever so slowly, she got up and got off the bed, got dressed, put her shoes on and walked out of the room without waking Katya. She moved on through the empty corridors of the hotel, took the lift down to the first floor and went out of the building and through a large car park. The street was quiet as the grave — there were no sounds of traffic or people talking, just the sound of the wind blowing through the trees in the nearby park. She put her hands in her pockets and walked down the empty street, listening to her footsteps and looking at the different buildings as she passed, first at the shops with their shutters down and then at the homes of people she had never met. She wondered who was in them and what their dreams were, what stories had they had to tell.

She walked up to the garage where she had seen the thief who called himself Mr Crow. Who was this, Mr Crow? As she looked down the dark alleyway, it gave off a foreboding sense of dread. Grabbing hold of her keys, putting each key between her fingers to use as a makeshift knuckle duster, she thought about walking down that alleyway. Still, for what reason, Lydia asked herself. It was early in the morning — the thieves were unlikely to be there, the door would be locked, and even if they were in and the door was unlocked, what would she do then? Hit them with her keys? No, she needed her grandfather's gun — there was no other way.

***

Peter was woken up by the loud knocking on his front door. Juno, who was in his bedroom with him, ran back and forth, barking in anticipation of finding out the mystery of who it was that was waking them up at the early hours of the day. "All right, all right, girl," he said to her while getting up out of bed, still wearing his white pyjamas. As he walked downstairs, the knocking got louder and louder. "All right, all right, I hear you," he yelled at the door before taking his keys from the small table just at the bottom of the stairs. He unlocked the door and opened it, seeing Lydia standing in his doorway. "Yes?" he asked her with a sigh, making it clear that her visit wasn't particularly welcome at that time.

"You sound so happy to see me. Your very own niece. I mean, can I not come and see my loving uncle?" she said bitterly.

"I guess so," he said as he got out of the way of the doorway, letting her into the house. "Do you have any idea what time it is?"

"Around half seven, and sorry if I woke you, but I need your help," she said as she closed the door.

"Right," he sighed as he walked into the living room with Lydia following closely behind him. "I'm having a coffee. To wake me up a bit, you want one?"

"No thanks," she said as she followed him to the kitchen and watched him switch the kettle on.

"What kind of help do you want?"

"I think you know, and I don't ask you for free. I want to make you an offer."

"Oh aye," he yawned and looked at her.

"I need granddad's gun, and I'm willing to buy it off you."

Peter folded his arms and looked at her. "Oh, this again, not a chance," he said, just before the kettle clicked off. He picked up the kettle and poured the hot water into the cup while letting out another yawn, which resulted in Lydia giving out her own yawn.

"You haven't heard my offer yet."

"What's your offer?"

"Five hundred pounds."

"No."

"I will pay you a grand for it then."

"No," he said as he walked past her to the fridge, taking out a bottle of milk, and walked back to his cup.

"Okay, how about one thousand five hundred pounds?"

"Nope," he said without looking at her, pouring the milk into his coffee.

"Two thousand," she said, getting more and more annoyed with her uncle.

Finally, he stopped what he was doing, turned to her and finally Lydia thought, *I've got the gun*, until he said that little word she was starting to hate — "Nope."

"Then what then."

"You can't have it. Do you think I would let my niece risk her life over nothing at all?"

"It's not nothing, and how about three thousand?" she told him as he put the milk back in the fridge.

"Lydia, you need to listen to me. I know since you have come back, we haven't seen eye to eye with one and another, but I'm telling you this because you are my brother's daughter, and you are all that is left of him and because I care. Forget it. Forget all of it. Go back to your pretty Russian and enjoy your youth because, believe me, it's not going to last forever." He picked up his cup and walked past her into the living room.

Lydia stood alone in the kitchen, thinking about what she should do next. He could be right, she thought — both Katya and Peter wanted her to forget it, but this was the last thing her father asked her to do, how could she refuse him. She thought of ways she could convince him to give her the gun, or perhaps there were other ways of getting firearms or some other type of weapon. Did she really need a gun? Maybe she could just break into the garage, but it was more than likely the dream recorder wasn't stored there? She walked back to the living room, seeing Peter turning the television on and lying on his sofa.

"What would you do if he gave you his last request?" she asked.

He turned around and looked at her. "I guess I would do it, but I'm an old man, not a young girl with her life ahead of her."

"And what life would I have if I spend the rest of it thinking about how I failed my own father? I am already drowning in the guilt of what happened to Vicky."

"That wasn't your fault. I was wrong with what I said last time."

"No, you were right, I want to do my family proud, and it was my idea to go to those woods that day in seventy-eight. You tell me I should just forget about it and move on with my life, but I can't do that without thinking about how I wasn't here for my dad or my little sister."

He sighed, looking over to Juno. "Why couldn't I just have been born in a normal fucking family."

Lydia smiled at that, finding it funny. "I'm always thinking the same thing."

"In my bedroom, there is a wardrobe, and in that wardrobe, there is a safe. Put in the code one, nine, zero, seven, and you'll find the prize that means so much to you."

"Thank you."

"Don't thank me for this."

She went upstairs to his bedroom and towards the large wooden wardrobe in the corner. Opening it, she found loads of shirts hanging on metal coat-hangers. Below them was the metal safe with its number lock. Getting on her knees, so she was now at face level with the safe, she put in the number Peter had told her. The safe opened, and inside were two shelves — the top one had three rows of £20 notes wrapped in a rubber band, and on the bottom was a plastic bag. She took out the bag and reached another hand inside, and pulled out the gun wrapped up in an old newspaper that had turned yellow with age.

A sickly feeling grabbed hold of her as she unwrapped the old yellow paper, revealing the dark Browning 9mm with its wooden grip. She stared at it with fascination and horror. *How many people did Granddad kill with this weapon?* she thought to herself. She pulled out the clip and checked it, seeing that it still had its bullets in it. She put the clip back in, wondering if there was somewhere she could see if it still worked without attracting any attention. Lydia was sure it still worked and was only planning to use it to scare the bastards. She didn't want to kill anyone, but the thought came into her head, *Could I kill if it came to it?*

CHAPTER 26

Emma knew Danny had to work nights, meaning there was no time for him to come over, but she did miss having his arms around her as she lay in bed. Unable to sleep, Emma listened to the sounds of Libby moving around in bed as she slowly closed her eyes, seeing the white corridor with the brown doors in her mind's eye. When she opened them again, she was back in her dark bedroom, listening to the sounds of footsteps coming upstairs. Her heart started to race as her door slowly opened. In horror, she sat up and stared at it, telling herself it was just the wind, but there was no wind — so if it wasn't the wind, what was it? It was a question that sent chills down her spine. It wasn't until the sound of heavy breathing came from the open door that she stopped telling herself that impossible lie.

Then she saw it. The jet black hand with long skinny fingers grabbing the side of the doorway. Frozen with fear, she only watched as a tall and overly thin man with a face that looked like it was stretched at the bottom and the top of it walked into the room. It had a bald head, a long smile with black lips and bright green eyes she had ever seen. It was the creature from Libby's nightmare — but what was it doing here, and why could she see it now? It slowly moved its long skinny finger to its long black mouth, simply making the sound 'shh' before walking back out of the room as the door slowly shut itself.

Then she woke up to the sound of Libby screaming. Jumping out of bed, she quickly ran as fast as she could into her daughter's room. She could see she had her eyes still closed, but she was screaming out loudly in pure terror. Emma called out her name as she sat on her bed, shaking her to wake her. Libby opened her eyes that were wet with her tears. "Mummy," she cried, wrapping her arms around Emma and resting her head on her shoulder.

"It's okay, baby, I'm here, I'm here," Emma said softly as if she was catching her breath.

"Why me!" she cried. "Why is it in my dreams?"

"I don't know, but I won't let anyone or anything ever hurt you," she told her, holding her even tighter. "I love you, monkey, and I won't ever let any harm come to the ones I love." And out of the blue, she thought that maybe she was focusing on the wrong thing when it came to Libby's dream. Perhaps the hallway meant nothing at all; the monster and the mysterious woman were the things Emma should be more interested in.

CHAPTER 27

D anny sat crossed-legged on the floor, much like Libby did the first time he was invited to Emma's home, staring at the television and watching his own dreams play out in front of him. The house could be burning down, and Danny wouldn't have even noticed. On screen, he could see himself. It had been some time since his recorded dreams were in his POV. He remembered hearing that seeing yourself in a dream meant that you felt that you were losing control of your life, but when was he ever in control was more the question.

In the dream, he found himself walking out of his house. He saw Edgar sitting cross-legged in the middle of the road. He was facing an old seventies' television with the grey screen surrounded by the wooden casing with three plastic nobs by the side of the screen, one to turn the TV on and off, one for volume and one for changing the channels. The video made Danny feel uneasy, primarily due to how Edgar was sitting just like him in the real world.

"Hello, Daniel," Edgar said, looking back at him. His face was white as a ghost. His eyes were also pale white like the eyes of a dead man.

"Hello," Danny replied, and with that, Edgar smiled and looked back at the television.

"You do know there's nothing on that screen, right?" Danny told him.

"Just because you can't see something doesn't mean that I can't see it."

Well, that is a good point, Danny thought, but it was the Danny in the real world. The one who was unable to be heard by the dead Edgar. If it was Edgar to start off with and not just Danny's twisted mind.

"You don't look so good, Daniel," Edgar said, never turning away from the television.

"You're the one to talk."

"You've seen it outside of dreams, haven't you?"

Danny didn't need to ask what he was referring to, and a chill ran down the actual Danny's spine. "Yes," he whispered to him. "What is it?"

"When you were a child, did you ever have a monster under your bed or see the boogieman?"

"No, I had real monsters in my childhood."

"Really. That is interesting," Edgar said, looking back at him with a questioning look.

"Just please tell me what the creature is," he begged Edgar

"I don't know for sure, but after my death, I gained more understanding of the world. The creature is a demon from the underworld."

"You mean hell?"

"In a way, yes, but not like you read in the stories with fire and brimstone. I can't tell you what the real underworld is like. No living man should ever know such things, but I can tell you this world that you live in is one of many dimensions. Some have great horrors and sometimes something can escape its dimension and not be able to find its way back."

Dream Danny then heard terrifying screaming coming from Emma's house. Quickly he turned around, looking at the house, which seemed no different than it did in the real world apart from a strange red glow coming from the windows. He turned back to Edgar only to find that he was standing in the middle of the road on his own. Even the old television had disappeared. As fast as Danny could run, he ran to Emma's house, kicking the door open with ease. The house's interior glowed red like the walls of hell itself, and chains like the ones you would find in a steel mill moved up and down the walls, for what purpose he couldn't say. Still hearing the screaming, Danny ran upstairs. Towards Libby's bedroom, where he saw Emma trying to wake Libby up with the creature, unbeknownst to them, standing by Emma's side, staring down at Libby. The video then stopped, and the screen went back to static.

"What the hell!" Danny cried out to the VCR, looking down when it had stopped at only 00.42.45. He tried pressing play again, but nothing happened, and then he moved back as he saw smoke coming from the top of the machine. "Shit, shit," he cried out and then quickly unplugged the machine and stared at the grey smoke coming from the top of it. He then jumped at the sound of someone knocking on his door. He dropped the plug down on the floor and walked to the front door, unlocking it and opening it to find Emma standing at his doorway. She looked as tired as him. There were small dark bags under her eyes, and her hair was tied up tight into a ponytail.

"Hey there," she said with a fake and tired smile. "Libby's at her dad's."

"Right," Danny said, feeling half asleep himself.

"Can I come in?" she asked, Danny then wondering why he hadn't invited her in in the first place.

"Yeah, sure, sorry," he said, bouncing back into life and reality. Walking into the living room, Emma could smell the burning. She looked back at him and asked, "You been smoking again?"

"No, my VCR has," he said, pointing to the machine which was letting out its last bit of smoke.

"What happened to it?"

"Hell, if I know. I was just watching something and bang, it started, uh, I don't know, just blowing up."

She looked closer at it and asked, "Were you watching another dream?"

"Yeah."

"What was the dream about?" She turned back to him, facing away from the broken VCR. She could tell by his hesitation that he didn't want to say, so she asked him another question. "Was Libby's monster in it?"

He sighed and slowly nodded his head.

"Yeah, I also dreamt about the monster last night," she told him as the image of the creature standing at her doorway re-entered her mind.

"You did?" Danny asked in surprise. "Only in your dreams?"

"Yeah, of course. Why do you ask that?" she said with an uneasy feeling, and Danny wondered how she would react if she knew what was going on in his head — would Emma be scared, run away and call him a mad man or would she support him? He didn't know. He decided to tell her a half-truth. "No reason, just a random question."

"Uh," she said, raising one eyebrow. But of course, Danny would be a fool if he actually believed that she believed him.

"There was no way you were going to believe that was just a random question, were you?"

"Not really, no." She looked at the broken VCR and back at him. "I'm already worrying about Libby. Should I start worrying about you too?"

He moved closer to her, softly touching her cheek, feeling her soft skin against his hand. "You don't ever have to worry about me."

She grabbed his hand and moved it from her cheek. "Then, for me, don't record any more dreams. In fact, don't even buy a new tape recorder."

"But what am I going to do with my Blockbuster card?" he japed, trying to make light of the matter.

"Don't joke about this, not about this. I don't know where you got that machine from."

"I told you."

"You told me a lie, and it is my hope that one day you trust me and that you will be honest with me," she said, sitting herself down on the sofa. Danny wet his lips, feeling uneasy once again, wondering how she would react when she found out what kind of man he was. Danny then thought that if he kept too much from her, he would lose her like he did with his past girlfriends. Emma was special to him, but Danny wasn't sure he could truly trust her. It could cost him dearly, but with a long sigh, he began.

"All right, I will tell you everything." She looked at him with interest. "First of all, everyone knows me as Daniel Greenway, but that wasn't the name I was born with. My birth name is Daniel Hammond, and I was born in the East End of London. I never knew my father, but my mother was a drug addict named Danielle. I guess she wasn't good at coming up with names," he said with a smile that quickly faded from his face. "My mum would rob people to feed her addiction. Once she went a little too far and killed someone in an off-licence. I don't know-how, and I don't want to know. But the idiot that she was, she left a load of fingerprints all over the damn place, and soon the police knocked down her door. They were greeted by filth, rotting food and used needles, and of course, another locked door. They had to see what was behind the door, so naturally, they knocked down that door as well. When they entered, they found a child's bedroom with a little boy who was all skin and bones, who barely had the energy to stand, wearing clothes full of dried food and

210

vomit. Holding the only toy he had, an old brown teddy bear. They later found my dear mother in the river. It seems as if she topped herself. The best thing she ever did for me."

"Then what happened to you after that?"

"I was put up for adoption, and I got adopted by a great couple who couldn't have children of their own. They moved me to this town and showed me love like parents are meant to do, so I took their surname, but I had too much of my mother in me. I started hanging out with this older kid Mark who I am still kinda friends with, and then the life of crime followed me. I became a thief like my mum, only I was good at it and not a drug addict, thankfully, unless you count the fags."

"So, you nicked the dream recorder?"

"Yeah, from a dead man," he confessed, and her eyes widened in horror. "I didn't kill him. We found him dead in his bathtub. Suicide, he cut his wrists open."

"Oh God," she whispered and covered her mouth with her hand. Then she moved her hand back down, but her mouth was still open as she said, "The day I invited you into my house. I had lost my pager, and you found it for me. Did you find it, or did you steal it?"

"Technically, I borrowed it." As soon he said that, she slowly stood up from the sofa. "I'm sorry I only took it, so I had a reason to talk to you."

"You steal from a girl to get her attention," she said with a confused look.

"I'm an idiot. I didn't know what else to do," he said, trying to convince her that he never wanted to hurt or steal from her.

"I'm gonna go home. I need to think things through," she told him as she walked past him.

"Emma, please, I'm sorry."

She stopped and looked at him. "I know, but I need time to think."

He stood in the middle of the living room as Emma left the house, wondering if he had made a foolish mistake.

CHAPTER 28

Lydia spent the day after her visit to the garage jogging in the morning. In the afternoon, she would go with Katya and take a train down to the Cornish town of Falmouth. She and Lydia looked at the windows of estate agents at the multiple homes for sale. Katya picked out a two-floor modern looking home with a view that looked out to the English Channel. She could see herself having a short walk from that house towards the beach, and once at the beach, she could imagine herself watching the sun go down while having a glass of wine. On days when the sun was shining, Katya would lie there, soaking in the rays, working on her tan. Lydia wondered if she could afford such a place; after all, her father was the wealthy one with the money to burn. Perhaps she could borrow money from one of her father's friends and start a business of her own. She was an intelligent woman, she thought, and she had money to invest.

Still, all the same, her mind kept going back to the thieves. Why, she would ask herself, why did she care so much? If she could talk to her father now, he would say to leave it and not put herself in danger. Lydia was barely listening as Katya spoke about the house and told her that they should go and visit it. Katya convinced her without much effort to go in and speak to one of the estate agents.

"I think Falmouth would be the perfect place for us," Katya told her as she grabbed hold of Lydia's hand. Lydia just smiled and agreed.

***

Emma found herself walking up and down her living room, thinking about Danny as the radio played a collection of her favourite songs. It was true that he was a criminal, and he stole from her. There was no way she could ever count what Danny did as borrowing, that would be absurd, and yes, she thought, to trust a thief like him would also be absurd. Now in the kitchen, watching the boiling kettle, batting her fingers against the counter, Emma thought about his smile and his eyes and how he'd nearly given over his secret before he actually did by telling her about the dream recorder. He did that in his belief that it would somehow help Emma to combat Libby's nightmares for her. If her life had taken another road, would she be a thief like him? Could she even do worse if she had to? Emma dreaded the thought, but she could not deny that she had a love for Danny.

Emma turned off the radio and stared at the wall that separated her home from Danny's. She closed her eyes, imagining his body, her fingers running down his chest as she reached out to the wall softly, putting a hand against it. As soon as she opened them, she knew that she needed him in more ways than one. She picked up her keys and marched out of the house, and banged her fist against Danny's door. When Danny opened the door to her, the look of shock was evident all over his face.

"Emma," he said, and he was about to try to explain himself, but the words were lost. Emma wasn't here for words anyway. There was no need for them here, no need whatsoever. She grabbed hold of his T-shirt and pulled him towards her lips. Her hand ran up his back as they moved into the house, kicking the door shut behind them. He moved from her lips and stared at her as he caught his breath. "I thought you would be mad at me."

"Shut the fuck up, Danny," she said, staring at him with lust in her eyes before going back in for another French kiss. "Let's go upstairs," she told him before she walked up the stairs.

Danny's eyes followed her while his legs and mind were still trying to process what was going on. Standing halfway up the stairs, she looked back down at him, calling out, "Well, come on then." His mind jumped into gear and told his legs to finally get a move on. Once he was on the top of the stairs, he followed her into the bedroom as she took off her top, throwing it on the floor next to his bedroom door. Once in the room, she turned to him, and his eyes went straight to her breasts which were still covered in her black bra. He took off his clothes as she pulled down her trousers, leaving herself in only her black underwear and white socks. They embraced each other before Emma turned them around and pushed him violently onto the bed, straddling him.

"I want to hate you, but I desire you too damn much," she told him just before he grabbed hold of her breast, and she unhooked her bra, pulled down his boxers, and she stood up pulled down her knickers. Taking hold of him, Emma put him into herself with a satisfying moan. He felt her body as she moved up and down on him. Her skin felt warm and soft against his fingertips. Just as he started to think that things were going right, he heard the heavy breathing of the creature. *Please God, not now*, he thought to himself as the walls around them seem to darken.

"I feel you too," he heard the croaky invisible voice say.

"Get out of my head," he whispered, making Emma stop and stare at him.

"What did you say?" she asked him.

"Nothing, don't stop," he told her, sounding out of breath, and she kept going, placing her hands on his chest and moving her hips. He looked at her face and at her body, trying to focus on her and nothing else, but in the back of his mind, he could hear the creature laughing at him.

"She's too good for you, boy," the voice taunted him as he tried. He closed his eyes, saying in his mind, *There is only you and Emma, you and Emma, you and Emma.* When he opened them, he saw Emma's brown eyes had turned yellow. Her once white teeth were darkened and rotten.

"No!" he whispered, but Emma kept going.

"Be quiet, lover," Emma said, showing her rotten teeth as she moved her hand on his chest. The pain hit

216

Danny. He felt Emma's fingers digging into his flesh, followed by the warm wet feeling of blood dripping down his side. He could feel her cold fingers now inside him, pulling at his rib cage. He let out a most horrifying scream of agony. Emma, not understanding what on earth was going on, jumped off him and stared at him in horror. He came back to reality, saw her naked at the end of the bed, looking at him with a scared look on her face and her body shaking. He quickly looked down at his chest and saw no wound and no sign of blood.

"I'm sorry, I, I can't do it. I'm so very sorry," he said, his eyes filling with tears.

"It's okay, you don't have to be sorry," Emma said, sounding sympathetic. But she worried not just for him but what had happened to make him this way. So she moved closer to him and was about to hold on to him when he shouted out, "No, please, just leave me alone!"

"If that's what you want," she said, getting off the bed and picking her clothes up off the floor. She put her knickers back on and picked up her bra before she stopped and looked at him again. "I need to know what happened?"

"I saw it!" he cried.

"The monster?"

He just nodded his head slowly before he told her, "It was you. You were killing me, and I knew it was in my head, but I could feel it as if it was real."

Emma was dumbfounded — she didn't know what to say.

CHAPTER 29

Emma called around for Danny, knocking on his door and even trying to let herself in, but all to no avail. She knew he was hurting and wanted to care for him as much as she did for her daughter. She had planned to find out about the creature with him. Instead, Emma just headed to the King George Mayfield Library alone; located in the town centre, it was a large building with a clock tower on top of it. It was built in 1764 and was one of the most well-known parts of the town, which wasn't saying much for Mayfield.

She walked into a large room full of bookshelves with signs on top of them telling visitors which genre of books was located on which shelves. At the end of the room, there was a row of computers with a map of the world pinned up against the wall behind them. Only one other person was sitting at the computers, playing what looked to be an 8bit video game where he was controlling a yellow spaceship shooting at other spaceships. He was a small red-haired man wearing a dark blue coat and baggy jeans. Emma sat on the fourth computer, moving the mouse to turn off the 3D maze screensaver only for it to become a log-in screen.

"You need to be a member of the library to use the computers," the man sitting on the other computer told her.

"Right, do you know how I do that?" she asked him.

"Yeah, you have to sign up to get a library card. Go and ask Mel to sign you up."

"All right, thank you," she said, standing up from the chair and walking from the computer, and the man then went back to his video game. Walking around, she found a woman with long grey hair, wearing a brown jumper, stacking the fantasy shelves and putting the books alphabetically, starting with the author's surname. "Excuse me," Emma called out to her.

She stopped what she was doing and turned to Emma. "Yes?"

"I take it you're Mel?"

"That's right."

"I was wondering if I could sign up for a library card?"

"Yes, of course, dear, if you would like to follow me," Mel said, walking away from the books and towards a small desk on the other side of the room.

"You just moved to Mayfield?" Mel asked her.

"No, I've been living here my whole life. It's just now I decided I want to make use of the library."

"Ah, I see," Mel said with a smile as she got behind her desk and opened a metal draw. Then, she pulled out a big green notebook that she opened up on the seventh page and put it in front of Emma and a silver pen. "If you would like to just put down your name and telephone number on here." Emma wrote them down and handed the pen back to Mel, who in turns handed her a card with the name of the library printed on it.

"Can I use the computers now?" Emma asked her.

"Of course, my dear, your username and password are just on the back of your card."

Emma turned the card over and saw 'WN2567' and under it, it said 'password: whiterabbit84'.

"Thank you," Emma said to the librarian before walking back to the computers and putting in the password and username, and then entering the web browser and quickly entering the search engine. She put her fingers on the keyboard and stared at the screen, not knowing what to type. The first thing that came to her was 'recurring nightmares in children',

The first website she clicked on told her everything the child psychiatrists had already told her. Useful for some, but it was no good for her.

Going off that, she went down the list of websites, and it was on the second page where she found a link about a dark man in your dreams. She clicked on it, and the first thing she saw was a painting of a tall man all in black standing over a sleeping woman with the name of the painter, Andre Faucheux, and the year he painted the picture, 1679. She moved the page down and read what was written under the painting. 'There are many sources of information on the dark creature throughout history — the earliest description was found on a tablet near the city of Rutba, Iraq. It is believed that it dates back to the 2nd century AD and that it describes the creature as a demon that appears as a tall old man.' She continued to scroll down, seeing the famous painting by Henry Fuseli that she remembered seeing in high school so many years ago. The picture was very similar to the one she had seen before — it showing a woman laying on a bed, but the woman looked like she was in pain with a small goblin sitting on her chest and a creepy-looking black horse in the background with white eyes.

"Are you searching for the deamhan dorcha?"

Emma heard the red-haired man say with a questioning tone to his voice. She slowly turned around and looked at him with a confused look on her face. "I'm sorry, what?"

"Is there a child you know who is having dreams about a tall man or woman?"

"Yeah, my daughter. Have you been watching me?"

"I used to have the same nightmares," he told her ignoring her question as he moved away from his computer and sat next to her. "A few of us did. It's the deamhan dorcha."

"A few of you had these dreams?" she said in surprise.

"Yes, Mayfield is a hot spot for the creature. Many people who dreamt of it as children don't talk about it. Others go insane before they even reach adulthood, spending their lives in asylums thinking that the deamhan dorcha is coming out of the walls." The look on his face told her that he instantly regretted what he said. "But I'm sure that won't happen with your daughter."

Ignoring that, she said, "You said Mayfield is the spot for the creature, but this site tells me they found a tablet about it in Iraq?"

"Well, yes, of course," he said as if what she had said was idiotic. "It has existed for a very long time — no one really knows how long, though. That tablet is the earliest information about it. Still, it is believed that it existed a long time before that tablet was ever created. There are hot spots for the creature all around the world, from the Americas to Asia. But of course, Mayfield isn't the only place in the UK. There is also a sighting of it in a town in Lancashire, I believe, and in northern Scotland, where it got its Gaelic name from, but you needn't worry, the creature does disappear when the child reaches puberty."

"But my boyfriend has been suffering from the same nightmares," she tells him.

"That's impossible — it only terrorises children. I never heard of it affecting adults."

So the dream recorder released it, she thought to herself.

"Is there anything else you can tell me about it?"

"Well, it wasn't just me who dreamt of the deamhan dorcha, but also my grandmother dreamt about it when she was a kid. She spoke about it at some length, and I remember how she described it. Slightly different to how I saw it."

Emma now understood why Danny said the creature sounded female — he saw something different to her.

"But affecting children the same way with nightmares and visions of itself. It has also been said it can possess those with weak minds, although I have never met anyone where that has been the case."

"Okay, but how do you get rid of it?"

"You can't. You just outgrow it, or it drives you into madness."

"That won't work. I can't tell you why that won't work but believe me, it won't work. There must be a way to kill it," she said in a panic.

"None that I know of, but I know someone who may know," he told her. He took a piece of paper out of his pocket and a pen from his other pocket and wrote down an address. "Go to this address and tell them Colin sent you. He knows much more about it than I do."

"Okay, Thank you for this."

"No problem."

"It's a strange coincidence that you would be here when. I am researching this," Emma told him with a friendly smile.

"Not really. I'm here every day. I can't afford a computer of my own."

CHAPTER 30

Danny and Emma stood in the kitchen as Emma waited for a pizza to cook in the oven. "I called around for you earlier, but I got no answer. Where were you?" Emma asked as she leant her back against the counter.

"I was sleeping," he replied.

"Well, as you were sleeping, I found a little more about the monster in Libby's dreams." With that, she got Danny's full attention. "It turns out that it is some kind of demon that has been terrifying children's dreams for many, many years. There was even a thing about it from the second century."

"Where did you learn this?"

"The library."

"And did you learn how to kill it?"

Emma didn't actually have to say a word. He could tell the answer from the look on her face.

"No, not yet. I was told that you just have to outgrow it."

"Well, that's good news for Libby. It was the videos that let it enter my mind," Danny said his worry for Libby now slightly diminished while his worry for himself and Emma slightly increased.

"Yeah, that's what I thought as well, but why has it not affected me in the same way as you?"

"Perhaps because I've watched more of them than you or perhaps because of my past," Danny said, and Emma could see the fear written all over his face.

"There must be a way to defeat it, though, and maybe the person whose address I have in my pocket could help us."

"Who?" Danny questioned.

"I don't know, I got it when I was at the library, but I'm going to find out after I have made Libby's dinner, I will drop her off at Mrs Peterson's house. I think she's a trustworthy woman, and I will go to that address. Will you come with me?"

"Yeah, of course, I will."

"Also, you know we could destroy the dream recorder. Maybe it is somehow tied to that machine."

"It would make no difference. As you told me, it was around long before the machine was invented and even long before you and I were born."

"But how do you know that. Seriously, how do you know?"

"Emma, the creature is already on the loose. Destroying the dream recorder would do nothing now. It's like trying to get rid of a poisoned banana by destroying its peel."

"That was a terrible metaphor, Danny."

"I know, but the point is clear," he said before they heard a kitchen timer go off. "The pizza is ready. Would you do me a favour?"

"Sure."

"Libby will be lost in her games, so can you go and get her?"

"Oh, yeah," he said nervously.

"Don't worry, she doesn't bite. It's only me who bites," she joked.

He gave a friendly smile pretending that she was actually funny. However, he did wonder if she was taking the piss out of him for the last time they tried having sex. *No*, he thought, *Emma wouldn't do that*. He walked upstairs to Libby's room, seeing the open door, and Libby sitting crossed-legged on the floor with the control pad in her hand, hearing the strange music and sounds coming from her television.

"Hey, Libby," he said, leaning on the doorframe. "What you playing?"

"Mario," she told him without looking away from the TV.

"Right, did you see the film?"

She paused the game and looked at him with a confused look on her face. "There's a Mario film?"

"Yeah, it was rubbish, nothing like the games. Listen, your mum wants me to tell you your dinner is ready," he told her.

She nodded her head slowly and just as he was about to turn around and go back downstairs, she said, "Danny."

He turned back to her, saying, "Yeah?"

"You will never hurt my mum, right?" She said it so quietly that Danny barely heard her.

Danny was also shocked by what she said. He slowly walked towards her and kneeled to get to her level. "No, I love your mother more than anything in the whole world. I would never hurt her or you. I understand it's scary for your mum to be dating someone you hardly know but believe me, you have nothing to worry about with me. I promise," he said.

She just stared right into his eyes and Danny could see fear there, but it wasn't fear of him but something else and then she whispered, "You've seen the monster, haven't you?"

He looked at her in shock, and in that shock, he could only say one word: "What?"

"The monster I have seen in my dreams. I think you have seen it too."

"Did your mum tell you?"

"No, she doesn't like talking about it."

"Then how do you know that?"

"Sometimes, I just know things," she told him, and questions flew into his head. *Can she see the monster right now? Can she read minds, or does she just know we recorded her dreams?*

"But how?" he said in confusion.

Libby's answer came with a shrug of her shoulders. "What are we having for dinner?"

Danny was busy thinking about what she had previously said and didn't pick up what she asked him. "What was that?"

"What's mum made us?"

"Oh, pizza."

"Are you having some?"

"If that's okay with you," Danny said.

She shrugged her shoulders again, saying, "It's fine with me," before walking past him.

CHAPTER 31

Emma and Danny took a taxi across town towards the address that Emma was given. They watched as they pulled up outside a row of terrace houses, one of which had the English flag up in the bedroom window while another across the road had boarded up windows from when some scumbag had smashed them, and they all had a small garden at the back. They were identically built across Britain and Ireland with thin walls and not much living space for the third-class worker ants of the Great British industrial revolution. "Thanks," Danny said, handing the taxi driver his fare.

"Cheers, mate," the driver replied as they got out of the car.

Danny asked Emma, "What number is it?"

"Thirteen."

"Of course, unlucky thirteen. That gives me hope," Danny said with a faint smile.

"I never took you as a superstitious man."

"Neither did I, to be honest. It's funny what a demon can do to your beliefs," he said as they walked to the door with number thirteen painted on the door with white paint. Emma wondered what happened to the little metal numbers the rest of the homes had. Had they been pulled off? If so, why? Danny knocked on the door, and after a few minutes, he looked at Emma. "Should I knock again?" She replied by just nodding her head. Then, just as he was to bang on the door again, he heard it unlock and took a step back as the door opened.

They saw a small south-east Asian woman with long black hair wearing a red woollen jumper and denim skirt, which showed off her skinny brown legs. She looked at Danny with suspicion while hardly taking notice of Emma.

"Hi, uh, we were told to come here," he said, lost for words.

"Colin sent us," Emma told her.

The woman put her index finger up, which they both took as one minute as she walked back into the living room, leaving the door wide open. They could hear her shouting to someone inside the house in a language they didn't know, but they took it as Thai or Vietnamese or somewhere around that area. A skinny white man with blond dreadlocks, wearing a dark green shirt over a black T-shirt and jeans that looked way too big for him, stood in the doorway with a strong smell of weed coming off his clothes. His eyes went to Danny and then darted to Emma as she told him, "Colin told me that you can help me understand my daughter's dreams."

"Maybe, come in," he told her, and just as they both were about to walk into the house. He put his arm toward Danny and said, "Not you."

"What?" Danny asked, and Emma stopped at the side of the man with dreadlocks.

"I said, you can't come in."

"Hey, albino Bob Marley, I don't trust you, so she's not going anywhere without me," Danny said, facing off against the dreadlocked man.

"Then sorry, love, but goodbye," the dreadlocked man said to Emma.

"No, please." Emma said in a panic. "Danny, I'm a big girl. I'll be okay. Just wait for me out here, yeah?"

"Are you sure about this?"

"Yes, I'm sure."

"All right, I'll wait here then. It's a good job it's not fucking raining," Danny moaned as they walked into the house, closing the door on him.

Emma and the dreadlocked man walked into the living room. The Thai woman was sitting watching the TV playing Bjork music videos on mute on a black and white television, and the walls were all painted red with a poster in the middle of one of a blue monkey-like creature wearing a golden triangular hat upon his head. It showed two large, sharp teeth coming from the bottom of its mouth like upside-down tusks. The woman could see Emma staring at the poster and told her in perfect English, "It's a Yaksha. They're famous spirits in Buddhist mythology."

"Are they good or bad?"

"They can be both. But they are very mischievous."

"I think I dated one once," Emma japed, which the woman didn't reply to or show any emotion to. Emma wondered if the stupid joke had offended her, "Sorry, bad joke," she said.

"Please take a seat," the dreadlocked man told her, and Emma sat next to the woman as the man stood over them. "You know you should be careful around that man," he told her.

"Who, Danny?" she asked him.

"Yeah, Danny," he confirmed.

"Why? He's a decent man."

"I am not speaking of his character, only that he has a demon attached to him to his soul."

"Deamhan dorcha," Emma muttered.

The man nodded his head before saying, "It is a rare thing for it to follow a fully grown man outside of his dreams."

"He got it after recording my daughter's nightmare." Seeing the confused look on their faces, she instantly regretted mentioning the dream recorder.

"What do you mean, he recorded her nightmare?" the Thai woman asked.

"Nothing, a figure of speech, I meant after learning about my daughter's nightmares."

"In any case," the dreadlocked man said, "the deamhan dorcha has him. A child can be fine after such a thing, but an adult would be driven into insanity, and death. For some people with a dark heart it makes them more violent with less care for human life. Let's hope he hasn't got a dark heart. There is worse. It can take control of a person's body."

"How?"

"If he gives it permission to do so."

"Well, I doubt Danny is that stupid to do that."

"Never underestimate the stupidity of man."

"But there must be some kind of ritual to get rid of it?" Emma said, sounding desperate for answers.

"A ritual," he replied as if it was the stupidest question he had ever heard. "This thing is from another dimension, nothing to do with any religion known to man or even scientific law. The only thing that mankind truly knows is that they know nothing."

"If we know nothing, then what am I doing here? Why have I come to speak with you?"

"You are here for hope, and there is still hope for your daughter."

"And Danny?" she asked him.

"His best hope is that he can keep the deamhan dorcha as just as a voice in his head, but that seems unlikely."

That was not what Emma wanted to hear. She sighed and prayed for the unlikely outcome of the creature just being a voice in Danny's head and nothing more. "There's another thing my daughter has been dreaming about, and that's a strange woman named Lydia who I don't think she has met in real life. I surely don't know who she is."

"A human mind is a great machine, but it can't create faces it hasn't seen before. So that woman could be someone she has seen while in school, or she could be someone she knew in a previous life."

Emma laughed. "So Lydia could be some girl she knew while she was fighting lions in the Colosseum?"

"I won't go that far back, but as I told you, there is more to our reality than we know about," he told her, and now she was thinking of how she was just wasting her time.

"Well, it's fascinating," she told them as she got up off the sofa. "But now I think I'd better go out to Danny."

"Do you want to know why I'm in Mayfield?" the Thai woman said, but Emma had just assumed she was a mail-order bride or had just emigrated to the UK. Nothing more to it. There were a lot of Thai women living in the town. After all, Emma's own mother was born in South Korea. Emma nodded her head, wondering what she was going to say. "Mayfield wasn't the first place in Europe I lived in after moving out of Thailand. I moved to Belgium at first but kept dreaming about this man," she said, pointing to the dreadlocked man, "and of this little town. After months of having these dreams, I decided that I had to find the town and the man, and when I did, I knew that was the exact place I belong and with the exact person I was meant to find."

"So, my daughter is meant to find this Lydia? If that is the case, then how do I find her?"

"She may find you, or you may both find each other by accident, but either way, your daughter is meant to find this woman," the dreadlocked man told her.

Emma, in her confusion, said, "But why?"

"Who knows such things."

234

"And earlier, you told me that the deamhan dorcha is from another dimension, so how on earth did it get into my daughter's dreams?"

"Most of the time, a dream is nothing more than your mind creating images for you but sometimes, they are gates into another world. These gates are always locked, just letting you get a view of what is on the other side but not letting you through."

"But the deamhan dorcha has the key?"

"It can enter a person's mind. Yes, it is far more powerful than any human being."

"And it can't be killed?"

"Some things are just immune from death."

"How exactly do you know all this?" Emma asked him, and the dreadlocked man sighed.

"Tell me what's the most famous murder case in Mayfield's history."

Emma had to think about it for a small town. There were quite a few murders in the town's history. There was a man from the Victorian era whose imaginary friend told him to eat his wife. She always remembered hearing about that one which made her feel sick to her stomach but surely, he couldn't be on about that one. Then she remembered about a little boy murdering his parents. "There was a boy who killed his parents in the fifties or sixties. I can't remember which."

"Sixties, the boy's name was Henry Winters. He was a quiet boy who didn't have many friends and suffered from the most terrifying nightmares. He was weak but also had a gift, you see, so the deamhan dorcha was able to use his body to murder the only people he cared about."

Emma looked at his hand, seeing it shaking to his side and came to the realisation that she was talking to that little boy. "You're Henry Winters?"

"I am."

Emma had no idea what to say. She couldn't believe that she was in the house of a man who had killed his own parents.

"I can sense your fear. However, you have no need for it. It wasn't me who murdered them but the demon controlling me."

"But why would it want to kill your parents?"

"For its enjoyment perhaps or perhaps because I have a link to the other world."

"What do you mean?"

"Sometimes I know things I shouldn't know, like your daughter's name, Libby Holland."

"You know my daughter?" she said in shock.

"Not personally. I remember a girl by that name in my dreams, and I knew as soon as I saw you that you were her mother."

"You told me earlier that you see strangers in your dreams because you have some kind of link to them, so what is your link to Libby?"

"I thought you would have figured that out. Unfortunately, she's just like me, which means you've got to be careful."

"Are you saying my daughter will try to kill me?"

"The deamhan dorcha took control of me. I see no reason why it can't do the same to Libby."

"This is insane," she called out. "Libby is not a killer, and she definitely wouldn't try to kill me. I'm sorry, I don't mean to be insensitive, but she's not you."

"My mother and father would have been saying the same thing about me."

When Emma went back out to Danny, she told him everything they said about Lydia but nothing about what they had said about him. In her mind, she felt it would be wrong to worry him.

CHAPTER 32

D anny waited in the alleyway next to the garage. Every now and again, he saw the figure of the creature from Libby's nightmares standing at the end of the street, staring at him. Each time, Danny told himself that there was nothing to be afraid of, but still, the feeling of dread filled his heart. He wondered who would come today — would it be Owen again? He hoped not. No matter how much Owen was willing to pay, watching his dreams again wouldn't be worth it.

"Are you on your own, Danny boy," he heard his mother's voice say in his head. He ignored it and kept walking back and forth from one wall to the other. "It's cold out here, Daniel, so very cold," the voice told him, and he felt a bitterly cold wind hit and started to feel the hairs on his arms raised and his body shake.

"Shut up," he whispered as he rubbed his hands together for warmth.

"You can't shut me up. I'm in your head, boy, and I will always be in your head from now on."

He took his hat off and ran his hands through his hair, wondering what he could do. Then he heard the sound of the metal door behind him unlocking quickly — he turned around and watched the door open. For a moment, he feared that the tall creature would come from the building, but instead, he saw Mark dressed all in black. "Mark, how long have you been in there?" he asked, feeling the shock of seeing him coming from the building, which he believed was empty.

"I just pulled up in the van. How the blue fuck did you not hear it?" he asked him, with a confused look on his face. It was a question Danny didn't have an answer for. "Are you feeling all right?"

"Yeah, I'm good," Danny told him, but Danny believed that Mark wasn't at all convinced by his answer.

"I hope so, mate, because I have a job for you."

"What kind of job?"

"Come inside, and I'll tell you."

"What about the Mr Crow work?"

"No one is coming today, mate, come on in." He held the door open for him. Danny stepped through the door and watched as Mark closed the door after him and locked it.

"Why the hell is no one coming? You remember you were meant to get the word out, and I'm the one who records the dreams and sells them."

"Well, not tonight."

"What are you talking about? I'm the dream merchant — I can't be the dream merchant if I haven't got any customers, can I."

"Yes, but the definition of a merchant is someone who sells things. Not someone who gives them away for free,"

Mark moaned, still feeling angry by what he saw as Danny's stupidity with Owen.

"I already told you. He will come back. It's a basic marketing strategy. You give someone a sample of what you are selling, and they get hooked on it," Danny told him.

"Sure, it is," Mark said sarcastically as he walked toward the van that was parked up in the garage near all the crates.

Danny thought to himself how glad he was that he had put the dream recorder in his coat pocket and not near the television as he had done before. He put his hand in his pocket and held onto the machine. "So why are you here then?" Danny asked him.

"I have been told about this bloke, a drug dealer. A right bastard from what I have heard."

"You should get on quite well with him, then."

"Shut up and listen. Monica's little birdy has told me that he keeps ten grand in his home. Of course, the money would be split between you, me, Monica and her mate who told us about this bloke. Now £10,000 divided by four is £2,500. That's not going to make us rich by any means, but it is all right for a day's work. Wouldn't you say?"

"And who is her mate?"

He sighed and slowly shook his head. "Oh, some black girl, I don't know, I forget her name. I think he cheated on her or something. I wasn't really listening when Monica told me."

"So, we're back to stealing then." There was a hint of disappointment in Danny's voice.

He gave Danny a look of confusion. "When did we stop that life? I didn't, and I know you haven't because mate, what else would you do? Be Mr Crow, the dream merchant? Please don't make me laugh."

"But we've been doing all right with it."

"Yes, you will go back to recording people's dreams. This just a one-time-only thing."

Danny thought about it, and yeah, £2,500, along with whatever items they could take, could make a good score. Mark picked up Danny's backpack from the floor and handed it to him. "Here, it's got all your lock picks and whatnot."

"So, we're going to do this now?"

"Yeah. Why, have you somewhere else you have to be?" Mark said, putting his backpack on.

"I don't think I'm dressed for it," he said, looking down at his old coat and feeling the fedora on his head.

"Oh, do you want to wear your little red dress, sweetheart," Mark said in a mocking tone, trying to sound like he was talking to a little girl. "We're going robbing a cunt, not going for tea in the bloody Ritz. Just leave that coat here."

Danny thought, *So your bitch of a girlfriend can steal the dream recorder.* There was no way anyone could make him part with the machine. "I think I'll keep the coat on, thanks," he said, touching the machine that was still hidden in his pocket. He took the fedora off, though and left it on one of the crates.

"As long as it's not going affect the job, then fine, whatever."

As Danny and Mark were talking in the garage, Lydia was on her way to the alleyway. The gun was resting in her coat pocket, and her fingers gently touched its handle. She ran through what she was going to say to Mr Crow when she finally got to him. It was like an actor trying to remember their lines. She only just managed to jump out of the way as a white van drove past her, almost splashing her as it went through a deep puddle.

"Fucking prick," Lydia yelled at the driver, who took no notice of her. She even pictured herself taking the gun out of her pocket and shooting at the van. A stupid thought, of course, and Lydia would have never done it. Perhaps it was the dark side of her personality that she would like to keep hidden from the world. The scary thought that entered her mind was what would happen if a violent fantasy became a reality one day. What if she did actually pull the trigger on Mr Crow? He must have friends and family, and murder wasn't something she could do. When she got to the alleyway, Mr Crow was nowhere to be seen. She slowly walked down the alleyway, hearing only the passing cars from across the street and the sound of her own footsteps. There was nothing there, just her and the metal door that Lydia knew Mr Crow would go into. Knowing that it was a long shot, she tried to open the door and failed and stood for a short moment thinking about what to do next — should she walk back to the hotel and to Katya or wait for him.

As the van passed, Lydia thought of them as just strangers, faces without a name and to Mark, it was the same feeling. Danny had another feeling towards the young woman walking on her own. He turned his head as they passed her, hearing her shouting at them, but he could not make out what she was saying. Danny felt like he knew her but didn't get a good look to see if he did or didn't for sure. As soon as the girl went out of his view, he felt a familiar feeling that something wasn't quite right. A feeling that something terrible was about to happen. He looked at Mark, who kept his eyes on the road and his mind on the job. Danny just couldn't understand why he was so nervous, given he'd robbed people since he was in his late teens. Perhaps it was the creature, he thought to himself, though he couldn't hear it or see it at that moment.

CHAPTER 33

Mark pulled up near a two-storey detached house with a silver Jaguar parked in front of it, which instantly caught Mark's eye. "Will you look at that beauty?"

Danny looked at the car, agreeing it was a beautiful machine, but still, he didn't want to be here. He wanted to be back in that alleyway, selling dreams. Danny looked at Mark, finding himself wondering if he still needed him, if he was, in fact, now holding him back. He then looked at the house, his eyes scanning it for CCTV cameras, guard dogs and anything else that could be a threat to them. He saw no cameras and no dogs, nothing.

"So, are you ready?" Mark asked him.

"You want to rob this place now?" he said, turning to him.

"Yeah, why not."

"It's a big house, nice car. I have to say I can't see any alarm system, but that doesn't mean there isn't one."

"Monica said he's new money, and from what I have heard, he isn't that smart," he said with a yawn. "So, are you ready?"

"Yeah."

"Then let's rock 'n' roll," he said just before both of them got out of the van and walked towards the back of the house. The back garden wasn't what Danny expected; there were hardly any flowers, and the grass was long and wild like it hadn't been cut for months, maybe years. Within the wild grass was a small pond with dead fish floating on the top of the water, along with a used condom and bottles of beer visible at the bottom of the pond.

"Think this cunt needs to get himself a gardener," Mark commented as Danny got down on his knees in front of the door, taking out the right lockpick. He put the lockpick in the lock and moved it about, trying to find the sweet spot and all the time worrying about the dream recorder, which was still in his pocket. He knew Mark could easily pickpocket him. He wouldn't put it past him to hit him over the head, knocking him out, and take the dream recorder for himself. Maybe that was why he was here; perhaps it was he who was the one being robbed, not the resident of this house. Danny moved the lockpick around, trying and trying to find the click that would open the door, but yet it would not come. Perhaps his mind wasn't on the job. Maybe he just wasn't ready.

"What's taking so long?" Mark asked him.

"Quiet. I'm trying to think," Danny hissed at him.

"Think about what? You've done this a million times."

"And a million times, I have told you that each door is different. It's like a woman — every one of them has their own sweet spot."

That statement made Mark let out a short hiss of laughter. "Now you have a girlfriend, you think you're an expert on women."

Finally, after moving the lockpick about for what seems like a good twenty minutes, he heard the click and pushed open the door. Entering the kitchen, they could hear the soft sounds of a man snoring. Danny moved ever so quietly into the living room and saw a middle-aged man lying on his back on his sofa. His hand hung off the side near where an empty beer bottle lay. Danny looked at Mark, who was standing behind him. He put his finger to his lips, telling him to keep quiet.

"You look upstairs," Mark whispered.

"What about you?"

"I'll look down here."

"Be careful."

"Yeah, sure and same at you."

Danny moved past the sleeping man. His eyes stared at his hanging hand before he left the room and headed upstairs. Upstairs, Danny could still hear the sound of the man snoring. He didn't know why, but fear had its grip on him like a cold embrace from an unseen entity. He felt as if something wrong was about to happen. Perhaps it was going to be the day they got caught. His hand reached into his pocket, feeling the dream recorder with the tips of his fingers. The first place he looked was the bedroom. It had a king-size bed, large walk-in wardrobes, and a photo of a smiling woman above the bed. She was next to the man who was sleeping downstairs, standing on top of the

Empire State Building with the New York City skyline behind them. He ignored the picture and started looking through the wardrobes and through the set of drawers. He was about to move when he picked up a pillow and felt something hard in it. He took the pillowcase off and threw it on the floor, seeing the twenty-pound notes duct-taped around the pillow. He smiled to himself before ripping the duct tape off the pillow and watching the money fall onto the bed. He picked up a handful of twenty-pound notes and put them in his pocket, feeling the dream recorder still in there. With the money in his hand, he moved to another pocket and placed them in there.

He stopped before picking up another bunch of twenties as he started to hear the dripping of a tap. He listened to the sound of the dripping water dripping into what seemed like a full bathtub and the man snoring downstairs. He quickly put more money in his pocket and ambled towards the bathroom, leaving only hand full still on the bed, thinking he would return for it after investigating the sound. His heartbeat increased as he pushed the door slowly open, seeing a bathtub full of dirty brown water. Danny stood in the doorway, staring at the dark water, wondering why it was here. What had the man downstairs been doing to get the water that dark and dirty? He started fantasising about unplugging the bath, a strange fantasy indeed, he thought to himself. He turned around and heard someone calling his name from behind him and within the bathroom. Turning around again, he saw nothing other than the empty bathroom.

"Daniel." He heard the voice again, but this time he could identify it as his mother's that voice, that croaky but somehow sweet voice. In the back of his mind, Danny knew that it wasn't his mother's voice, but the impulse to walk into the bathroom and look into the dirty water was too irresistible. Slowly he moved to the bathtub, looking into it, still hearing the voice from inside. "Daniel, do you see me?" A whispering voice came from the dark water without any suppression of the sound. The other voice inside his head told him to move away, but as if his legs were glued to the floor, he could not move.

With a loud splash, a green-skinned thin arm came out of the dirty water, grabbing hold of Danny around the throat. He found it hard to breathe as he felt its long nails digging into his skin. The voice changed to the very similar croaky voice of the creature, saying, "Your mummy never loved you," then he was pushed back with some force, making him fall on his back with a loud thud as he hit the floor. Rubbing his neck, he stood back up, looking at the now clean and empty bathtub. The voices were now gone but replaced with faint voices coming from downstairs. *Oh God*, he thought — the sleeping man downstairs had woken up.

Mark was looking through a small set of drawers under the television. He saw random and useless objects — a roll of Sellotape, photo albums and CD cases without the CDs. He then heard a loud thud coming from upstairs, the sound of something heavy falling on the floor. "Fucking idiot," Mark whispered to himself. He didn't know what had fallen on the floor, but he knew it was Danny's fault.

"Who are you?" He heard a terrified but angry voice coming from behind him. He turned around and saw the once sleeping man standing in front of his sofa staring at him, his eyes wide and full of confusion and fear.

"Uh," Mark said, lost for words as his hands moved to the flick knife he kept in his trouser pocket, and his eyes moved to the glass bottle in the man's hand.

"What are you doing here?" the man demanded of Mark, as he held tightly onto the neck of the bottle. "I asked you what are you doing here?" the man yelled at him as Mark's fingers continued to feel the flick knife. The man took a step towards Mark, and quickly he took out his knife and flipped it open, revealing the silver blade.

"We're only here for your money, not your life," Mark told him, showing him the knife, making sure he knew he had it.

"You think I'm going to give some prick my money? You'd better leave now," the man hissed.

"Mate, you've got a bottle. I have a knife, and a mean and angry cunt is just upstairs right as we speak. I know who my money would be on. Or should I say, yours." Mark then noticed the man's eyes move from him to the doorway. Mark, without thinking, turned around to look behind him, seeing Danny with a worried look on his face.

"Watch out!" Danny shouted to Mark. Mark, without a moment's thought, quickly turned with the knife in his hand. He came face to face with the shocked looking man.

He heard the glass bottle fall to the floor. Mark looked down at his hand and saw the knife stuck in the man's chest. At first, Mark was shocked by what he had done, but as the man coughed up blood, a killer instinct in a very literal sense came to him. It was his fault, Mark told himself — it was him that ran at me. He pulled the knife out and watched as the man fell to the floor. He looked at the blood on the blade not with horror but with fascination.

"What the hell have you done?" he heard Danny gasp behind him as both of them looked at the man lying on the floor, taking his last breath.

CHAPTER 34

"It was a mistake but one that isn't just on me, but on you too," was the first thing Mark said to Danny as he saw the body of the man they were robbing.

"On me, how?" Danny said in shock.

"You woke him up by doing whatever the hell you were doing up there," Mark yelled, pointing his bloody knife towards him.

"I was finding the money," Danny said, panting as if the horror of the evening was exhausting him.

"And where is it?"

"Where's what?" Danny said, his mind and eyes on the dead body and his hand in his pocket feeling the dream recorder.

"His porn mags, did you find any?" Mark said sarcastically before raising his voice. "The money, you moron!"

Danny nodded his head. "Some is in my pocket the rest is still upstairs in the bedroom." he said in what was almost a whisper.

"All right, good, now listen to me," Mark said before noticing that his eyes were glued on the body. "Hey," Mark yelled at him, bringing Danny out of his daydream and getting his full attention. "Wake up and listen to me and listen good, mate, because shit has got really fucking serious. So, first things is first. We get what we came for."

"What?" Danny whimpered. "What about him?"

"I'm getting to that. Then we'll take the body into the back of the van, and we'll drive to the woods and bury him somewhere no one will ever find him. There is a shed out back, you remember it?"

"I remember."

"We get in there and see if there is a shovel." They did as Mark said and walked upstairs to get the rest of the money.

As Mark put the last set of notes in his pocket, he looked at Danny, and Danny looked back at him. "What was the thud?" he asked Danny.

"What are you talking about?"

"I heard a loud thud coming from upstairs. Like you dropped something."

"It was me. I tripped over my, uh, shoelace," Danny said with nerves still shaking.

"Your shoelace?" Mark questioned him as he looked down at Danny's tied shoes. "Listen, mate, you better get your head out of your fucking arse and start acting like a professional again because I can't work with amateurs. You know that." His eyes were glued into Danny's eyes.

"I know, and it was just a mistake, that's all."

"No, a mistake is burning the toast, putting orange juice in your tea — this isn't a mistake, it's a fucking disaster which you are responsible for." There was a moment of silence as Mark stared at Danny, and Danny started to wonder if he actually knew his friend. "It's not just me who has blood on his hands. You understand what I'm saying?"

Danny clearly understood what he was saying, and he knew he had no choice but to help Mark bury the body. They went back downstairs, and Mark looked in the dead man's pockets and found a set of keys. With the keys, they walked to the wooden shed at the end of the garden. They tried three of the keys until they finally got the right one. Mark shone his torch into the shed and saw it was full of power tools and cobwebs, but it didn't take him long to find what they were looking for. He shone the light towards the shovel resting against the back of the shed. "Get it," he ordered Danny, who did as he was asked, picking up the shovel.

After putting the shovel in the back of the van, they moved back into the house and picked up the body, Mark grabbing hold of the shoulders and Danny the legs. He was a lot heavier than Danny thought, and touching a dead man made him feel sick to his stomach. They put the body in the back of the van, and Danny waited for Mark to climb over it to exit the vehicle's rear. They shut the van's back door. Danny reached in his pocket to grab a cigarette, only then realizing he hadn't got any. His mind for only a moment went off the body in the van, the dream recorder and the monster to wondering when the last time he had a cig was. Had Daniel Greenway actually quit smoking without even realising it — if so, how was that possible?

Besides the power of recording people's dreams and putting monsters in his head, he didn't think the dream recorder would help one to quit smoking.

Mark tapped Danny on the shoulder. "Come on, we'd better get moving. The sun will be up in a few hours."

On the short drive into the middle of the woods, neither of them said a single word to one another. In the van's headlight, Danny kept getting visions of the tall, dark creature watching them. They stopped in an area surrounded by tall trees. Mark kept the lights on, shining it into the place they were going to dig, handing the shovel over to Danny, and saying, "You dig."

"Why me?" he protested.

"Because your stupidity is what killed the man."

"I wasn't the one who stabbed him, was I."

"No, you weren't," Mark said, and he pulled out the knife, flicked it open. "And you know what, I still have the knife."

Danny looked at the blade and saw the blood still stained on it. "So, you're gonna stab me now?" Danny bickered.

"Well, it has been a funny kind of night, hasn't it? Who knows what's going to happen next."

Danny sighed, grabbed hold of the shovel's handle, and began to dig and dig as Mark watched.

"You know what," Mark said, sitting on the ground watching his friend dig the grave. "Killing someone isn't as difficult as you would think."

Danny stopped and looked at him.

"We'd better keep digging, mate, it's not long until sunrise."

"You mean I'd better keep digging," Danny hissed, feeling the sweat dripping from his forehead. It was no good, he thought. Danny had to take his coat off before he fainted. He took it off along with the shirt he was wearing underneath, leaving him topless. He thrust the shovel into the ground, and Mark, seeing that Danny's attention was on the digging, turned to his coat, seeing the dream recorder sticking slightly out of the pocket. He quickly looked back at Danny, who was still busy digging. He stood up and moved slowly to the coat, taking the dream recorder out of his pocket and looking at the small black object with its wire hanging from it.

"Put it down," he heard Danny hiss in anger. He turned around seeing Danny standing in the grave, holding the shovel as if it was a shotgun.

"I was just looking at it. Don't worry, I wouldn't steal off a mate," he said, putting the machine back in Danny's pocket. It was only when Mark walked away from the coat and the machine that Danny kept on digging. Once the grave was deep enough to hide a body, Mark gave him a hand out of the grave, and they both threw the body in, covering it back up with dirt. Once the grave was covered and they were satisfied that it would be hard for any nature lover and dog walker to notice it, Danny finally got to have some rest. Catching his breath, he stood over the grave, wiping the sweat off his forehead while Mark listened to the birds singing to bring in a new day.

"I think maybe I should say something," Danny said.

"What you on about?"

"Uh, you know, like a prayer," Danny panted.

"I didn't know you were religious."

"I'm not. I'm just trying to be decent, you know."

"You're a thief like me — we're not decent people."

"Oh yeah, well…" Danny sighed, staring down at the dirt in front of him. "Uh, shit." Lost for words, he looked up at the dark sky and then back down at the grave and heard the creature's voice.

"There is nothing decent about you. You are scum just like your mother."

He ignored the voice and stood still and quiet before realising that he didn't know any prayers. There was nothing for it, he thought, he would have to make his own, "Sorry you're dead, and I hope there's a heaven, and I hope you're in it, amen, I guess." If there was a heaven and hell, he knew he would end up in the latter and he even told himself he would deserve to burn in it.

"Wow, that's so beautiful, really beautiful. Have you thought about writing poetry?" Mark said sarcastically before walking back to the van, leaving Danny standing next to the grave. "Are you coming or what," Mark shouted back to him.

Once Danny returned home, he jumped into the shower and washed all the dirt from his body. He looked down at his hands as if he could see the blood still on them. The blood that could never wash off. Sure, he didn't kill the man directly but caused the death and hid the body in a strange case of causality. He felt the hot water washing over his body, and he felt like the bathroom was darker than it actually was. He looked down at his toes and saw five small cockroaches climbing from his drain. He didn't get scared or jump out of the shower — instead just closed his eyes, and when he reopened them, he saw that the cockroaches were gone, as if they ever existed in the first place. When out of the shower, he saw the dream recorder resting on his bed. He had almost forgotten he put it there.

The day before, he had got a new VCR as he knew he couldn't quit the dream recorder. It had replaced his last addiction that was cigarettes. Maybe one day, he would have no desire for anything else, not even Emma, only for the dream recorder. He lay in bed, still unable to believe that his friend had killed someone, and that was when a memory came into his head.

He was twelve years old, and he was reading a Batman comic in his bed as he heard something hitting against his window. At first, he ignored it, just thinking he was hearing things. Until he heard whatever it was hitting his window once again. Finally, looking out of his window, he saw Mark, aged fourteen, with a full head of messy brown hair. Danny opened his window, shouting down to Mark. "Hey, what are you doing?"

"Your mum won't let me in. Come out. I want a chat."

"All right, hold on," Danny shouted back to him. He moved downstairs, hearing his adopted parents watching *Coronation Street* in the living room. He slowly opened the front door so they wouldn't hear him, and he stepped outside where Mark was waiting for him, Danny only then noticing his blackened eye.

"Come on, let's go to the park," Mark told him, and Danny as always just followed. The park was in the centre of the town, not too far from the cul-de-sac where Danny and Mark lived. Mark and Danny sat on a bench in front of a duck pond for a moment. They just sat there not saying anything before Danny asked him the question he already knew the answer for. "Did your dad do that to your eye?"

"What do you think," Mark replied bitterly. "The bastard was drunk again. I guess that's no surprise, eh." Danny didn't say anything as he had no idea what to say. "Sometimes I think of running away from that arsehole and from this fucking shithole town."

"I like this town," Danny told him.

"Well, you would you are from some nob cheese area of London. Actually, you know what I really want to do?" he asked Danny as he pointed his fingers at one of the ducks like his hand was a gun. "I want to fuck this town up, burn it to the ground."

"Like Nero watching Rome burn while playing the flute."

"God, Danny, you are a geek but yeah, just like that."

"Maybe we can eat marshmallows while doing that. Cook them on the school," Danny told him, and Mark smiled.

"Have a barbecue on the library."

"If we had the Death Star, that would be even better," Danny said with a smile.

"Yeah, I could be Darth Markus the feared, but no, I'm serious. I want to fuck this place up, destroy it all, I think you are the only person I like in Mayfield, and you're not even from here," Mark told him, and this time Danny didn't make any jokes. He wanted to say something comforting, maybe telling him about his mum would help, but for whatever reason, the words just refused to leave his mouth.

CHAPTER 35

After giving Danny a lift home, Mark drove straight back to his own flat. He looked at the sun rising in the sky and wondered how long would it take for anyone to notice that the man he killed was missing. Had Danny hidden the body as well as he thought — would he be finding himself in a prison cell by the time the week was out? He parked the van in the garage and went on a short walk towards his flat. When he got to his floor, he unlocked and opened the door before he slammed it shut.

Monica woke up. "For fuck's sake," she called out as she jumped out of bed, wearing her pink pyjamas. "What the hell is going on?" she cried out to him as she stood in the doorway, her hair looking wild and her acne that she would always hide with makeup on full display.

"The job didn't go as well as I hoped," he told her calmly before he wet his dry lips.

"Did you get the money?"

"I did."

"Was you caught?"

"Kind of."

"What do you mean kind of, you was, or you weren't? There is no kind of," Monica puzzled.

Mark answered the only way he could think of by taking out the knife and showing her the stained blood on the blade. He didn't need any words; the bloody knife spoke as loudly as any words could ever do. She put her hand over her mouth like she was going to be sick.

"Oh god," she whimpered.

"It's all right. There's no need to worry. We buried the body. No one will find it."

"You killed him," she screamed.

"Hey, a little louder I don't think they heard you in France," Mark moaned at her.

"Listen to me," she said, now more calmly, but her eyes showed how afraid she was. "That man was Lucy's ex-boyfriend — when the police come looking for him, who do you think they will ask first, and do you really think Lucy can keep her mouth shut? I sure as hell don't think she will."

"Don't worry about it. She will keep her mouth shut. I'll make her keep it shut," he said, looking at the knife.

"Oh yeah, will you kill her too?"

"Perhaps."

"So, you're a killer now, eh?" she questioned him

"I'm just a man who does what he has to do."

"What about Daniel?" she said in almost a whisper.

"He's, my friend. I have known him since I was a lad."

"Lucy is my friend," she said, moving towards him. "But when shit hits the fan and I believe shit has hit the fan and it has hit it hard, there are only us two who matter, no one else." She touched his warm face softly.

"I should have taken the dream recorder," he said, closing his eyes and imagining himself holding the machine in his hand. Monica removed her hand from his face before saying, "What do you mean?"

"I had the perfect chance to take it."

"But you didn't take it?"

"Obviously not"

"You complete fucking moron," Monica hissed.

"Don't call me that."

"Do you not realise that machine could be our ticket out this shitty flat? Live wherever we want, do whatever we want but no, like the moron you are, had to just fuck it up."

With that, Mark couldn't take any more, and he grabbed hold of Monica's throat, pinning her against the wall with one hand and with the other, he held the knife close to her right eye. Monica, for the first time she had known Mark, felt afraid of him.

"I told you not to call me that," he said.

Monica's eyes were wide, not just in shock but in horror. "Okay, I won't," she whimpered.

He moved his hands, letting her go and exhaled like he was catching his breath. "I'm gonna have a bath. Would you be a doll and make me some breakfast?" he said to her.

She slowly nodded her head before walking to the kitchen. He thought about catching up with her and apologising to her, but he found himself unable to do so. Monica was the only woman he had ever loved, but he was also enjoying the power the night's events made him feel.

He put the knife back in his pocket before walking into the bathroom and ran a bath for himself.

CHAPTER 36

While Lydia went on her morning jog, Katya wondered how good the breakfast at the small café across the street was. She had told Lydia that they should have breakfast there many times. Lydia said to her that she remembered going there before she left the UK and that the food tasted like cardboard but all the same, Katya just liked the look of the place. The café had three sets of chairs and tables outside with flower baskets hanging near the sign that said its name, 'Little Coffee House', which was an odd name. It wasn't really a big café, but it was definitely not the most petite café she had come across.

She went inside and ordered a cup of coffee, a bacon sandwich and a croissant. Although the weather was pretty cold, she still sat outside as she ate her sandwich and drank her coffee.

"Katya." She heard Peter's voice calling her. She looked up, seeing Peter walking Juno on a lead; the dog was panting, her long pink tongue sticking out of her mouth.

"Peter, what are you doing here?"

"Just walking the dog." Katya found this explanation to be a little suspicious as it was a long walk from his home. "You mind if I take a seat?"

"No, not at all." He sat at the table across from her. "You don't want to order anything?"

"No, not really. I won't be here that long. By the way I have been wondering where you learned English?"

"School. People think that we weren't allowed to learn other languages but Russian in the Soviet Union, but many people learn English, French and German. I always was interested in the west. My mum and dad only wanted to visit other Eastern Bloc countries. I would save up my own money so one day I could visit the west."

"Did the Soviet government let you go to western countries?"

"Yes, but it was frowned upon and you need to get permission. Anyway, that didn't matter. I only started travelling after the collapse."

"I see," he said as he scratched Juno behind her ear. "You have any siblings?"

"No, there is just me," she said, remembering that as a child wishing that she could have a little sister.

"I'm the youngest out of three boys."

"Three," she said in confusion, thinking that there was only him and Edgar. "Yeah, Benjamin was my other brother's name. He died in the war. I was the only one of the Knightley brothers who didn't fight. I was too young. I guess that was the reason why I always wanted to be the one to keep my old man's shooter."

"Shooter?" Katya asked.

"A gun, the same gun Lydia has." He could see the shock on Katya's face. "You know Lydia, she's impulsive, highly tenacious, and she isn't as smart as she thinks she is. She's going get herself hurt."

"I know," Katya said with a heavy heart. "I mean, it is what I am afraid of."

"Me too. You know I never thought I would ever get to meet a lesbian Russki, but I'll tell you what, I'm glad I did, and I'm glad Lydia did too," he said with a smile. Katya didn't know how to reply to that, so she just watched as he stood up from his chair. "Well, we'd better be going, hey girl," he said to Juno, and he walked off with Juno at his side.

"Peter," Katya shouted to him. He turned around and looked at her. "We have plans for the future. Even a baby, of course, the baby can't be completely mine and Lydia's, but all the same, when we have the baby, I would want you to be the godfather."

"Thanks, sweetheart," he said, smiling back at her. "I would like that, but I doubt it would happen, but if you get that baby, don't let them grow up in Mayfield. This town has a darkness to it."

"What do you mean, a darkness?"

"Nothing. I'm just an old man saying strange old man things. Do svidaniya, Katya." He walked off, leaving Katya wondering what on earth he meant by a darkness.

CHAPTER 37

Emma noticed something different about Danny as they sat in her living room watching TV. She could see that his eyes weren't on the television but staring out at nothing. "Danny?" Emma said, and he blinked, bringing himself out of his daydream.

"Yeah?"

"You all right?"

"Yeah, it was a long night, last night."

"Why, what happened?"

"You don't want to know."

"Yes, I do. Tell me," she told him, wishing that he could just open up to her. She loved him, and she didn't believe or just refused to let herself believe that he was a danger to her as Henry told her, but all the same, the way he was acting was starting to worry her.

"Just difficult clients, need the loo." As he stood up from the sofa walking upstairs, Danny noticed Libby's door open once again, seeing her sitting on the floor playing on her video games. "Hey," he said to her, and she looked over to him, pausing the game.

"Hey," she replied.

"Can you see the monster now?" Danny asked, wondering if because he can't see it or hear it at that moment that it was actually gone. Was he momentarily free of it? The uncertainty seemed to terrify him even more than if the creature was in his direct eye-line.

She shook her head before saying, "That doesn't mean it's not here, though."

"Right, can I come in for a minute?" Libby nodded her head, and Danny stepped into the room, looking at the paused game, which looked to be a 3D platfomer. "When did you start seeing the deamhan dorcha?" He asked.

"What?" Libby replied. Danny then realised that she may have not even heard that name before.

"The monster."

"Oh, I don't know, for a long time now, but I have always been a freak."

"What do you mean?"

"That's what everyone at school calls me. I guess they're right."

"Hey," he said, kneeling down to face her. A way to be on her level to make it easier to be more comforting as he remembered his adopted parents doing to him so many years ago. "Don't tell yourself things like that. You are not a freak. Ignore those fools at school or wherever. Some people are so sad and weak-minded that the only way they can make themselves feel good is by being mean to other people. So, it doesn't matter what they think. Fuck them, what I say." Danny suddenly noticed he had just said fuck in front of his girlfriend's daughter. "Do me a favour, don't tell your mum I said a bad word, yeah?" he said nervously.

Danny then saw something quite rare, a smile on Libby's face as she said, "I won't tell her." But the smile quickly fell from her face as she asked, "Do you think the monster can hurt us?"

"No, no, I don't think so," he said, for how could he say yes to such a question when asked by a little girl? Then he noticed Libby staring at him with a worried look on her face. "What?"

"Something bad has happened, hasn't it, something you feel guilty about?"

A chill ran up his body as she said those words. "A friend of mine did something terrible, how do you—"

"Danny?" he then heard a voice say from behind him before he could finish what he was saying. Turning around, he saw Emma standing just outside the doorway. "What are you two talking about?"

"Video games," Libby told her mum, which Danny knew Emma would know to be a lie. He got up and walked out of the room. Once they got downstairs, she turned to Danny. "What were you really talking about?" She moaned at him.

"The deamhan dorcha," he said as he once told himself that he would tell Emma no more lies. Plus, she had a right to know.

"Jesus, Danny. You don't talk about that kind of stuff with her," she yelled at him.

"Libby knows more about the creature than I do, and I need to learn what is haunting me."

"She's a child," she barked back at him.

"She's seen more than you and me. We've been dealing with this for a month. Libby has been dealing with this for years. Not days nor weeks, years."

"She's my daughter, and I say what you can and can't talk to her about."

"Libby is special and not like other children, and we need her help."

"What do you know about her? Nothing, and I'm the only one who should talk to her about that thing." She said the last word in disgust, like it was leaving a foul taste in her mouth.

"Then tell me please everything that Henry told you."

"I already told you what he said."

"You didn't tell me everything, though, did you. I want to know the real reason why that weirdo didn't let me into his home."

"How about because you're a lowlife thief, Danny," she yelled, and that was a hit he didn't expect and one that hurt more than anything even though he could see the regret on her face.

"Is that how you really see me?"

She sighed and shook her head. "No, it isn't. I'm sorry."

"Please, I need to know."

"He told me that you are a danger to me, but I don't believe him."

Danny felt the heavyweight of anguish fall on him. He closed his eyes and thought about the man Mark killed and how it would have never happened if he didn't fall, and that was when he knew Henry was right about him.

"But I don't believe him," Emma repeated, blinded by love, Danny assumed. "He's insane."

"No, he's right," Danny told her with a heavy heart.

"No, he's crazy. He's been locked up in the looney bin for God only knows how many years."

"I know, but that was because of the deamhan dorcha."

"Oh, come on." She sighed. "You are not Henry Winters."

"I'm not yet. Listen, I love you, Emma," he told her, touching her cheek. "But I should leave. I could be a danger to you and Libby."

"No," she said in shock. Her eyes narrowed on his face, checking if he was serious to both of their despondency. He was deadly serious.

"Until I find a way to get rid of this thing. You should stay away from me," he said, opening the front door.

"You're leaving me?" she cried.

"I have no choice. I'm sorry," Danny whimpered as he left the house and closed the door after him.

He could hear Emma yell through the closed door, "Then fucking go," as his heart fell to pieces. He told himself it was for the best; it was the only way to keep them safe until he could find a way to get rid of the creature that was haunting him.

CHAPTER 38

When the sun went down, Danny had the first client of the night, a tall muscular man he knew as Arthur. Mark once told him that Arthur wasn't his real name but didn't bother telling him what his real name was, not that Danny really cared as long as he got paid. Arthur wasn't a fascinating one. He just dreamt about having dinner with his long since deceased grandmother. It was the second time with him, and the second time he dreamt about her. She must have been a good woman for him to be still dreaming about her after all those years. Danny ejected the video with it being twenty minutes through and handed it over to Arthur. "Thanks, man," Arthur said, giving him his payment which Danny put in his pocket without counting something Arthur found a bit odd. "You're not counting it?"

"Oh, yeah, shit," Danny said, now remembering to do so. He took the money back out of his pocket and started to count it.

"You all right?" Arthur asked him.

"Yeah, I'm good. It's just one of those days, you know," Danny said as he put the money in his pocket.

"Yeah, I know," Arthur said, nodding his head. "Say, have you ever tried recording a dog's dreams?"

"Why would I record a dog's dreams?"

"I don't know, out of curiosity."

"No. I haven't. They would just dream about sniffing arses and running in fields but if you want me to record a dog's dream, then bring one in, but it would be the same price as a human."

"Would it work?"

"I can't see why not."

"Mmm, interesting, well, I'll be seeing you, Mr Crow," Arthur said as he walked out of the garage. Danny soon followed him out on the cold rainy night.

He stood in the rain, his hands in his pockets, his fingertips again touching the Dream Recorder as he stared down at his feet. As he did, he heard the sound of footsteps coming ever closer to him. He looked up, seeing a skinny figure with his hands in his pockets his face covered with his hood.

"Mr Crow," the figure said, and Danny knew the voice belonged to Owen.

"Owen," Danny replied with disinterest.

"I want you to record my dreams."

Danny took a deep breath, remembering what he dreamt about last time and remembering seeing the sight of that little girl and hearing the sound of her screaming. He hoped that he would never see that face or hear those screams again. "I don't know, you have some twisted dreams, you know that?"

"I know, but I have to see more," Owen begged of him.

"Why?" Danny said, his anger getting directed towards him.

Owen quickly looked behind him, and when he looked back at Danny, he could see the worry in his eyes. "I have a horrible desire. I try to fight against it, but I know that the video you created can help me."

"Hey," Danny yelled at him in anger. "I don't create the video, some poor bastard in a factory in China creates the tapes, and it's you that creates the footage on them, not me."

"Right, yes, of course," he said, sounding like he was actually scared of Danny. Could that be true though, no one had ever feared him before? "But please, you have to help me. I have the money, see" He pulled out a roll of twenty-pound notes that was held together with an elastic band from his coat pocket.

Danny looked at it and back up at him, taking the money straight off him without hesitation. He dropped the elastic band on the wet floor, counting the money in his hand. There were a hundred pounds there, much more than he would typically charge people. "How did you get this money?" Danny asked, and before he answered, he told him, "You know what, I don't care. Come on." He opened the door that led into the garage. Owen followed him in as Danny shut the door after him. When Owen walked towards the bed, Danny was able to see what he believed to be a look of worry on Owen's rigid, square, Frankenstein's monster looking face.

"On the bed," Danny told him, pointing to the bed as if he thought that he had forgotten what a mattress was. Owen sat on the bed as Danny moved a water bottle that was resting on top of one of the crates. Danny picked it up and passed it to Owen, giving him the water along with two sleeping pills. "Here," he told him before he walked back, sitting on another crate, waiting for him to fall asleep. Owen took both of the pills and washed them down with the bottle of water.

"Have you ever acted on your desire?" Danny asked him.

Owen looked at him, and there was a short pause where everything was silent before Owen replied. "No, never," but Danny didn't know if he should believe him or not.

"Right, just lie back and let the drugs do their work," Danny told him, and Owen did as he asked. Danny waited for around twenty minutes, almost falling asleep himself, until he heard the sound of Owen snoring. It was time, Danny told himself, jumping down off the crate. He took the dream recorder out of his pocket and stood with it in his hand as he stared down at Owen.

"Are you really going see his dream again, you sick bastard?" the voice of Danny's mother said in his head. "Oh, I know what you are thinking." Of course it did, it was in his head, but surely, he couldn't go through with it. Looking towards the closed door that led into the alleyway, he saw that little girl from Owen's dream yet again staring back at him.

"He wants to hurt me, don't let him hurt me," the little girl moaned. He put the dream recorder down on top of the television. He struggled to pull the pillow from under Owen without waking him. He eventually got the pillow and stared at Owen, fearing that he would have woken up but to his relief, he was still sleeping like a baby. Now with the pillow in both hands, he held it above Owen's head, staying like that for a few minutes, thinking, "I can't do it."

"Please, he will hurt me again," the girl cried.

"Do it," he then heard the creature say in his mind. "Just do it." then he thought, *Perhaps I would be doing the world a favour in killing him, perhaps by taking his life, I would be saving the lives of children*. It was then he placed the pillow over his head, holding tight as Owen's body kicked and shook, fighting for air; still he held onto the pillow even tighter. If Owen could look into his eyes at that moment, he would have seen the look of pure hate upon Danny's face. Danny just stared down at his hand on the pillow until Owen finally stopped kicking. He left the pillow on his head and took a step back, not believing what he had just done.

"Well, that's that, you're a murderer now — before you were just responsible for a man's death, but now, now you killed a man with your own hands. Murderer," he heard his mother say.

"The world is a better place without him. He deserved to die," he said to what would have looked like an empty room.

"And you don't?"

That was now a question that ran through his mind. Did he deserve to die like Owen? Wasn't he a sinner as well? Sure, he had no twisted desires like Owen, but he was a sinner all the same. "Sinner," he said to himself — it was a word he didn't remember ever using before. He thought, *I'm concentrating on the wrong things. I need to think about what to do with the body.* He then remembered that some of the crates were empty. He grabbed the crowbar from the floor next to one of the crates. With the crowbar, he opened the first of the large boxes. Inside he found a television covered in bubble wrapping. He went to the next one, and opening that one, he found a desktop computer; it was the third one he opened that was completely empty.

Considering the recently deceased Owen, he wondered if he was strong enough to pick Owen up or if the crate was big enough for him to fit into, or would he have to cut him up. He really hoped he wouldn't have to do that. He picked up the body, and thankfully for Danny, he didn't weigh as much as he thought, but still, he had to just drag him across the floor towards the crate. The thought had entered his mind of asking Mark for help, but he remembered Owen being a friend of his, so he thought better of it.

While Danny was hiding the body of the man he killed, Lydia was walking towards the alleyway with the gun in her coat pocket. She banged her fist against the garage's metal door, not knowing what had happened moments ago beyond that door. Lydia waited for a short moment, but there was no answer, So she had to bang her fist against the door again and again. Lydia wasn't going back empty-handed, not again — she couldn't.

CHAPTER 39

D anny had just lifted Owen's body into the crate before the banging on the door started to drive him mad. "All right," Danny yelled at the door, picking up the lid and placing it on top of the crate. He would nail it shut later, he thought, as soon he got rid of whoever was knocking. He walked towards the door and opened it while shouting "What?" in frustration. Then the frustration and even trepidation dissipated for a short moment upon seeing the woman at the door. She reminded him a bit of Emma, but he didn't know why. This woman didn't really look like her — the height was more or less the same. Perhaps Emma was a bit smaller, but her face was completely different, with Emma having a round face with a bit of button nose. This girl had more of a long face and nose. Even her colouring was different — Emma had jet black hair but pale skin, and this girl had light brown hair and tanned skin like she had spent a lot of time in a hot climate, and her eyes were green, not brown. So why, he wondered did she remind him of Emma. *Where do I know her from?* he thought, to himself, almost forgetting the body he had left in the crate.

"I'm here to see Mr Crow," she told him. He couldn't imagine Mark knowing a girl like her, but he had seen her face, and she knew Mr Crow's name. She had to be someone Mark knew. Perhaps she was a buyer of stolen items.

"Yeah, that's me," he told her.

"I want to see my dreams," she told him, and he did nothing but stare at her. Should he let her in was now the new question in the deep ocean of questions in his mind. "I have the money," she said, taking out a handful of twenty-pound notes.

He took them out of her hand and counted them like he had hours before with Owen. He looked back at the crate that contained Owen's body and was reassured that it seemed no different from the rest of the boxes with its lid on. Danny smiled at her and welcomed her in. The woman stepped in, closing the door after her. Danny was still wondering where the hell had he seen her before. She soon saw the dream recorder resting on top of the television. Knowing where her eyes were directed, Danny rushed in front of her, grinning like an idiot.

"Can I just ask, have we met before?" he asked her with a questioning look.

"No, I think I would remember you," she answered him, looking past him and at the dream recorder. "I take it that is the machine that records one's dreams."

"Yeah."

"How does it work?"

"Do you mean how do you use it?"

"Yeah."

"Well, you put it on someone's head, hit the little button, then just wait for it to record. After you plug it into your VCR and record it to a video. Bob's your uncle. You have a dream on a video," he explained to her, and then his eyes widened, and his jaw fell open. It finally hit him like a brick in the face. He knew where he knew her face from, but it was impossible. Could it be the bald woman from Libby's dream? But she had hair — surely, he thought he must be mistaken. There was only one way he could know for sure. "Lydia?" he said, gauging her reaction.

It was now Lydia's turn to look surprised. "How do you know my name?"

"Do you know a little girl name Lib—" He stopped and said her full name, "Elizabeth Holland?"

"No, never met anyone by that name."

"She dreamed of you."

"About me?" She spat the words out with shock and confusion. "How can someone I have never met have a dream about me?" she said, the confusion apparent on her face.

"I don't know," he said, walking towards the dream recorder, now turning his back on Lydia. "I wish I knew, but to be honest with you, I know hardly anything about this machine."

Lydia pulled the pistol out of her pocket and pointed it at Danny as he picked up the machine. He turned around with a shocked expression on his face as he saw the barrel of the gun pointing right at him.

"You want to know who I am. I am the last living daughter of Edgar Knightley — do you even know who that is?" she yelled at him.

"Yeah, I know. The old man who invented the dream recorder," he said, the words full of guilt and melancholy.

Lydia had expected to hate him and expected her anger towards him to get the better of her, but when she saw him and looked in his eyes, it gave her another emotion: pity. She actually felt sorry for him, but she refused to let him know that.

"That's right, and I bet you know why I'm here."

"I think I do," he said, looking back down at the machine that was now in both of his hands like a priest would hold a bible.

"So just throw it down on the floor, and I will take it, and I'll leave here, and you never have to see me again."

"You don't know what you are asking."

"Don't fucking test me," she yelled, her hands shaking as she held the gun towards his head.

"Why because you'll shoot me? Then go ahead," he told her calmly.

"You don't think I will. Then it's evident you don't know me," Lydia threatened him.

"You are right, I don't know you, but all the same, I want you to know I didn't kill your father."

"I know you didn't, you moron, but you did rob him."

Danny ignored that and continued with what he was going to say. "It was this machine that killed him, like it's killing me. There is a power in this little plastic box that I can't even begin to explain. It scares me, but it's also so exhilarating it's like a drug you just can't quit."

"Then give it to me, and I'll destroy it," she said more calmly, trying to sound like she wanted to help him.

"I wish it was that easy, but it will destroy you too. You know I used to smoke like a darn chimney, but I haven't touched a fag since…" He stopped himself and tried to remember the last time he smoked, but failing that, said, "Since I don't know when. My addiction has been replaced with this. When I see my girlfriend, well, now ex-girlfriend, I no longer think about a future with her like I once did. I just wonder what she is dreaming of, and every moment of the day and night, I think about the world this box shows me. It's even put a demon in my head." He said the last part with a laugh over how absurd it all sounded. He looked at Lydia, who just stared back at him. "You asked me earlier how to use the machine. Which I think means you know nothing about it."

"I know I'm meant to destroy it. So, give it to me, or I will be forced to pull the trigger."

"Do what you want because you'll not be getting this." He showed no fear of Lydia and her gun and realising this, Lydia lowered the weapon. Danny believed he had finally got through to her and that she would leave without the dream recorder. He was wrong.

Lydia wasn't lowering the gun at all, but in fact, aiming it down at his foot. She squeezed the trigger with a loud bang that echoed throughout the garage, and in intense pain, Danny screamed out and fell to the floor, dropping the dream recorder. As quickly she could, Lydia fell onto her knees, grabbing hold of the machine. Danny ignoring the burning pain in his foot, reached out, grabbing hold of Lydia's wrist, feeling the bone and beating pulse under her soft skin.

"It's mine," he yelled out at her, his face red with pain and rage. She moved the gun around in her hand, and with all her strength struck him on top of the head with the butt of the weapon, knocking him out cold. Now free of him, she stood up, staring down at the unconscious body lying in front of her. Then she looked at the dream recorder in her hand, a bland little thing, she thought. She could do it here — destroy the thing finally, completing her father's last wish, but she found that she couldn't do it. Instead, she found herself putting the machine into her pocket to take back to the hotel with her.

CHAPTER 40

Lydia had finally got the machine. Her hand held it tight in her coat pocket. In contrast, her other hand held onto the gun, which was in the other pocket, and she thought about Mr Crow while entering the hotel entrance and making her way up the lift. When she opened the door into her room, she found Katya sitting on the bed staring at her. She had what could only be called a look of disappointment on her face. "Where have you been?" she asked her in a dry cold way.

"It's over. I finally have it," Lydia said, taking the dream recorder out of her pocket.

"Good, then destroy it," Katya said, her eyes on the machine, thinking how it looked nothing like what she had expected. It was a kind of boring and ugly looking machine, she thought.

Lydia put it on the table and stared at it. "How?" she asked Katya, her eyes glued to it, mesmerised by the power that it held inside it.

"Shoot it," Katya suggested.

"I don't know how things are in Russia, but here in Britain, it's not a good idea to fire a gun in a hotel full of people."

"Then I don't know. There are many ways to break things. I mean, try putting it in the toilet. That's how my cousin broke his Gameboy."

"It's not a Gameboy, Kat. And how did he end up dropping it down the toilet?" she questioned.

"I don't know, I didn't ask him. Maybe you can just stamp on it."

Lydia gave that a try, throwing it on the floor and stamping on it repeatedly with the heel of her Doc Martens' boot, but it didn't even make a dent in the dream recorder. "No, it doesn't work."

"Then hit it with a hammer."

"I don't have a hammer."

"Drop it out of the window," Katya told her, and Lydia walked to the window and looked down at the hotel's car park. She was about to open the window and drop it when she realised that someone out there could steal it if it didn't break.

"Wait a minute," she called out. "Britain is an island — we can just throw it into the sea. All we got to do is rent a boat and drop it in the ocean."

Katya shook her head. "I don't like boats, they freak me out, and it is easier and cheaper to hit it with a hammer."

Lydia sighed, staring at the machine. "I guess you're right."

"Are you not tempted to try the machine?" Katya asked her, noticing that her eyes had hardly been off the device.

Lydia looked at her, shocked by what she was saying. After all this dream recorder had done to her family. She wanted to be angry with her, but the strange truth was the answer to Katya's question was yes, she did want to try it, at least just once, to see what it was like. She wondered what would she see — perhaps her father, her sister or maybe the monster that haunted her nightmares as a child, the same monster that may have haunted her father's. No, she quickly decided, we can't use it. "That machine was the reason why my father took his own life," she told her.

"Yes, of course, but to see your dreams on film... well, that would be very interesting, don't you think?"

"No," Lydia said simply before lying down on the bed.

"But think, this is once in a lifetime thing. It can be something spectacular, if that is the right word? Yes?" she asked Lydia.

"Yes, that's the right word, but you are still wrong. No one else should ever be able to use that machine. It has to be destroyed because it is far too dangerous. It's like the ring from the Tolkien books."

"Okay," Katya told her. "But what's a Tolkien?"

Now Lydia was speechless. She thought even behind the Iron Curtain, she must have heard of Tolkien. "You don't know Tolkien?"

CHAPTER 41

Danny woke up on the floor of the garage in pain in both his foot and his head. He groaned with pain as he tried to stand back up but ended up falling back down as he tried to put weight on his injured foot, letting out a cry of pain and anger. Danny was angry not with Lydia but himself for letting her get away with the recorder. He crawled to the bed, using it to aid him in lifting himself up. He sat down on the bed quickly, looking at his foot. It felt wet and sticky inside the shoe, and he could see the bullet hole and bloodstain around it. His attention moved from his foot over to the crate where he'd hid Owen's body. He breathed a sigh of relief when he saw the top still on it.

"You let her take it," he heard his mother's voice say.

Danny wheezed as he lifted his leg over his other leg and started to untie his shoelaces very slowly. He slowly pulled his foot out of the shoe. "Fuck a duck," was the strange phrase that he moaned through his pain, dropping the shoe on the floor and staring at his white sock stained red with his blood. He knew he needed to cover the wound but with what? Just as he thought of getting up and struggling his way to the bathroom to get some toilet roll, the garage's large door started to open.

The bright light of Mark's van filled the garage as they slowly drove in. Danny could see Monica's pale face with a disgusted expression on it staring at him through the passenger side window. They parked up near the crates as the garage doors started to go back down. After turning the engine off, Mark and Monica got out of the van and quickly moved towards Danny.

"What the hell happened to you?" Mark called out with a shocked look on his face as he stared at Danny's bloody foot.

"I've been shot in my foot," he said, the red-hot pain still driving him into despair.

"I can see that, but how and by who?" Mark asked.

"How. A bullet flew out of a gun, and by who? Lydia Knightley," he wheezed.

"Who's Lydia?" Monica asked him.

"Edgar's daughter."

"Edgar's daughter? You mean the dead old man?" Mark asked.

Danny nodded his head before saying, "Can you please get me something to stop the bleeding before I pass out?"

"Yeah, sure," Mark said, taking off his shirt, leaving him with just a white tank top which let him show off the black snake tattoo on his upper arm. Mark put it around Danny's foot, tying it as tight as he could as Danny moaned in pain.

"Don't be such a baby," Monica said with a grimace.

"I'm not being a baby. It fucking hurts. Do you want me to shoot you in the foot so you know how it feels?" Danny hissed at her.

"Shoot me in the foot, and I'll make you wish you'd never been born. You stupid prick."

"Monica, will you shut the fuck up," Mark screamed at her.

"He has just threatened your girlfriend, and you tell me to shut up?" she argued back at him.

"He hasn't got a gun, so it's not a real threat, is it? And you're the one who started it."

She spat on the floor before saying, "Well fuck you both," and stormed out of the side door into the alleyway.

"Sorry about her," Mark then told Danny.

"It's all right," Danny said, moving up the bed and lying down on it. "But I can't see what you see in her."

"Don't start, mate. Sure, she can be a bitch, but I love that bird, so don't."

"Sorry," Danny wheezed.

"So, tell me, has she got the dream recorder?"

"Yeah."

"Fuck!" Mark screamed out in anger. "That damn bitch. She's going to pay for that, you know." He calmed himself down and said, "So what happened? How did she get in here?"

"I let her in. I thought she was a client that you sent to me."

"Jesus Christ, Danny. You well and truly fucked up." Mark sat on the end of the bed, passing his hand over his bald head and thinking for a short moment while letting out a long sigh. "I have a mate who has a mate who works as a detective for the Mayfield police. I've told you about him before, remember? I was told there was a detective, who is now dead. Not the bent one, another one who was speaking with the daughter of an inventor, and I bet my right arm that's our girl."

"How did he die?" Danny asked.

"Who, the detective?"

"Yeah."

"I don't know, I forget," Mark said without a moment's thought.

"What was his name?"

"I fucking forgot, all right," Mark yelled at him. "Anyway, the reason I'm talking about this is that maybe, just maybe, I could get information about her, perhaps where she is staying. What did you say her name was?"

"Lydia Knightley"

"Lydia Knightley." He repeated it out loud.

"But she told me she's going to destroy the machine, so we have to be quick."

"Oh well, that's just fucking great, isn't it," Mark moaned. "What about that notebook? Does she have it?"

"No, it's back in my house, but it doesn't matter anyway. It doesn't say how it is built, but just tell me how long you think it will take for you to find her?"

"I don't know — hours or maybe even a day."

Danny closed his eyes and slowly nodded his head in defeat. "And do you really plan to kill her?"

"You bet your fucking arse I do," Mark told him.

After what Danny had seen a few days ago, he believed him, and to Danny's horror, he didn't know how he felt about it. There was a part of him that wanted it. He imagined Mark cutting her throat, and there was a sick feeling in his stomach at the thought of it, but he knew he needed the machine back at any cost.

CHAPTER 42

It was mid-afternoon, and DCI John Gallaway was sitting at his desk, reading through his notes on the missing case of Antony Matthews. He had questioned his girlfriend, Lucy, who seemed to say she knew nothing about his disappearance, but John had no trust in the girlfriends or boyfriends of missing people. Going by Matthew's history of narcotics, it seemed to him it would be doing the world a favour to let the cunt stay missing. Perhaps someone had finally put a blade or a bullet through him. His mind was taken off the case by the ringing of his telephone. He sighed before picking it up. "DCI John Gallaway speaking."

"John, it's me," the Irishman said the other end of the line.

"Yeah, what do you want?" he said, leaning the phone against his shoulder and ear as he picked up his cup, putting it to his lips and taking a big gulp of now cold coffee.

"Was you on the case about the death of an Edgar Knightley?"

"No, that was Williams who is no longer with us, sadly." He said the word sadly, but he didn't really care about the death of his colleague. The man was driving too fast and lost control of his car. In John's eyes, it was his own fault for driving at such a speed. The rest of the station was worried about him in the days before his death. Still, John had more important things to worry about other than some fat detective who could no longer handle the job. They should have kicked him off the force a long time ago before the man became too fat to see his own prick. "It was an open and shut case. Mr Knightley lost his mind and committed suicide. Neighbours and friends had often worried about his mental state. Although there is something about some weird videotapes. So why do you ask?"

"A friend of mine wants to find his daughter, a Lydia Knightley. Do you think you can find out where she lives?" the Irishman asked.

"Is she going to end up joining her dear dad?"

"Do you care?"

"Not really, but another death means more paperwork for me, so if your friend wants to have that information, it's going to cost him — let's just say around five hundred pounds."

"I see. I will ask my friend, and we'll see what is what."

"You do that," John said, putting down the phone and going back to his notes on the disappearance of Antony Matthews, reading about the rumours that were going around about him cheating on his girlfriend. Her name, Lucy O'Brien, came into his mind as a possible suspect.

She did away with him, I know it, he thought to himself before the phone rang again. He picked it up. "DCI John Gallaway speaking."

"Yes, John, it's me again."

"Well, lucky me, what did he say."

"He will pay for it, and I will give you the money first thing tomorrow morning."

"All right, just give me a moment or so, and I'll find out where the bitch is," he told the Irishman before putting the phone back down.

***

In the morning Lydia got a hammer from the closest DIY shop and quickly went back to the hotel with the thought of destroying the dream recorder clearly in her mind. When she got back inside, she put the machine down on the desk and held the hammer over it. Memories of the video that Williams showed her ran through her mind, mostly images of Victoria. It would be like heaven for Lydia to see her again.

"What's wrong?" Katya asked, seeing Lydia's hand shaking as it held the hammer above her father's machine. Lydia lowered her hand and let the hammer fall from her fingers, hitting the floor with a loud thump and perhaps scaring the guests below them. "I can't do it," she said, sounding shocked by her own weakness.

"Why, I thought you wanted the thing destroyed?"

"I did, but the thing is it's my father's legacy, and it can show me. my sister, again." She looked at Katya, who looked back at her. "I could see my sister's face again and not just a photo of her."

"But it won't be your sister, just your mind creating images of her."

"Yes, I know, but even so, I can't destroy it, not yet anyway. You are right. We have to try it."

Katya smiled to herself, happy that she had finally won her over. "Great, but didn't you say we need a blank video?"

"Not a problem, there's a supermarket just across from here. I can get a video and be back in a jiffy."

"What's a jiffy?"

"A short period of time," she said, grabbing her coat. Then, she turned to her and gently kissed her on the lips.

"So, see you in a jiff," Katya told her.

"It's a jiffy," she corrected her. "You want me to pick you anything else up while I'm there?"

"No, I have everything I need," Katya said with a smile.

"All right, I'll see you in a bit," she said, kissing her on her soft lips before leaving the room and leaving Katya sitting on the bed on her own.

CHAPTER 44

"Five hundred pounds I had to pay out. I can't fucking believe it, five hundred. How did you let that bitch trick you, eh. Really how stupid can you be, Danny." Mark moaned the whole way to the Britannia hotel where Lydia Knightley was staying.

"How was I meant to know who she was?" Danny hissed, his foot still aching as he looked out of the window, seeing Owen and the little girl in the dress standing side by side on the pavement watching the van drive past. He quickly moved his head, not wanting to see those two together. He hoped to God it was the deamhan dorcha playing tricks with his mind, and they were not actually together in what he could only say was the afterlife. Danny still didn't know if the little girl was real or made up, dead or alive.

"Five hundred pounds, though. I could have used that kind of money to be resting in Spain with some hot Spaniard with a nice arse or a big fucking television. but no, no, I'm using it to find out the location of some toff bitch," Mark said before they entered the hotel's carpark.

"We need to be careful — remember she does have a gun, and we only have a knife," Danny told him, feeling worried for the safety of everyone who was going to be involved in this madness.

"You scared of a little girl?" Mark mocked him.

"No, I'm scared of a gun and the bullets that come out of it. You know, being shot isn't a nice feeling."

"Neither is paying out five hundred quid but don't worry. I won't give her a chance to pick the weapon up, never mind use it," Mark said, putting on some white latex gloves, making Danny feel more and more nervous. He hated the thought of another person dying because of him, but he needed the dream recorder back at any cost.

Finally, they both jumped out of the van and walked towards the hotel. Mark looked at the pained expression on Danny's face after every step he took. "Are you going to be all right?" he asked Danny.

"I'll be fine," he replied.

Mark took the piece of paper out of his pocket and read Lydia and Katya's room number.

"We're just going to scare her, right?" Danny murmured then.

"Danny, don't you dare go chicken on me," Mark said, stopping and pointing his finger at him like he was a child being told off for staying awake over his bedtime. "And are you sure you can do this with your foot and all that?"

"Yeah, I'm sure."

"You'd better be, mate, because I won't let you slow me down. You hear? I won't let any cunt slow me down."

Danny didn't really know what he meant by that, but he had a good idea. When it came to Mark, money and success came before friendship, and well, before anything if the truth was told. Danny knew Mark would sell his own mother for a few quid. Loyalty was never one of Mark's vital attributes.

"Yeah, I understand," Danny told him.

"Good, so let's shut our traps and get this job done, yeah?"

As Mark said those words, he saw the angry look on Danny's face just before he told him, "You know you should be more grateful."

"What the fuck are you talking about?"

"How many times has it been *my*, lockpicking skills that have made us money and who was it who picked the dream recorder up in the first place, me. So how about you be a little more grateful."

"Fair enough, I'll get the lube, you drop your trousers, and I'll show you how grateful I am." There was a moment of silence as they stared at each other before Mark said, "No? Well, in that case, let's just get a move on, eh?" and with that, Mark walked off, and Danny sighed and followed after him.

***

Katya sat in the hotel room with a cup of tea watching a strange TV game show called *Knightmare* about a child going into a virtual world while a man with a big black beard told him what to do. *Brits watch some weird shit*, she thought to herself, but still, she did actually enjoy it. Katya kept wondering what was taking Lydia so long. Just as her eyes begin to feel heavy and she felt that she would fall asleep, she heard a loud knocking at her door. Katya looked towards the door as if expecting it to be knocked down. Picking the remote control up from the side of the bed, she turned the television off, not really knowing why, as if it was just an unconscious reaction. The loud knocking came again, and this time she shouted to the door, "What do you want?"

"It's my wife, she's a diabetic, and her blood sugars are extremely low," the male voice explained from behind the door. "Do you have anything high in sugar like chocolate or something like that?"

Katya looked to a packet of chocolate biscuits next to the dream recorder on the top of a desk. "Why don't you call the front desk?" she shouted back at them.

"We tried. They're not picking up. Please, miss, we need your help," the man said, sounding like he was about to break down right in front of her door. She knew it could be the thieves, and they could be tricking her, but there was a chance the man behind the door was telling the truth, and someone's life was really in danger. "Please, we need something like biscuits or chocolate, anything really that is high in sugar," the voice begged of her.

She let out a big sigh before shouting, "Okay, just a minute." She opened the set of draws under the television and took out the pistol hidden under Lydia's dark green shirt. She held it in her right hand as the left picked up the packet of biscuits.

"Thank you, thank you so much," the voice behind the door cried.

Katya slowly moved to the door as she held the gun behind her back with her finger gently resting on the trigger. Opening the door, she expected to see an overweight middle-aged man with a panicked look on his face but what she saw was two men in their late twenties. One was a tall, bald man standing in front of a skinny blond man who looked to be leaning his back against the corridor wall with a pained expression on his face.

Without any warning, the bald man punched her in the face, knocking her back into the room and knocking the gun and biscuits out of her hands. Katya's nose began to bleed as she crawled towards the weapon that had fallen near the legs of the bed. Just before she got her hand on it, the bald man's foot stood on the gun and slid it away from her. "I don't think so, sweetheart," he told her as he picked the gun up and looked at it. "God, this looks older than my nan. Where did you get this relic?" he asked as he pointed the gun towards her head.

"From an antique shop," she told him while covering her nose with her hand, which made him laugh at the absurdity of getting a functional firearm at an antique shop.

The blond quickly noticed the dream recorder in the room and moved past them both, picking it up.

"You never told me she was Russian," he said to the blonde man.

"That's not her."

"No? Well, who are you, my little comrade?" he asked Katya, still aiming the gun at her head.

"Fuck you," she told him with no idea where that courage came from. Maybe her newfound loathing for the man who just entered her life was outweighing her fear of him.

The bald man laughed before looking back at his accomplice. "She's got some spirit on her. I'll give her that. Where's the other girl?"

"I don't know. She left me," Katya said, still holding her bloody nose and feeling the overwhelming feeling of all-out dread for her own life but also for the life of the woman she loved.

"You're lying to me, Natasha. Not that it matters anyway, we've got what we came for," he said, putting the gun in his pocket. Then, just as Katya thought it was all over, the bald man pulled his knife out of the same pocket.

"What are you doing?" the blond man asked him with trepidation in his voice as the bald man knelt down in front of her, putting the knife to her face.

"You are a pretty little thing, aren't you. I always had a bit of a thing for Eastern European girls." He said it in a soft and gentle sounding voice, and Katya felt the blade touching her cheek but tried her best to show no fear and spat out blood into his face, hitting below his right eye. He wiped it off with the back of his hand, saying, "That's not very ladylike, is it?"

"Come on, what are you doing? Let's get out of here," the other man moaned.

"All right, I guess this is where we leave you, my sweet little Lenin girl," he told Katya, and then he drove the knife in Katya's heart. She let out a grunt as she coughed up blood and her eyes widened, looking into the cold eyes of the man who had claimed her life. For the moment before Katya took her last breath, she thought of Lydia and the danger she was now in.

"Oh god, why did you do that," Danny cried, and Mark stood up, took the gun out of his pocket and pointed it towards Danny's head. Danny feared that poor Lydia would be finding two bodies when she came back, but he also thought that Mark pulling the trigger on him would be a blessing.

Mark smiled and put the gun back in his pocket. "Just kidding with you. I had to kill her because she saw my face. Come on, we'd better be getting out of here."

"What have we become," Danny cried, looking down at Katya and thinking about Owen's body in the garage. This wasn't him. He wasn't a killer, nor was Mark. Had something changed Mark Long, had his true nature, his real wickedness, finally been released. Danny now believed his dream of being a good man had died along with the Russian girl.

"Danny, get a move on, would you," Mark moaned as he walked towards the door.

Lydia felt happy as she walked back to the hotel. She had finally got the dream recorder. They could watch one dream with it and then destroy it and never have to think about it again, as long as it didn't take hold of them as it had with her father. She would be okay from its influence after just one video. Her father and Williams watched too many; that was their problem — one would be just fine. As she entered the car park, she noticed a white van pulling away from one of the parking spaces and watched as it drove off down the street away from the hotel. Many people drove the same white van as the thieves. Lydia realised she had never memorised the license plate number. There was a sickening feeling in her stomach then, as if she knew it was the thieves.

Lydia quickly ran into the hotel, past the reception and rushed into the lift. There was a feeling of dread as she walked towards her room. She put the key in the door and opened it, seeing what she feared the most, her partner's pale body lying on her back with a stab wound in her chest.

"No, please God, no!" she cried, falling to her knees. Her heart broke, and the pain of it filled her mind as she knelt next to Katya, looking into her dead eyes. "No, no. I'm so sorry," she whispered to her body as her voice broke and her eyes fill with tears. She took hold of Katya's cold dead hand. "I love you, Kitty Kat, I always have, and I wish, wish I told you more often when I had the chance." She then heard a scream coming from behind her. She turned around and saw an overweight blonde woman looking at her through the doorway. It was the woman staying next door.

"Oh my god," she cried before running back to her room, more than likely phoning the police. Lydia looked back down at Katya's eyes, moved her hand slowly over them to shut them, shutting them forever. Mr Crow had taken the woman she loved, and now she didn't give a damn about the dream recorder or her father's dying wish. She only wanted to see Mr Crow dead.

CHAPTER 45

Monica waited in the garage, just walking around while listening to her CD Walkman, which played her collection of pop music from the seventies. She stepped back and forth, bored out her mind, looking at the bloodstain that was on the floor as Harry Chapin sang to her. Monica even found herself wondering how painful it was to get shot in the foot. *Incredibly*, she thought, *but not as much as being shot in the kneecap, that would be worse. They say giving birth is the most painful thing a woman can go through — how funny it is that women crave babies when they cause so much pain*. Then she started to ask herself if she would one day desire to go through that pain — perhaps once she and Mark had made money with that dream machine thingy if the thing actually did work. What would she name the child — Charlie after her dead brother, who died from a drug overdose seven years ago, and maybe Charlene for a girl as it sounded a little like Charlie. The child could have Monica's surname of Wisniewska, as she believed Mark's surname of Long was way too ordinary and way too boring.

The garage door began to open, and she turned her Walkman off and moved out of the way, standing next to the wall as they drove the van in. They parked it up, and Mark came out of the van with a smile on his face. "I've got it, baby," he told her in delight, as Danny stepped out of the passenger side of the van while Monica took out her earphones and put her Walkman down on one of the crates.

"You took your time," she told him in disappointment, angry that he'd made her wait in the cold garage.

"Well, good to see you too," he said, taking out the gun from his pocket and showing it to Monica. "Would you just look at this old beauty? I think it's from the Second World War."

"Let us have a look," she told him, and he handed it over to her with a lot of hesitation. She looked at it with a childlike fascination. She looked at its detail, its wooden handle and dark metal shaft, and she felt powerful holding a device that could take life with a pull of a trigger. "Is it real?"

"Yeah, and it's loaded, so you know, be careful with it."

"I will," she said, looking at Danny, who was now standing behind Mark with his hands in his pockets. "Danny, do you know how the dream recorder works?" she asked him.

"Sure," he told her.

"Then how?" she said, expecting him to have told her already. Mark looked back at him, and he looked back at Mark.

"Go on, tell her," Mark said to him, but Danny didn't want to tell them how to use the machine because he knew

308

as soon as they knew they wouldn't need him any longer. But the scary thought was, it wasn't such a complicated device to operate — they could kill him and figure it out themselves. Not even Monica and Mark were that stupid. After getting fed up with waiting for an answer, Monica pointed the gun at him, with Mark taking a few steps back, not wanting to get caught in the crossfire.

"Tell me, Daniel," she said, trying to aim the weapon at him.

"This is the third time I have had that gun aimed at me, and each time I give a similar response."

"It will be your last time," she hissed at him.

"Don't piss about, Danny. Give us the machine," Mark said, holding his hand out to Danny.

"So, what's going on here?" Danny asked him.

Mark sighed. "Well, your idea of selling people's dreams was a good one. One that Monica and I are going to adopt, but we came to the agreement that you just slow us down and fifty-fifty cuts better than uh, shit…" Mark stopped himself, trying to find what the percentage would be; maths was never his strong suit.

"A thirty-three each cut," Monica told him, still pointing the gun at Danny.

"So, this is the way it goes, eh? You stab your friends in the back?" Danny asked, his tone revealing his feelings of disgust with them.

"You never had friends. Everyone has been trying to use you," his mother's voice said inside Danny's head.

"Shut up," Danny replied out loud, making Mark look at Monica in confusion.

"It's nothing personal, mate," Mark told him.

"Nothing personal?" Danny said in shock, and to everyone's surprise, he started laughing to himself like a mad man. "We have been friends since we were kids, way before you ever met that bitch."

"Hey, I'm the bitch who still has the fucking gun," Monica yelled. Both of the men ignored her.

"You used to be like an older brother to me. All the things we have been through together, all the ups and the downs, are just going to end here. It's completely absurd," he told Mark, actually getting into Mark's cold heart. He remembered the times they spent as children, running around stealing from local shops, the times they would play soldiers through the fields or when they would play football even though Danny couldn't hit a ball straight to save his life. For better or worse, primarily worse, Mark had made him into the man he has become.

Reluctantly Mark moved towards Danny. Mark was putting his hand in Danny's pocket just as his fingertips touched the machine. Danny turned to him, punching him square in the jaw and knocking his head to the side and then they heard a loud bang. Danny fell to his knees, feeling a searing, burning pain in his stomach. He moved his hand to his stomach, feeling the warm blood coming out of it. He knew he couldn't survive this but didn't know how long it would take before he finally died.

"Jesus, Monica, what the hell" Mark screamed at her, seeing her holding the gun with its barrel still smoking.

"He attacked you," she answered.

Mark looked down at his old friend, now horrified by what was going on. He thought he would be okay, that seeing him die would be like seeing the other people die, but it wasn't. This was his friend.

"Come on, grab the machine," Monica ordered him, now with the gun lowered by her side. Mark reached into Danny's coat pocket, pulling out the dream recorder, thankful that at least that wasn't destroyed.

"You idiot, you didn't even ask him how the thing works," Mark shouted over to Monica as he took the machine to her.

Danny now could barely hear what they were saying to one another as he lay on the floor dying. From the corner of his eye, he could see the tall, dark figure slowly moving towards him. He turned his head, seeing the creature smiling down at him with long sharp teeth. "You're dying, little boy, you're dying," the creature told him in a whisper just before it disappeared and turned into his mother, who kneel by his side.

"Your good friend killed you, my sweet little boy, but not to worry, Mummy can save you, and I can release you from the pain," she said ever so softly.

Danny made a wheezing sound that was meant to be the word 'how' — a human being wouldn't be able to make out what he was saying, but Danielle Hammond was dead and what she really was, wasn't human. It was something unearthly.

"Tell me that you want this, and your pain will come to an end," his mum said, and Danny didn't have any idea what he was talking about, but he didn't trust the creature, not one bit. Yet the red-hot pain was agonising, and the thought of it just stopping was so very tempting to him. Danielle was now on all fours like a dog, her head so very close to Danny's. "I see your pain. Let me ease it for you, my sweet, sweet boy." Danny just stared at her, not knowing what to do. Finally, Danny slowly shook his head.

"You fool. Do you not see that they will kill Emma and Libby after your death," she told him, and Danny thought to himself that his mother was dead, and it is the deamhan dorcha, but still, it could be right? Mark and Monica may try to kill anyone who knew about the machine. He couldn't let them get anywhere near Emma and Libby, so he slowly nodded his head, and the smile came to Danielle's face before she put her hand over Danny's mouth. The pain Danny was feeling gradually disappeared, and he slowly shut his eyes, wondering what would come next.

CHAPTER 46

Mark felt, for the first time in a very long time, the pain of guilt. He thought he didn't need Danny any more, but he changed his tune after seeing his girlfriend shoot him.

Monica stood in front of him, still with the gun in her hand, and loved the feeling of power. She had taken a life. That was something she had always dreamed about doing, something she would never tell anyone, not even Mark. She wondered to herself if she was psychopathic — but really, what did it matter if she was? A lot of psychopaths became very powerful people — she had read that somewhere but had forgotten where. Mark was staring at the dream recorder in his hands. It looked to Monica like he was reading something on it, but there was no inscription on it as far as she knew.

"I think you tie it to your head and press the button. It seems simple enough," he told her.

"What about putting the dream onto a video?"

He held a wire up, showing her the little metal bit that plugged into the VCR. The look on his face was what she should have expected — it was the look of someone who had just seen his girlfriend kill his best friend. Monica walked towards him, softly touching his hand where he still held the machine.

"This is what we wanted, isn't it? This is our dream for the future, right?" she said so very softly.

"Of course," he said with a fake smile.

"Now it's just you and me against the world. We're going to be rich. We're going to have a big house, multiple cars and a big swimming pool. Have you fucked in a swimming pool, Mark?" she whispered into his ear before kissing his neck.

"No, but there is a first for everything," he told her.

"That's what I always say," she said, smiling at him, but then her eyes went to Danny's body which was shaking behind him. Was that normal? It couldn't be normal; she'd never heard of a body shaking like that. *I should have shot him in the head*, she thought. *But it's not too late*. She could just walk up to him and pull the trigger, nothing to it. Monica walked closer to the shaking body with the gun in her hand. She felt fear that she had never felt before — like the fear of spiders or clowns, something that felt irrational and very real at the same time. Monica heard a very faint croaking sound coming from his mouth. "He's still alive," she whispered to herself. She aimed the gun down at his head as Mark turned away.

Danny stopped shaking and just remained lying on the floor, looking like he was just sleeping. "I think he's finally dead," she said, not really to Mark, more to herself. Staring at him, she found herself amazed by how peaceful he looked and wondered how much pain was he in towards the end. Just as she was about to walk away, she noticed something quite peculiar — Danny's chest was moving slowly up and down. He was still breathing. So, he was still alive, she thought, and that thought was confirmed when Danny's blue eyes quickly opened and stared at her. A shot of horror ran through her body like electricity, and Danny's hand quickly grabbed her arm — the touch of his fingers was so very cold. She screamed, and Mark turned around, not believing what he was seeing. Monica pulled the trigger of the gun, but it only made a click, and she felt his nails digging in her skin as he pulled himself up.

Mark ran towards them, but before he got to them, Danny was back on his feet. He punched Monica in the nose, knocking her down to the floor, the gun flying out her hand just as Mark had done to Katya. As quickly as she fell, Danny was on top of her like a lion attacking its prey.

"Get off her," Mark screamed, running towards the gun, but it was too late — as soon as Mark picked up the gun, he heard a horrifying high-pitched scream of agony coming from Monica. Holding the gun towards them, Mark could see Danny on top of Monica with his thumbs digging into her eyes. Her legs kicked, and hands grabbed at Danny's arms and still, she let out her horrifying cries of pain. Mark then pulled the trigger, but as it had for Monica, all he heard was a click. With the gun in his hand, Mark ran as fast as his legs could take him towards Danny, hitting him across the head with the butt of the gun, knocking him off Monica. He looked at Monica and saw the red holes where her eyes used to be. She was still screaming in pain, touching her face near where her eyes would have been.

"Fucking bastard," Mark cried as Danny stood back up with a look of pure hatred. He tried once again to hit him with the gun, but Danny was too quick, grabbing hold of his arm with one hand and with his other punching Mark in the eye and blackening it and then once in the nose, busting it. Mark got his leg behind Danny and pushed him down on the floor while getting on top of him, punching him in the stomach where the bullet had hit. If he'd had time to notice, he would find it shocking that Danny was no longer bleeding. Grabbing hold of Mark's head, Danny pulled him down towards him and bit down hard on Mark's ear. Mark felt his teeth ripping into the flesh and felt the warm blood going down the side of his face as he cried out in pain as Danny pushed him off him while spitting out something that looked like a chunk of meat. He put a hand to where his ear used to be, feeling nothing but the wet warm feeling of his blood.

"My ear, you bit off my ear," Mark cried. It was then he knew he wouldn't win the fight with Danny, and he started stepping back with a deep fear of his old friend along with the warm wet feeling of urine going down his leg. "Hey, come on, mate. We're old friends, remember," he begged of Danny as Danny grinned an enormous and terrifying grin, with his white teeth and red gums above them showing.

"Then come on, give your friend a hug," Danny said in a deep voice that was not his own, as they heard Monica's continuous bone-chilling screams behind him.

CHAPTER 47

The sky was bright and blue, the sun was shining, and Lydia wondered, *How can the sun shine, children play in the park and bees make honey on such an awful day?* Lydia didn't know what to do as she walked down that alleyway with a knife in her pocket. Her anger was outweighing any common sense that she still had. As soon as she got to the door, she took the knife out of her pocket and slowly opened it, at first thankful it wasn't locked, but not in her wildest nightmares did she expect to see what greeted her in that garage. The white van was gone, but what remained horrified her.

She could see a woman's body lying on the floor, her head caved in — any semblance of what she would have looked like was now lost as her skull was crushed with splatters of blood around what was left. Across the room, Lydia could see a man sitting on the floor, with his back leaning against one of the crates. He had a black eye, broken nose and severed ear. She believed he was dead already until he moaned and slowly moved his head up to look at the figure standing in the doorway.

When he woke up, Mark saw a beautiful woman holding a large knife in her hand, which she put back in her pocket as she noticed him still alive. He wondered if he was just hallucinating or was she really here — perhaps she was an angel, and he was already dead. As the woman moved closer to him, walking around the body of Monica, he looked into her green eyes, filled with disgust. He knew who she was, no hallucination and not an angel, just the daughter of a dead man and friend of a dead woman.

"What happened here?" she said, standing over him as he looked up at her.

"Daniel Greenway happened here," he wheezed, and that was when she noticed that his bloody hands were holding his stomach. She didn't know the name Daniel Greenway, but it wasn't hard for her to put two and two together. Daniel was Mr Crow's real name. "He's not human," he said, coughing up blood that stained his teeth dark red.

"Where is he?" she hissed, taking the not human part as a figure of speech while getting down to her knees to face him directly.

"You're the daughter. That was some invention that your dad made." He smiled, showing his bloodstained teeth. "I'm dying. It's a strange thing to know you'll be dead in a few minutes."

"Where is he?" she asked him, this time with more anger in her voice. She didn't care about this man's pain. She didn't know him, but she knew that he was one of the thieves or why else would he be here.

"I don't know."

She sighed, thinking of how she had lost both the dream recorder and her girlfriend's killer. She looked at him and came to realise the possibility that she was, in fact, in front of the man that murdered Katya. She looked into his eyes. Those eyes that were full of pain.

"But I know where he lives," he then wheezed out.

"Where?" she said with exuberance.

"Seventeen Dingwall Street," he hissed through his pain. "I told you what you wanted to know now. Please put me out of my misery."

"Out of your misery?" she said, raising one eyebrow as she said it. "What about the misery you and your friend put me through. Tell me now, was it you or he who murdered Katya?"

"I don't know what you are talking about," he said to her, his head slowly falling to one side as if he was getting too weak to keep it upright. Lydia sighed and got up, and just as she turned around, he called her back. "Wait."

"You're talking about that Russian bitch?" He could now see the anger on her face. "It was me, and I would have fucked her too if I had the time. I always had a thing for eastern European tarts. You know you're fit," he coughed and continued, "but a girl like that still could have had better." He hoped that she would finally kill him out of rage, but she just closed her eyes and took a deep breath.

Lydia opened her eyes again and spat in his face, the little bit of spit now resting just below his one good eye. "You deserve this, and I hope it hurts, I hope it really hurts," she told him before she walked towards one of the crates on the far side of the room, which had a black pen and a Walkman lying on top of it. Mark watched her as she walked off, then his eyes moved onto Monica's lifeless body, thinking of how things could have been so different. He started to feel very tired, his vision started to blur, and the garage seemed to darken as the pain eased. His hand dropped from his stomach, revealing the large cut that Danny made into his belly. He took one last deep breath, and his head fell down, and all turned to black.

Lydia stood next to the large crate, writing the address to Danny's house on her hand. She looked at the address questioning, herself if it was actually correct. "Is it Dingwall or Dingwell?" she asked, not knowing that he was now a corpse. When Lydia didn't get an answer, she turned around and saw his head was down as though he was asleep. There came a whisper from her mouth saying, "Doesn't matter, there can't be a Dingwall and Dingwell in this small town," before thinking, *Who the hell am I talking to now*.

Lydia would find him, but what was she going to do when she did? She looked at the two dead bodies — if he could do that to them, what was he going to do to her?

Lydia knew that the intelligent thing to do would be to just phone the police and let them deal with Daniel. Perhaps they would destroy the machine, and maybe she would finally be able to end all of this. Perhaps, Lydia needed to make sure the machine had been destroyed, and Danny, what would she do to him? She had never killed anyone — there was nothing but her anger making her think she could kill now. Knowing the pen she had just used would have her fingerprints on it, she put it in her pocket. She moved in front of Mark again, her heart full of anger, now wishing that she had killed him or perhaps tortured him just before his end. It didn't matter any more — he was dead, and so was Katya. He died a painful death, and perhaps that was good enough for Lydia's vengeance or maybe not — only time would tell.

Days later, the police would find not just two bloody bodies but another one inside a large crate. It would make the front page around the country. The garage would be forever known as the haunted place of a gruesome mass murder. Along with the death of a young girl from Russia, it would be something the citizens of Mayfield would talk about for years to come. The garage would be left abandoned, only being the home to rats until it was finally knocked down in 2009. A small park dedicated to the three people who lost their lives there was built a year later.

CHAPTER 48

Danny found himself in a cold and strange place, a forest full of trees with no leaves, just a weird black tar dripping from their branches. The sky was a peculiar dark purplish colour. No stars could be seen, but there was a white light in front of him. Danny thought it was the gates of heaven until he noticed Edgar holding an old lantern in front of him as he walked towards Danny.

"Where am I?" Danny asked him.

"You're in our world. The deamhan dorcha brought you here."

"How do I get out?" he said in a panic.

"You can't just leave," Edgar told him.

"Is this hell?"

"No, you're not dead, Daniel, not yet anyway."

"Then where is the deamhan dorcha?"

"In your world wearing your skin because you give him permission to do so."

Danny thought back, remembering the deamhan dorcha telling him that he could ease his pain if only he would allow it, which he did. What a fool, he told himself and thought about Emma and Libby. "I thought I was trying to save them, and now I've put them in even more danger," he told Edgar his heart aching with that knowledge. "Libby," he called out with excitement.

"What about her?"

"She has kind of a, I don't know, supernatural power. So perhaps you can warn her."

"It doesn't work like that."

"Then how does it work?"

"Libby's mind must be open to this world and there are times it is and times it is not. Sadly, at this time it is not."

"Shit," he whispered while running his hand through his hair before he heard a child crying. Looking behind him, he found a small square building with white walls and one door. "What's through that door?" he asked Edgar without looking at him.

"Only the past."

Danny walked slowly towards the brown door with its golden handle and golden number seven nailed upon it. He opened it, and he found himself in the corridor from Libby's dream. At the end of the hallway, Danny saw the little girl from Owen's dream pointing to one of the doors as if she was a cardboard cut-out sign pointing out directions in a theme park. He turned back around and found himself alone. With no idea what had happened to Edgar, he walked towards the girl, who disappeared into thin air as soon as he got close.

Danny looked to the door, slowly opened it, and walked into a child's bedroom where the walls were grey. The bed had just a mattress stained with urine. The

324

window at the end of the room that looked out to the night sky had metal bars over it, and below it lay a dog's water bowl.

"Mummy," he heard a little boy cry. He turned around, seeing a boy banging his fist against the door, crying for his mother. Danny knew who this child was, for it was himself at six years old when his mother left him locked up in his room. How long was he in that room without food? The six-year-old Danny stood back as he heard a loud banging against the other side of the door. The door then swung open, and two policemen wearing their seventies' dark blue uniforms and the old custodian helmet with the metal emblem of the Metropolitan Police Force made their way in.

"What've we got here then?" the first policeman said, looking at young Danny. "It looks like a boy."

"It does that, a pretty disgusting one, I may add."

"True that. No one is going to want a boy like that."

"No, no one at all."

"There's only one thing for it. I'd better put it out of its misery," the policeman said, taking out his truncheon.

"Yep, it's the kindest thing to do," the other said, taking his truncheon out too.

"No," Danny screamed, jumping in front of the two policemen. "Leave him alone." The two policemen looked at each other and walked out of the room, leaving them alone as Danny demanded of them. He heard loud laughter coming from behind him. Turning around, he saw to his horror that the room was covered in what looked like black tar and he noticed something strange, something unearthly coming from the tar. It had a long black and slimy neck coming from the ceiling with the upside-down head of his mother laughing at him, showing her yellow teeth and a dark green drool coming from her upside-down mouth. He took two steps back before feeling someone's cold hand grabbing hold of his arm and pulling him out of the room. It was Edgar, and as soon as Danny was out of the room, the door slammed itself shut, or perhaps it was Edgar who closed it. Danny couldn't say for sure.

"Stay away from them," Edgar told him, and Danny noticed something strange about Edgar's eyes. They were yellow like that of a cat.

"You're not Edgar Knightley, are you?" Danny said in surprise, not knowing why he didn't figure that out before.

"Edgar Knightley is in the afterlife. I'm the same as the deamhan dorcha, only I'm here to help you." Danny didn't know if that was true or not, but what other options did he have other than trusting him. "Close your eyes."

"Why?"

"Do it."

Danny dubiously did as he was told and shut his eyes but didn't find darkness; instead, he saw through his own eyes once again as the deamhan dorcha used his body. It was driving Mark's van towards the street where Henry Winters lived. He didn't know if it knew he saw through its eyes, or he should say his own eyes, as it parked up and got out of the van with Mark's knife in his hand. It opened

Henry's front door, and the Thai woman came running out of the living room shouting, "What are you doing here? Get out." The deamhan dorcha replied by quickly cutting open her throat. But it didn't wait around to see her die. Instead, it went upstairs towards a small room where Henry was sitting on a desk chair staring at it.

Danny could see the fear on his face as Henry said, "I knew this day would come."

"I know you did, for as you know, there is no escaping me," the deamhan dorcha said.

"You need to fight the fear, Danny."

"Danny is already lost," it said, walking towards Henry. Danny quickly opened his eyes, bringing him back into the corridor as he didn't want to see yet another death by his own hands.

CHAPTER 49

L ibby hadn't seen much of the monster; there were nights where she wouldn't even dream of him but dreamed of other things, mostly of things that were nonsensical in her waking mind. Although the monster featured less in her nightmares than it did before, she didn't feel safe from it, and her mother was still worried about her, and not just that she knew that something was running through her mind. Something was scaring Emma, and Libby wished she knew the right thing to say to her mother — she had asked if she was okay, and of course, the answer that always came back was, "Yeah, I'm fine." Libby knew she had no skill in expressing the right words to people. Due to her social anxiety, she chose not to confront her mother with her worries. Instead played on Mario Cart 64, struggling to stay focused on the game — her mind kept going back to her mother. There was also something else that worried her, but it was nothing more than a feeling, a sense that something truly awful was about to happen. She had her sixth sense she didn't understand, and she didn't know why or how this dreadful thing was going to happen, but it had something to do with Danny.

Libby no longer hated Danny. In fact, there grew a bit of a fondness for him, and she didn't think he would ever have the desire to hurt her or Emma, but there was a sense of danger around him. She tried to ignore the feeling of dread and tried again to focus on the colourful cartoony world of the game. Yet each time, she found that she would crash the cart and lose every race she played. It was then that she heard the sound of a real engine outside her window.

Pausing the game Libby stood up and looked through the window, staring down at the road in front of her front garden. Libby saw a taxi pull up next to the house and saw a woman who seemed oddly familiar to her come out of the passenger door. It was a woman with brown hair wearing blue jeans and a brown jacket. She stood in front of Danny's garden, staring at his door, looking like she was afraid to knock and too scared to see what was in that house. The woman then took a few steps forward into Danny's front garden and stopped and looked up at Libby's window, noticing Libby staring back down at her. The woman gave her a shy smile before walking closer to Danny's front door.

Lydia thought as she set foot into that garden how average the home of Mr Crow was. She had expected it to be in some run-down location with pavements decorated with used needles and condom wrappers. She thought she would find herself being watched by crackheads and drug dealers, that being in the street would be a danger, but it wasn't the case at all. All there was, was a curious little girl that watching her. His garden seemed a little unloved and overgrown, but that was about it. She turned her hands into fists and banged on the door, moving her other hand to the knife she kept in her pocket. Again and again she slammed her fist against the door until she heard a woman's voice tell her, "He's not in," from the garden next door. Lydia turned around and saw a woman who looked to be in her mid to late twenties with dark hair — she was obviously the mother to the little girl in the window.

"Do you know when he will be back?" Lydia asked.

The woman stared at her with a face full of puzzlement and took a quick look up at the child's window but saw nothing apart from her closed cream-coloured curtains.

"Are you okay?" Lydia asked her, wondering if the woman was on some kind of drug because of how she looked at her.

"I'm fine, but why do you want to see Danny?" the woman replied quickly.

"We have some unfinished business to deal with," Lydia told her, but she still found it strange how this woman stared at her like she was trying to look through her. The woman's attention then moved to her front doorway, where she could see her daughter standing watching them both.

"Libby, go back in," she told her, and Libby turned around to walk back into the house. That is when something clicked in Lydia's memory, the name Libby.

What did Mr Crow say about that girl? She remembered he asked did she know her because the little girl had a dream about her. *But why would anyone dream of me*, she thought to herself.

"Is that your daughter?" Lydia asked her.

"Yeah, my little angel," she said before biting her bottom lip, wondering what to ask next.

Lydia needed to know more about this strange woman and try her best to determine why the little girl she had never met would dream about her.

"You got any children?" the woman asked Lydia.

"No, I haven't, my partner and I had once planned to adopt, but things didn't work out."

The woman could see that subject had hurt her but didn't know why. "Oh, you broke up then?"

Lydia looked at her and shook her head. "She's…" It became hard to say the four-letter word, but the word came out in a croak, "Dead," through her heartbreak.

"Oh, I'm sorry."

"Yeah, so am I."

"Say, do you want to come in for a quick drink?" Emma asked, wondering as soon as she asked the question if it was the right thing to do. She felt a need to learn more about the woman inside Libby's dream, but what if she was dangerous. She didn't look like someone who would want to hurt a little girl like Libby, she thought, but looks can be deceiving. In the end, she decided it was best for them to sit down and have a chat.

It seemed as if Lydia agreed with her as she answered her question with a quick and unenthusiastic, "Sure."

In Emma's living room, Lydia sat on her leather sofa with a cup of coffee with two sugars and a small amount of milk. In contrast, Emma sat on her armchair with a cup of tea with no sugar.

"So, what kind of unfinished business do you have with Danny?" Emma asked.

"Oh well," she said with uncertainty, "he did a favour for me, and I just need to pay him back for it."

"Ah, I see," Emma replied, watching Lydia drinking her coffee. Wondering, what kind of favour did he do with this girl — whatever it was, it must have been recent. She would have assumed that Danny would say something or given a hint that he knew the woman in the video unless he had cheated on her with this woman. But if it was indeed the woman in the video — she couldn't be sure without watching it again. "Sorry, I didn't think to ask your name?"

"It's Lydia," she said with a friendly smile. So, Emma thought, *I was right*. How was it possible, and what was so special about her?

"And what is your name?" Lydia asked, sounding disinterested like it was a scripted question.

"Emma," she replied quickly and coldly. "Can you just excuse me for a minute? Nature calls." Emma got up off the chair and walked out of the room, and went upstairs to Libby's bedroom, where she noticed Libby sitting on the floor like she was meditating. "Libby, do you know that woman downstairs?" she asked her softly.

"I've seen her in my dreams, only she didn't have any hair in them."

"Why?" Emma asked, standing over her.

"Why what?"

"Why didn't she have any hair?"

"I don't know."

"Do you know if she was good or bad?"

"Good, I think," Libby replied, but the tone of her voice told Emma that she wasn't at all sure.

"Libby, I need you to really think, okay. Why was this woman in your dreams?" she asked, accepting the answer that she would surely get, and of course, the answer was a confused look with an,

"I don't know."

"Does she do anything in your dreams?"

"I can't remember?" Libby answered with agitation in her voice. This was a subject that was starting to become both confusing and scary to her. The questions rolling around in Emma's head — she wondered if she would ever find any answers to them.

"Is there anything that you can tell me about her, anything at all?"

There was a long pause before Libby shook her head. It was true. She had nothing to tell Emma — her memories of Lydia were very vague, more like little snapshots of her not doing much. Emma smiled down at her daughter, trying to hide her disappointment. "Okay, monkey. Do you want to wait here for a bit, and if you're good, I'll buy you a new game or a toy when I get the chance, okay?"

"Okay," Libby replied, with no enthusiasm — it was not that she didn't care about getting a new game. Having no friends, games, books, movies, and toys were her only means of escapism and fun.

Emma walked back downstairs into the living room. She saw that Lydia was now looking at a photo of Libby as a baby, sitting on the floor surrounded by soft toys. She turned and smiled at Emma. "She's a beautiful kid."

"Thank you, she sure is," Emma replied.

Lydia then looked at her guitar, pointing at it like a child would point at an animal in the zoo. "Do you play?"

"Yes," Emma said with a smile — she always loved the opportunity to tell people about her old band. "I used to be a guitarist in a band called the Devil Kats, but we broke up many years ago."

"Kats?" Lydia said, and Emma noticed that a simple little word had caused some distress in her.

"Yeah, but spelt with a K instead of a C. It was kind of a punk rock band," she told her as she sat down on the leather sofa.

"That's really cool."

"Do you play?" Emma asked her.

"No, my dad tried to get me into the violin, but I couldn't get into it. So I guess I'm not that musical."

"I see," Emma replied, before saying, "Listen, this is going to sound strange, but I need to ask you something." Lydia sat back on the sofa, giving her full attention.

"Have you met my daughter Libby, or Elizabeth, before?"

"No, never," she answered. "But I think I know why you asked me that."

"You do?" Emma said in surprise.

"I think so. You've watched your daughter's dreams, haven't you?"

A strange feeling ran through Emma's body. Had Danny told her about the dream recorder? If so, why? "How do you know that?"

"The machine that allows you to watch a person's dream was invented by my father, but don't ask me how, because I don't know, and to be honest, I don't care. I just want the thing to be destroyed, and I would have already done it if that bastard hadn't stolen it."

"Have you used it?" Emma asked.

Lydia didn't know why but for some reason, the question took her by surprise. "No."

"It drives people insane. Think what you want about Danny, but he's not a bad man, and this machine has done awful things to his mind. He sees a demon or a boogieman, whatever you want to call it in his mind, as clear as day. The very same creature that we saw in my daughter's nightmare."

"Was it a tall looking anthropomorphic creature?" Lydia asked, remembering the creature both in her childhood memories and on the video of her father's dream.

Emma just looked at her with her face full of confusion. She hated making herself look stupid but needed to ask, "What's antrop—"

"Anthropomorphic means human-like."

"Yeah, it was. You've seen it as well?" Emma asked in excitement.

"I have, yes. I was just a bit older than your daughter is now when my sister died, and for years after that, I would have wild dreams about that creature. But then, I got older, and those dreams started to slowly dissipate, and I never thought about it. It was only when I watched one of my father's dreams that I saw the deamhan dorcha again."

"Yeah, I spoke with Henry Winters. He told me much about it."

"Henry Winters?" Lydia said in surprise. "The kid who murdered his mum and dad?"

"It wasn't him, or it was, but he wasn't in control of himself. It's able to possess people like in *The Exorcist*," Emma said,

"Not human, he said," Lydia whispered to herself.

"What?"

"Never mind, sorry thinking out loud, can I just ask what kind of relationship you have with your neighbour?"

Emma didn't know what to tell her — she worried how this strange woman would react if she told her the truth about her and Danny's relationship. She sighed and finally decided to tell her the truth. "He was my boyfriend before we broke up."

"You're better off. Did you know he was a thief?" Lydia asked, and it was a question that Emma didn't appreciate.

"Not at the beginning, but what does that matter. Danny is a good man — he treated my daughter and me well. He never got the chance to learn to play the violin or live in a big house in the country. He had to learn to survive on his own," Emma said bitterly.

"Did you meet his friend?" Lydia asked grudgingly.

"No, I never met any of his friends."

"Well, his friend was the man who killed my girlfriend, and your sweet Danny was there when he did it, and he did nothing to stop him."

CHAPTER 50

The police were on the lookout for Mark Long's white van. John Gallaway knew, of course, that the death of the Russian girl was his fault. It wasn't the guilt about her death that worried him. It was that the crime could lead back to him, and there was confusion about why they'd killed the Russian girl. Katya Smirnova was her name. She was twenty-five years old and from a city named Sochi in the southwest of the country. What was she doing here in Kent? For once, John, who had a young daughter of his own, felt terrible, not for the girl but her parents at home in Russia, not knowing that their daughter had died so far from home. So, every police patrol car now had the van's licence plate number.

It was around three o'clock in the afternoon when the report of the burnt van came in. The vehicle was found in the woods just off Rose Hill Road, close to where Andrew Williams died. It had to be the vehicle they were looking for, but the whereabouts of the owner or driver was still unknown. Gallaway knew he had to get his fellow officers off the scent, for this was one criminal he couldn't afford to catch. Still, John Gallaway had to look like he was trying to find him. Perhaps he thought he could pin the blame on Lydia Knightley, but first, he had to find her. Lydia could have gone mad with her father's death; her worried friend could have confronted her about her mental illness. What if she snapped and lost control? Some of the cops wondered why they weren't told to watch the Knightley house.

He drove to the old house — it was a long shot that the girl would be there, but it was worth a try. When he parked just outside the house, he thought to himself, this was going to be the last time he would ever deal with the Irishman again. He sat in the car, staring at the house before opening the glove box and taking out a container of aspirin and taking two pills, washing them down with a bottle of Irn-Bru that had now gone flat after days of resting in his warm car. He got out of the vehicle. He walked to the house, thinking what a nice place to live, it's out in the middle of nowhere and it's a decent-sized property. He would like something similar if he had the money.

Gallaway moved towards the door, noticing to his surprise that the door was unlocked. He pushed the door open and stepped into the hallway leading to the living room and the kitchen. The only noise to be heard was the sound of his own footsteps. He ever so slowly opened the door into the living room and looked around at the pieces of furniture, which were the only things left. The television, pictures and ornaments were all gone. Then all of a sudden, he heard something moving around upstairs. Was it Lydia Knightley who was up there, or was it the killers? The Irishman had never told him the name of his client. Would it be better if it was him upstairs or Lydia? He wasn't too sure, but he knew how dangerous he was if it was the killer.

He took out his police CS spray from his inner pocket and moved out of the living room, and slowly went upstairs, which seemed emptier than the downstairs. He walked past the bathroom, where he knew Edgar's body was found. Standing on the landing, he looked towards the open door that led into an empty room with a blue carpet. He felt like he was being watched, and though Gallaway believed in that kind of sixth sense, he didn't believe in ghosts and other things that go bump in the night, so he knew someone was in that house with him.

"Hello," he called out. "I'm with the police. If you are here, Miss Knightley, I would just like to ask you a few questions, that's all." But there was no answer. He started to think he was just paranoid until a hand quickly covered his mouth. Someone had sneaked up on him, but who? He didn't know, but he knew it wasn't Lydia as it was a rough hand, a man's hand with his fingers pushing into him so hard he started to feel that they could crush into the bone. He felt another hand on his forehead, and before he could work out what was going on, his head was twisted violently to the side, and he fell down onto the floor.

Danny looked down at the body that now lay in front of him. He didn't want to kill him, but he no longer had any control of his own body. It was like Danny's body was now a machine that was being operated by the deamhan dorcha. He kept watching as it moved to the far end of the room and got down on all fours, feeling the carpet.

"What is it doing?" Danny asked Edgar while seeing through its eyes but got no reply from him. The deamhan dorcha then found a small cut in the carpet where he pulled it up, finding a loose floorboard. He then pulled it up and threw it to the side, finding another notebook with no writing on its dark blue cover. It opened it up, seeing detailed drawings and instructions on how the dream recorder was built.

Danny opened his eyes, finding himself back in the corridor, standing in front of the fake Edgar. "He's going to create more of them," Danny said in a panic.

"The recorder gives it more power hence the reason why the gun failed to work for Mark and Monica, so what if every nation on earth had a dream recorder," Edgar told him.

"More of its kind will walk the Earth," Danny answered.

"Yes. It wants its kind on your world."

"How do I stop it; how do I kill it?" he asked in a panic.

"There is no way one can kill a deamhan dorcha but you can stop it, but you wouldn't like how."

"Just tell me."

"By shedding blood, your blood."

CHAPTER 51

L ydia stood staring out of Emma's window, waiting for Danny's return with her arms folded in front of her.

"Do you plan on killing Danny?" Emma asked her.

She sighed, not knowing the answer to that herself, but she gave her the response of, "I just want what he took from my family, that's all."

"It's completely mad, isn't it," Emma muttered, and Lydia slowly turned around and looked back at her, saying,

"What is?"

"All this over a bloody tape recorder, it's ridiculous. I suppose it says a lot about human nature — we all fight over that something new."

"That's quite hypocritical of you, Emma — after all, didn't you use the machine on your own daughter?" She said like it was a question, but she knew very well she did.

"I thought it would help her, but it just made things worse for everyone. I learnt more about the monster in her nightmares, but that was it. I still don't understand why she dreamt of you or what the hallway was all about."

"That's your problem — you are trying to rationalise dreams. They are, in fact, completely senseless. Now I have to admit that your daughter dreaming of me gives me quite an odd feeling and something that I cannot explain. Still, I believe most of what we see in dreams is meaningless, just your mind creating images like a film."

"How can you say that?" Emma moaned at her. "What about the deamhan dorcha? You told me it was in your nightmares like it's in our Libby's."

"I was a child who had just lost her little sister. Of course I had nightmares and would have seen monsters. My head was all fucked up from what happened to my sister. The same thing could happen to any child in that kind of circumstance. It doesn't mean me and your daughter have been seeing the same monster."

"But you asked me if the creature was human-like?"

Lydia didn't say anything to that — it was true she said that, and yes, she did actually believe in the creature. *Perhaps it's nothing paranormal, just an idea that fills some people's minds.*

"You could see it because you are like me," they heard a soft and sweet voice say from the living room's doorway, where Libby was standing looking at them both.

"I told you to stay upstairs," Emma moaned at her daughter.

"What do you mean, we are the same?" Lydia asked her.

"The monster that scared you when you were little is the one that I see in my dreams."

"And how would you know this?" she asked, speaking to her like she was an adult.

"I see things," Libby said, and she shook her head before saying, "but only sometimes, not all the time."

"You mean the monster?" Lydia asked, and there was a worried look on Emma's face.

"Sometimes, but I've also seen you. Your full name is Lydia Helen Knightley, and you were kind to Vicky because you loved her, and your heart was broken on the day she died. You always blamed yourself for her getting hit by that lorry, but it wasn't your fault," Libby said, and Emma looked at Lydia, whose eyes were starting to water.

Emma, with her mouth slightly open in shock, looked back to Libby. "How do you know all that?" she asked.

"I don't know, I just do," Libby said, still standing in the doorway.

Lydia was trying to not show her feelings as she'd already cried that day and really didn't want to cry again. "Does Vicky talk to you?" she then asked Libby.

"No, not really," Libby told her.

"Are you asking if my daughter sees ghosts?" Emma queried.

"After everything she has told me, do you think her seeing a ghost is really that hard to believe?"

"Listen, I am sorry about what happened to your sister, I really am, but I don't want you to have this type of conversation with my daughter. She's just a child. She shouldn't have to deal with ghosts and demons and shit like that," she told Lydia.

"You're right. I'm sorry," she said and looked back through the window, still waiting for Danny.

344

Libby finally walked into the room, sitting on Emma's lap. "Am I still getting a game or a toy?" she asked her mother softly.

"No, I told you, you could get one if you stayed upstairs — that was our deal, and you broke that deal," she moaned to her.

"He should have been back by now," Lydia whispered to herself.

"How long did it take your dad to make the dream recorder?" Libby asked Lydia, and Emma sighed quietly — so the secret was up, she knew about it. No doubt she had been listening in on their conversation. *Only a child would take something as crazy as a dream recorder at face value*, Emma thought to herself. Still, she was surprised that she wasn't upset about having her dreams recorded. Emma guessed at such a young age you always believed your mother knows best.

"A very long time. Years actually, maybe decades of testing and researching this and that," Lydia told her and then turned back around to face them, giving Libby a smile that was filled with sadness. "I still remember in his study that the walls were full of notes and..." She stopped herself, her eyes widening as though something had just come into her mind, and it had. If the deamhan dorcha was real, it might know everything that her father knew, such as the location of all his notes on the creation of the dream recorder. "Oh god," she whispered.

"What?" Emma asked.

"He isn't going to come back home. Did you say there are more of those monsters?" she asked Emma.

"Oh, so you believe in them now."

"Just answer the question, please," Lydia moaned, and Emma looked at Libby, who was still sitting on her lap listening to what they were saying.

"Yeah, a few all around the world."

"The dream recorder gives the creature more power — what if he was somehow able to create more of them and sell them in every corner of the world?"

"Danny wouldn't be stupid enough to do that," Emma said in a matter-of-fact tone before saying, "unless it had possessed him."

"I don't think Danny is Danny anymore," Lydia said, as once again the images of the massacre in the garage ran through her mind. The words of 'the scumbag', as she called Mark, were also embedded into her mind. Lydia knew then the real reason her father told her to destroy the machine. Yet, even with that information, her heart still felt heavy about the death of Katya. *I should have forced her to stay in Greece*, she told herself.

CHAPTER 52

"Why can't I go with you," Libby moaned as Emma held her hand, dragging her across the street towards a row of houses that faced her own. All the while, Lydia waited for her outside Emma's house, thinking how she wished she had told Emma no when asked to come back to the old house with her. Lydia didn't think she could deal with another death on her conscience, especially the death of a woman with a child. Perhaps Lydia could just run away while Emma's back was turned. She was a fast runner, coming third place in the 1993 Mayfield marathon, and Emma would be too busy dealing with her daughter. She wouldn't even notice, but it was a long way to travel, and it was some distance into the town centre where she could find a taxi.

"Because where we are going is no place for little girls," Emma said to Libby as they entered Mrs Peterson's garden, which had little ornamental frogs that covered the grass, each of them doing their own activities such as fishing or sunbathing with a red bikini on; another was sitting on a bike. Mrs Peterson was a neighbour who Emma trusted. Although she would be the first to admit that she could hold the Guinness World record for trusting the wrong people, she doubted that little old sweet Marge Peterson would do any harm to anyone. Just as Emma was about to knock on the door, Libby cried, "But I can help you!"

"No, you can't."

"I'm not a baby anymore," she yelled at Emma, and it was the first time she had ever raised her voice to her. "Let me help you."

"I know you're not a baby, Monkey," she said softly. In any other circumstance, Libby would have been in a lot of trouble for yelling at her mother.

"I'm not a monkey either," Libby moaned.

"All right, all right, you're not a monkey, but I need you to wait here, not for you but for me. I love you more than anything in this crazy world, and if anything happens to you, then I wouldn't be able to live. So, you understand that just spending a few hours with Mrs Peterson is what is going to help me."

There was a short pause as Libby thought it through before saying, "But Mrs Peterson smells of pee."

"Libby, come on, that's not nice." Emma turned to the door, and just before knocking, she said to her, "Okay, she does smell a bit funny, but she is a lovely lady who is also very old. So, don't go telling her that you think she smells of pee and especially don't tell her that I agree with you." She pressed the doorbell which played a little tune of Frere Jacques. Mrs Peterson was an old woman with thick curly grey hair and big milk bottle glasses. She was wearing an orange jumper and a skirt with tiny pictures of roses on them. As soon the old woman opened the door, they could smell that awful smell of urine.

"Oh hello," Mrs Peterson said, acting like she was happy to see them both. Perhaps she was — the woman may have been in her eighties and didn't get many visitors that Emma knew of after the death of her husband.

"Hi, Mrs Peterson," Emma said with a big smile on her face. "I was wondering if you could do me a huge favour?"

"What's that?"

"Can you take care of Libby while I nip out for a few hours? I will try to be as quick as I can," Emma begged of her.

Mrs Peterson looked at Libby, who was just standing at the side of Emma, staring up at her. "Yes, sure," she told Emma with some uncertainty.

"Thanks, thanks a lot. You wouldn't believe how much of a help this is to me."

"Oh, no problem whatsoever," she said in her friendly tone while Libby sulked at the side of Emma.

"Right, Libby, be good for Mrs Peterson, okay?"

"Okay, bye then," Libby replied under her breath, walking into the old woman's house.

"Once again, thank you so much," Emma said, giving Mrs Peterson a big friendly smile before rushing off back towards her own house where Mrs Peterson could see another woman waiting for her.

"Who's your mummy's friend? Dear?" she asked Libby.

"Lydia, a lady who was in my dreams. They are going to destroy a machine that let monsters out of people's nightmares into the real world," Libby told her, like it was nothing, even though she didn't really know if the facts were correct.

"Oh, that sounds nice, dear," Mrs Peterson said with worry in her voice.

Lydia and Emma sat in the living room, waiting for a taxi to take them to Edgar's old house. Lydia walked back and forth like an angry lion in a cage, impatient that the cab had not yet arrived. "Why don't you own a car?" she muttered to Emma.

"Why don't you? You're one with the wealthy father," Emma said.

"I sold my car just before moving to Santorini," Lydia explained.

"Where's that?" Emma asked.

"Santorini?"

"Yeah."

"It's an island in Greece."

"Why did you move to Greece?"

"It's sunnier and more relaxing than Mayfield," she told her, but the truth was she was running away from her past. It's funny how such things catch up with you. She sighed before saying, "I went travelling through Europe using the money that my dad gave me. You'd be surprised how fast your money disappears when you're travelling."

"Is that where you met your girlfriend?"

"Katya, yeah, in a bar in Rome. She was so beautiful but also so innocent at that time. I fell for her as soon as I heard that Russian accent. I thought she sounded cool like a villain in a bad action movie," Lydia said, making herself smile. "That was a funny thing to think as, really, she was the least villainous person I have ever met. She didn't have a single bad bone in her body. I should have been the one to die, not her."

"It seems you really loved her," Emma commented.

"I did. Do you love Mister Crow?"

"Who?" Emma asked.

"Sorry, I mean Danny."

"Oh yeah, I think I do," she told her, and Lydia turned back to the window as they heard the sound of a car pulling up in front of the house. "The taxi's here," she then told Emma. "Are you ready?"

"Of course."

Together they walked out of the house, Emma locking the door after them, and then they took the taxi to Edgar's old house, not knowing if Danny was already there or not. Lydia hoped to God that he wasn't because she knew that he still had the gun. She didn't know how she would be able to defend herself against him if he had the gun. How many bullets were in it? Surely, she thought, there weren't many but as she thought back to the two dead bodies in the garage, she remembered that neither of them looked like they had been shot. *Should I tell her about the gun and the bodies?* she wondered as they sat in the back of the taxi,

Emma sitting quietly by her side looking at the passing buildings through the window.

When the taxi pulled up at the house, there were no cars to be seen, making her think that the house was completely empty. After all, Danny was driving a white van and that van was nowhere to be seen. Lydia paid the driver and walked towards the house's front door with Emma walking by her side.

"Is this where you grew up?" Emma asked her.

"Yeah."

"Very nice," Emma said, looking at the old Tudor home and the pleasant green fields and hills around it.

"It was all right, it was just home, I guess," she told her as she got to the door and took her keys out, putting them into the lock turning it, but to her surprise, the door was already unlocked and she had just relocked it.

"What's wrong?" Emma asked her as she noticed the worried look on her face.

"The door was unlocked — it might be nothing, but we should be careful," she told her as she slowly opened the door and looked back at Emma, putting a finger to her lips. Emma didn't understand why she was so worried — it sounded like there was no one in there. In fact, it sounded like there was no one for miles. Everything was just still and quiet, apart from the sound of the birds singing in the trees, but still, she thought, what is it they say? The calm before the storm, perhaps that was what was happening here.

CHAPTER 53

Danny, with the deamhan dorcha controlling his body, drove Gallaway's car towards the road near the field behind Edgar's house. It reminded Danny of the first time he was here with Mark, checking out the house and seeing the old man in his garden. They had thought it would be an easy job — there would be nothing to this one. Not in his wildest dreams, would he ever have believed that things would turn out the way they did. How he wished more than anything that he had simply died instead of taking the creature up on his offer. Living with the deamhan dorcha controlling your body was no way to live. He got out of the car and opened the car boot where Gallaway's body lay, his eyes still open like he was staring into the abyss. It didn't have a clue what it was doing, Danny thought, as he picked the body out of the boot and put it over his shoulder like it was nothing more than a rolled-up rug. Anyone could drive past them and see what they were doing. He threw the body over the wall which separated the road from the field.

Again, Danny thought about how stupid this was. There were a hundred and one ways for them to get caught carrying a dead body out in the daylight. He dragged

Gallaway by the legs across the field towards a large lake with an English walnut tree in front of it. It kind of reminded Danny of the dream he had when he was talking to Edgar. The lake looked the same, but in the dream, the English walnut tree was a giant Japanese maple tree. He clearly remembered renaissance style statues out in a very grand looking garden. Yet neither the statues nor garden were anywhere to be seen. Instead, there was a little wooden paddle boat next to the tree. He lay the body in the boat and put rocks into the dead man's pockets, then dragged the boat into the lake. Just as it sailed off, he jumped in with it, almost tipping the boat over.

"It's a fool. It's hiding a body in daylight," Danny told Edgar, still with his eyes shut, still looking at what the deamhan dorcha was doing with his body.

"Perhaps it doesn't fear the consequences of a poor body disposal plan. After all, if it gets caught for murder, it isn't it that would spend the rest of its days rotting in prison," Edgar told him.

The deamhan dorcha sailed into the middle of the lake, taking the oars out of the water and putting them in the boat with him as he picked up the body. The boat rocked, making Danny think that he would fall in the lake, but the boat remained upright on the water as he threw the body in. Then, as the deamhan dorcha watched the body disappear into the depths of the lake, it said with its own voice, "I know you are watching, Daniel. Did you enjoy watching me use your body for murder? I'm sure you enjoyed the death of Monica and Mark. I wonder how much you will enjoy the death of Emma Holland and her daughter?"

"Please do what you want with me but leave them alone. I beg of you," he cried.

"They must die."

"Don't you dare touch them," Danny screamed out loud in anger, forgetting that he had nothing to threaten it with.

The deamhan dorcha laughed. "You can't threaten me. I am the one in control. You need proof?" it said, making Danny in his world grab hold of the little finger of his left hand and pull it back, creating an awful cracking noise, followed by a sense of pain that he could feel in the other world. Danny opened his eyes, seeing the panicked look on Edgar's face as Danny still held his hand in pain. Then heard what Edgar heard, the loud banging against the door. He knew it was the tar creature trying to force its way out of the room.

"What is that thing?"

"Another lifeform of this world. It feeds on misery and fear."

The door then flew off its hinges and hit the wall on the other side of the corridor. "Run."

"What about you?" Danny said, panicking.

"Don't worry about me. It can only give me pain, not death," he said as the creature squeezed itself through the door and it began moving towards them. The face of Danny's mother grew from the tar and screamed like it was in pain like a mother giving birth.

"Run," Edgar screamed at him.

Danny ran as fast as his legs could take him past Edgar. Finally, he made it to one of the wooden doors. Before going through it, he looked back at the fake Edgar, seeing the old man had been replaced with a creature that looked very much like the deamhan dorcha but with pale white skin and long white hair. A dark hand came out of the tar creature, grabbing the fake Edgar's hand as another came out, grabbing his other hand. It picked him up with both hands, stretching his arms out wide to his side like a man being crucified.

"Run" Edgar screamed through the pain as the tar creature ripped off both arms of the fake Edgar like a cruel child pulling the legs off an insect.

Danny quickly opened the door, jumping through it and ending up in the dark forest, where he found the oak tree next to the lake and in the middle of it an old wooden boat resting on top of the water with the deamhan dorcha standing in the middle of it, staring right at him. Danny was frozen with fear, just looking back at it as it hissed, "Remember I have you."

CHAPTER 54

"There's nothing here," Emma told Lydia as she looked through every room in the house, slowly moving around, trying to listen where the floor creaked a little more than usual. They went through every corner of the living room and the kitchen, checking every bit of furniture that still remained in the house but finding nothing.

"This could take us all day," Emma moaned.

"Then go home," Lydia snapped.

"I told you this is just as important to me as it is to you. More perhaps, so I'm staying here."

"Then just quit your whining."

"I'm not whining. I just feel like this could be a complete waste of time," she said, walking around the room and checking if any of the floorboards are loose.

"Anything?"

"Nada," replied Emma.

"All right, let's try upstairs," Lydia said, walking past her and upstairs with Emma following closely behind her. They walked into the room that was once Edgar's bedroom, and Emma quickly noticed a tiny red stain on the blue carpet.

"Lydia?"

"What?"

"Look," she said, pointing toward the stain. They both moved in closer until they were standing over it. They knew that stain was blood, but whose blood was the question.

They had similar ideas, but they didn't know for sure. Lydia thought it could be Danny's, that he'd got injured during his fight with the two thieves in that garage. Emma also thought it might be Danny's blood, but she didn't have Lydia's exact details.

"He was here," Lydia whispered, fearing that he still could be somewhere in the house. Emma turned away from the stain. Looking towards the window, Emma saw that the carpet in the corner of the room seemed to have been slightly pulled up. "Lydia, I think the thing we're looking for could be over there." They both moved to it, and Lydia pulled the carpet up, seeing the loose floorboard underneath it.

"Bingo," she whispered before removing the floorboard and picking up the notebook. With a lick of her lips, Lydia skimmed through the pages, seeing quickly the details of the making of the dream recorder. She didn't give herself any time to read what was written or take in any diagrams. Still, she knew unequivocally it was the right notebook.

"Is that what we came for?" Emma asked.

"Yeah, it is," she said before standing up and holding it in her hand. "Come on, we'd better get out of here," she said and as soon as she said that, they heard a door downstairs open and shut. "Oh no," Lydia whispered — with all the furniture upstairs gone, there was now nowhere to hide. She looked at Emma, putting her finger to her lips. The only hope they had was to be as quiet as the grave, or they would end up in one. She moved ever so quietly and put the loose floorboard back in place before retreating to the wall next to the open door. Emma still didn't realise the danger, but Lydia surely did with what she had seen in the garage. They stood in silence, listening to the footsteps downstairs.

"Listen to me," Lydia whispered to Emma. "Danny isn't the man you once knew. He's that thing now. We have to be really quiet."

Emma replied by just nodding her head. She knew the creature was dangerous, but just not how dangerous. As they heard the sound of footsteps making their way upstairs, they stood up as straight as the walls with their backs against them. The fear on Lydia's face made Emma feel an awful sense of dread, just like her. Danny walked through the door and straight past them. Lydia covered her mouth and nose with her hand, and Emma followed him with her eyes as he walked towards the loose floor. Emma's eyes moved to Lydia, who signalled her with her eyes to move out of the room while Danny's back was turned away from them. As he knelt down, both of the women slowly began to move out of the room.

Just as they thought they had made it out without being noticed, both of them heard the click of the gun.

Straight after it, they heard the deamhan dorcha's voice saying from Danny's mouth, "Little Lydia, oh how I have missed you." They turned around and saw Danny pointing the gun at Lydia, ignoring Emma like she wasn't even there. Emma noticed his little finger on the left hand sticking up and bent unnaturally back. "Look at you all grown up, but still, I can taste your fear like I could the day you first saw me." It was an unreal feeling for them to hear the creature's voice coming through Danny. "You remember, it was only a few days after you killed your sister." Lydia felt a rush of regret wash over her, thinking, *He's right, It was my fault*, before she remembers what Libby told her.

"Danny, please just lower the gun," Emma begged.

Danny's eyes finally moved to Emma as he said with the creature's voice, "Quiet, whore, Daniel has no control here." Then, his eyes went back to Lydia, and he gave her a big smile. "This seems so very familiar, doesn't it? Only your places have changed."

"I am not scared of you anymore," Lydia said, trying to act tough in the face of danger, but it knew, as did everyone else in the room, that was a lie. "Daniel, do you remember what little Lydia did to you the last time you saw her? For I do." He aimed the gun down at her legs. It stood there aiming the weapon for a few seconds before saying out of the blue, "Leave them alone after what she did to you?"

Lydia quickly looked to Emma, who said, "Danny, are you in there?" which got no reply. Lydia knew it wasn't going to just let her go, so she closed her eyes and then heard the bang and the scream coming from Emma. She quickly fell to the floor, crying in pain, as she heard Emma running out of the room.

The deamhan dorcha in Danny's body jumped on top of Lydia, his hands around her throat, choking the life out of her. "Are you ready to die, little Lydia, I enjoyed watching your father die, and I'm going to enjoy watching you die," he hissed through Danny's teeth.

Emma, who was now downstairs, stood in front of the front door. She wanted to run for her life and never look back, but even though she barely knew Lydia, she couldn't just leave her to die. She looked back up the stairs and whispered to herself, "Oh bloody hell." And then she looked back to the door, and she sighed the words, "I'm sorry."

Lydia couldn't breathe as she realised that this was it, this was the last moment of her life. But she would not go out without a fight. Lydia couldn't just let it win. Reaching into her coat pocket, she pulled out her knife and stabbed it into Danny's leg, but it had no effect on him.

Emma quickly rushed upstairs and saw Danny on top of Lydia, his hands around her throat and the gun resting near them where he dropped it. She promptly ran as fast as her legs could take her towards the gun and picked it up, aiming it at Danny's head.

"Get off her," she yelled at him.

Danny released his grip on Lydia's throat and looked at Emma. "Emma," he said now with Danny's own voice. "It's me Daniel, you won't hurt me, not the man you love."

She looked down at Lydia, who was gasping for air on the floor. "Let her go," she told him as her hands shook — she hadn't thought what she would do after getting the gun. She knew she couldn't bring herself to kill Danny, so what was she going to do.

Danny got up, and Lydia crawled out of the way and sat in the corner of the room, holding her throat and catching her breath.

"Come on, please," the creature cried, still using Danny's voice. "I love you, Emma."

Emma started to lower the gun. If Lydia could still speak, she would scream at her, *no, he's tricking you*. The creature made Danny smile a joyful yet sinister smile. Walking closer to her it then slapped her across the face with the back of his hand, knocking her down on the floor, knocking the gun out of her hand. Danny picked the gun back up and stood above Emma.

Emma looked into his eyes, those blue eyes that she had got to know so well. "This isn't you, Daniel. You don't have to do this," she cried out.

"I told you, you fool, he has no control here." He spoke again with the deamhan dorcha's voice as it aimed the weapon at her head.

"You do have control, Daniel!"

The deamhan dorcha just laughed but knew he did have some control; it was the only reason she was still alive. Still, Emma believed this was the last moment of her life, and she would never see her girl again.

CHAPTER 55

D anny, who was still in the other world standing by the lake with his eyes closed, begged the deamhan dorcha, "You have me, just please leave them alone."

"Leave them alone after what she did to you?" the deamhan dorcha questioned with the women hearing it in his own world.

"Danny, are you in there?" Emma asked.

"Yes, I'm here." Danny cried out, but Emma couldn't hear him. Then all of a sudden, he heard a loud banging, bang, bang, bang. Danny opened his eyes and looked at the small white room where he had left the fake Edgar, still hearing bang, bang, bang. That tar creature was coming for him. He looked around the dark woods, knowing he could run away, but if he did, he would not be able to see into his world and see Emma. His heart raced, his breathing became heavy, he knew it was going to break through the door, and it was going break through it soon. Quickly looking back into the woods, he asked himself, *Do I run to safety or keep my eyes closed and see what is happening with Emma and Lydia.* He realised he had done enough running and he closed his eyes seeing Emma begging, "Please don't do this."

Danny wanted to scream at her to run away.

Lydia closed her eyes and then heard the bang and the scream coming from Emma. She quickly fell to the floor crying in pain. Emma finally did as Danny wanted her to and ran out of the room and down the stairs. The deamhan dorcha in Danny's body jumped on top of Lydia, his hands around her throat, choking the life out of her. "Are you ready to die, little Lydia, I enjoyed watching your father die, and I'm going to enjoy watching you die," he hissed through Danny's teeth.

As he did, Danny got strange visions, where he was sitting on the floor in a child's bedroom seeing the deamhan dorcha under the bed smiling at him. Then in the woods with children laughing and playing tig, all of them dressed in seventies fashion. He watched as a little girl with a red T-shirt, no older than seven or eight, ran through the trees onto Rose Hill Road. He heard a girl scream out, "No," through his own mouth as a lorry headed towards the girl with the red T-shirt, the tyres letting out a scream as they marked the road with two black lines. There was a thud, and the lorry bounced horribly as the little girl's tiny body fell under the wheels, her bones crushed.

Danny realised then it was Lydia's memories. The deamhan dorcha could see their past traumas in its very own memory recorder. He opened his eyes again, seeing the cracks in the door; the tar creature was coming, and soon he would be face to face with his mother again. *Run away*, he told himself, *that's the smart thing to do*, but he found he couldn't do it.

Instead, he closed his eyes again, now seeing Emma standing in front of him with the gun in her hands as the deamhan dorcha used his voice. Begging her to put the weapon down. "No, don't listen," Danny screamed out but couldn't be heard, and then he heard the door breaking open and coming off its hinges. He opened his eyes and watched as the tar creature, still with his mother's face, squeezed its way through the doorway. Danny was frozen with fear as it made its way towards him.

Another face grew out of the tar monster, the face of Mark Long. He then remembered what Henry said before he died: "Fight the fear." Danny took a deep breath and stepped towards the tar creature. "Come on then, I'm not scared of the fucking blob," he said, thinking of the 1958 monster movie. The tar creature got close to Danny putting its face that still looked like his mother near Danny's, and it spoke with her voice. "Mummy doesn't love you; mummy wants to see you die."

But then he started to hear another voice coming from nowhere. It was the voice of Emma Holland. "Your name is Daniel Greenway." He closed his eyes and saw Emma in front of him and his own hand holding the gun to her head. "It used to be Daniel Hammond, but you changed it to the name of your foster parents. Your mother was a drug addict, and you always were afraid you'd turn out like her, but you didn't. You are a good man, Daniel. The man I love." He reopened his eyes, still hearing Emma's voice as he looked into the eyes of his mother. "You're a good man Daniel Greenway; you're not your mother or this thing that wants to control you. You are the man who I love, who I have loved since the second I saw you." Danny smiled at it, showing it that he wasn't afraid. The head of Danielle Hammond went back into the tar creature, followed by the head of Mark Long as it moved away from Danny.

Danny could hear the deamhan dorcha's voice screaming in his mind in fear and mostly desperation. "I have you. You are nothing but a voice in my head, in my head, you useless scum."

"No," Danny cried out, and to Lydia's surprise, he cried it out loud with everyone in the room able to hear the real Daniel breaking through the deamhan dorcha's control. The tall figure of the deamhan dorcha materialised in front of him, quickly grabbing him by the throat and lifting him up off his feet. Danny felt its long sharp nails digging into his skin as he fought for air. He couldn't see what Emma was doing now but he hoped she was running out of the house.

"I own you," the deamhan dorcha hissed. Danny quickly thought of Henry's words once again: "Fight the fear." And now accepting his fate, he put his hands on the deamhan dorcha's face, putting his thumb to its right eye. *Karma for Monica*, he thought as he pushed his thumb into the deamhan dorcha's eye, pushing it in, feeling it squish against his thumb.

It screamed out in pain, an awful high pitched cry that hurt Danny's ears. It dropped Danny, and he found himself back in his own body in his own world. He was free, but for how long. He moved his hand to his face and turned to Emma, putting her arm around Lydia, trying to help her up.

"Emma," he said before looking down at the gun in his hand. Emma looked back at him; her jaw opened in surprise. He didn't know how but he knew that she knew it was the real him. Inside his head, Danny heard the deamhan dorcha screaming in pain. He felt it grabbing hold of him, felt the warm burning sensation as it entered his body. He knew then he would never be rid of it until Emma, Libby and Lydia were dead.

"Danny," Emma called back to him.

"I love you; I always have," Danny said as the finger of his left hand began to move on its own.

"I love you too," Emma replied. A tear rolled down Danny's cheek as he knew there was only one way to be rid of the deamhan dorcha. He aimed the gun up under his chin thinking, *I can finally die as a good man*, and he pulled the trigger.

"No," Emma yelled out with a horrifying cry but was silenced with a loud bang as the last bullet in the gun went through Danny's head, and his body fell to the floor. With the creature in Danny's body, Lydia came to the conclusion that it was dead along with Danny. She looked to Emma, who just fell to her knees, her mouth and her eyes wide open in shock and horror, still not able to process what had just transpired.

CHAPTER 56

Emma didn't have much time to grieve, although her heart truly ached for the death of the man she loved, and Lydia was in a bad way, still finding it hard to breathe. The bullet in her leg ached and made walking extremely difficult. Emma took her shirt off, revealing the grey T-shirt underneath, which had dark sweat stains under the armpits. She put it around Lydia's leg and tied it tight, ensuring it would stop the bleeding. Emma didn't know if you were meant to take the bullet out or not — before this, she hadn't even seen a firearm, never mind had to deal with someone being shot. Emma looked back at Danny's body lying on the floor, blood coming out of his head, and she felt tears roll down her eyes.

"Emma," came a croaky whisper from Lydia. "We need to destroy the machine."

Emma looked into Lydia's green eyes that now looked bloodshot. "I need to get you a doctor," Emma told her.

"No, I will be fine," she croaked. "We need to burn the machine and the book."

"I don't know where the machine is."

"It's got to be somewhere in this house. Just look for it. You'll find it," Lydia told her, but Emma looked back at the dead man lying on the floor behind her. "Emma." She turned back to Lydia. "He sacrificed himself for us. You were right about him, and I was wrong. He was a good man, and I won't ever forget that."

"Thank you," Emma cried before standing up.

"If you need time, I understand,"

"No, let's just get this done." *I can cry later*, she told herself, before going off and checking each room for the dream recorder. It didn't take Emma all that long to find the machine. The deamhan dorcha had left the dream recorder resting on the floor of the living room. *That was easy to find*, Emma thought. Emma, for just a moment, didn't think of her grief and thought, Perhaps it had kept it in Danny's pocket but took it out. *Maybe because it knew that Lydia was upstairs and worried it may have been damaged while trying to kill her*. Then, just as the sun was starting to set, Emma picked the dream recorder up off the floor and looked at it before she sat down with her back resting against the wall. She wanted to wait until she got home where Lydia wouldn't be able to hear her but couldn't, and began to cry, thinking of the short time she'd had with Danny.

While Emma was away, Lydia looked back at Danny's body and saw the tall, dark figure of the deamhan dorcha standing over him and smiling at Lydia. She had wondered before it appeared if it was dead or still alive, but there was something different about it. It was transparent. She could clearly see the window and the wall behind it like looking at a reflection in a window.

"Still here," it hissed so quietly that it was almost a whisper.

"Maybe, but you have no power, and I'm not afraid of you. No one has to be afraid of you now," she said, only realising after she said that it could mean she was still here, not it. The deamhan dorcha said nothing and just disappeared like it was never really there, to begin with. She knew then that it wasn't disappearing for good. Danny didn't kill it along with himself. He just weakened it, and she knew that soon it would be visiting another little girl or boy. She wondered was there some way she could help those children. Still, right at the moment, she would settle just for helping Emma as she was feeling useless sitting on the floor, trying her best to stand up but falling back down again, moaning in pain. Lydia prayed that she would still be able to use the leg in the future as she heard Emma walking up the stairs.

"I have it," Emma told her as she walked into the room.

"Good, you need to get the book, too," Lydia said. Emma looked back at Danny's body. "Emma, I know how you feel, and I would get it myself, but I can't walk on this damn leg, and we need to put an end to this."

Emma moved slowly to Danny's body, looking down at the blood that had come out of his head and stained the blue carpet. Then, feeling the heartbreak in seeing him once again in such a way, she knelt down.

"Make sure you don't touch him," Lydia told her, thinking about the fingerprints that could be left behind.

370

Emma picked up the book and give it to Lydia. "Right, do you think you can help me get downstairs?"

"I think so," Emma said, putting her arm around Lydia and helping her back to her feet. She once again moaned in pain as they struggled to descend the stairs. Emma made a small pyre out of wood she had got from the shed in the garden and some from the nearby woods, and by the time she had made it, it had become dark. Lydia sat on a plastic chair that Emma has also found in the shed. It reminded Lydia of the days these plastic chairs were used when her father had friends and family over for a barbecue or a garden party. Then, using a lighter that was found in the kitchen, Emma lit the pyre. Both of them watched as the fire rose. Lydia then handed her both the book and recorder, and Emma threw them in the fire.

They watched the flames as they took hold of the machine. It had caused Lydia so much misery. It should have been a joyful experience for her, but it was quite the opposite. Seeing the melting plastic of the machine that her father built filled her with melancholy. This was her family's legacy, the thing that could have put the Knightley name on the world stage. Yet, there it was, melting away in front of her. What would she do next; would she still move to Cornwall; would it seem right without Katya by her side? She knew one thing, she wouldn't be staying in Mayfield. That was for damn sure.

CHAPTER 57

Emma sat on a bus wondering how Lydia was doing with her leg. She remembered Lydia telling her that she would be fine, although she may have a limp from now on. That was two days ago, and she hadn't seen her since and didn't think she would. Emma's eyes and mind then moved to an old woman across from her reading *Mayfield Daily*, the local newspaper with the headline 'Petty thief turned mass murderer' with a picture of Danny under the headline. She sighed as it still made her sad that the town pinned the deaths on him, but who would believe her if she told people the truth. She turned her head away from the newspaper, looked out of the window at the passing houses, and thought, is there a child in one of those who is now seeing the deamhan dorcha like Libby once did. The bus stopped near a post office with a pie shop at the side of it.

"Excuse me," Emma said to a middle-aged man who had just walked out of the post office. The man stopped and looked at her. "Can you tell me where York Close is?"

"Yeah, just head right from here. It's three streets away."

"Thank you," she said as she headed down the road where the man directed her to a cul de sac surrounded by orange brick homes with small gardens in front of them. She walked up to the house with the number seventeen on the door and knocked. An elderly woman opened the door, looking at her with suspicion. "Yes?" the woman said.

"Mrs Greenway, I'm Emma Holland, a friend of Danny's."

"Ah, yes, he told me about you before he stopped coming to see us. Please come in," she said, letting her into the house.

"Thank you." Emma walked into the living room, where she found Paul Greenway sitting down next to an oak fireplace with a picture of himself in his thirties, his wife to his side laughing and Danny as a child on his shoulders on top of it. The picture made Emma smile as she saw a joyful grin on the young Danny's face.

"Paul, this is Emma, Danny's friend," Mrs Greenway told him.

"Have you heard what they have been saying about him?" he said, picking a newspaper up from the side of the chair.

"I have, and it's not true," Emma told him as she sat on the sofa across from them.

"He was so shy when we brought him back from that orphanage. It took him days to have the courage to say more than two words to us. What his biological mother did was sickening," Paul told her.

"She was no mother to him. A mother is meant to love and protect their child. Like you two did. I have a child of my own, and I will die for her."

"Libby." Mrs Greenway said.

"Yeah," Emma said, surprised that she knew her name.

"Why are you here, Emma?" Paul asked her.

"Because I think you should know your son wasn't a murderer. Yes, he was a thief, but he atoned for the bad things he did. He saved my daughter and me in more ways than one. So, I owe him and knowing Danny, I think he would want you to know what really happened to him."

Emma told the Greenways everything about Libby, Lydia, the dream recorder and the deamhan dorcha. It was hard for anyone to believe, and she thought surely, they would think she had lost her mind, but deep down, they would know their son died a hero.

EPILOGUE

2019, Mayfield, Kent, UK

It had been twenty-two years since Lydia had gone back to her home of Mayfield. She never felt any love for the place, although she did admit that sometimes she missed the simpler days when she was a kid, back when Vicky was still alive.

The first thing she did on entering the town was to visit the graves of her father Edgar and her sister Victoria. The second thing was to see her Uncle Peter, now in his seventies and living in a care home. She apologised for the way she treated him back in those days, and he apologised for the awful words he said to her. He told her how sorry he was when he heard about the death of Katya.

Katya was a woman she never really got over. She did get into other relationships after her death, with both men and women — she even had a son who was sixteen years old. He lived with her in Cornwall, but his father had abandoned her months before he was born. Peter and Lydia hugged and forgave each other for the fighting in the past.

She drove her black Land Rover to an address she put into her GPS. It took her to the Frankston district on the far north-western side of the town. She had got the address from a private detective. She had no idea how the now thirty-year-old Libby Holland would take to meeting Lydia again, or even if she remembered who she was.

After all, Libby was very young, and Lydia looked like a completely different person than she did back in 1997. For one, she had more wrinkles, and she had to walk with a cane thanks to her encounter with the deamhan dorcha. She was wearing a white shirt and a grey pencil skirt and had thick dark hair. Lydia parked next to a shop that sold mystical objects such as healing crystals, incense sticks, replica medieval swords and shields, books on witchcraft and interpreting dreams.

The smell of incense struck Lydia as soon as she entered the small shop, and her eyes quickly went to a replica of a medieval long sword hanging from the wall. She walked to the shelves in the middle of the room. She looked at a Lord of the Rings chessboard with 3D characters as the pieces. Lydia pictured herself playing it with her son and thought it would make a nice gift for him. She also looked at a crystal skull, but that was only out of curiosity. In the corner of the room was a counter where a long-haired man stood reading a Spiderman comic.

"Excuse me, how much is the chessboard?" Lydia asked him.

"Three hundred pounds," he answered back without looking away from his comic.

"I'll take it."

"All right, that one is just for the display. I'll get the one from the back for you," the clerk told her as he put the comic down on the counter.

"Okay, but before you go, can I ask, does a girl named Elizabeth Holland work here?"

"Yeah, she's in the back."

"Can I speak to her, please?"

"Sure," he said before walking towards the back door behind the counter. A few seconds later, a young-looking woman with long blonde hair and a nose piercing that looked like a golden ring hanging on her nostril came out through the door. She was wearing a black T-shirt and a long purple silk skirt. She may be thirty years old now, but Lydia could tell it was Libby from her eyes and the fact that she had more than a passing resemblance to Emma.

Libby looked at her and smiled a friendly smile. "I was wondering when I would see you again."

"I'm surprised you still remember me," Lydia told her.

"Of course I remember you, Lydia. I remember everything about that time. I have to work, but there's a café across the street called Trajan's. Do you want to meet me there at five?"

"Yeah, okay, perfect."

"All right, I'll see you there."

The long-haired man came back with the Lord of the Rings chess set, which he put in a plastic bag and Lydia put into her car boot.

Five o'clock came, and Lydia made her way into the café, where Libby sat next to the window waiting for her with a cup of green tea and a chocolate muffin. Lydia sat next to the window, and as soon as she entered the café, Libby's eyes went to the dark red cane that she carried. "I like the colour," she commented.

"Oh yeah, my son made me get the red one. He said it was like Daredevil's walking stick or something, I don't know. I'm not really into comics, so it was all alien to me."

"You have a son?" she said with surprise in her voice.

"Yeah, a teenager now called Nathan. What about you, got any kids?" She didn't know why she asked that as Lydia learned through the detective that she didn't.

"No, and I don't want them to be honest."

"And what about your mum?"

"Yes, she's got a daughter. Me." Libby smiled.

"No," Lydia said with a giggle. "I meant, how is she doing?"

"Oh, she's good. She got married about seven years ago. The guy is all right. He treats her well, and she seems happy with him, but to be honest, I think she still kinda misses Danny even after all this time."

"I see."

"Lydia," Libby says, leaning over the table and touching her hand, which Lydia thought of as a little strange. "Why don't you tell me why you really sought me out."

Lydia sighed and looked around the café at the other customers who were not paying a bit of attention to them.

"I need to talk about the dreams you had about me. Remember when you were a kid you dreamt of me?"

"I kinda remember," Libby says, removing her hand from Lydia's.

"I need to know what happened in those dreams," Lydia said, and it almost sounded like she was begging.

Libby took a sip of her tea and gently placed the cup back down on the table. "I don't remember what happened in them. The tape that Danny had made went missing years ago. Maybe my mother has it, maybe not. Although she tells me, she hasn't, but I don't know."

"Okay, but in your dreams, I was bald, right?"

"Yes, I think so," Libby answered with uncertainty.

"What happened to me in those dreams? Did I die?"

"Again, I can't remember. Why are you asking this now after all these years?"

Lydia took a deep breath and moved her hand to her dark hair, pulling it off and revealing that it was a wig and showing her now bald head underneath it. "I lost my hair due to the treatment I have been having to fight my cancer. I've always been the type of girl who is afraid of looking afraid, but I will tell you with all honesty I'm scared. This disease is eating away at me. I know it's going to kill me sooner or later." Lydia looked out of the window, unable to make eye contact with Libby. "I don't want to die."

"For years, I questioned why I dreamt of a woman I didn't know, and when I was twenty-three, I became friends with a girl who said she could hypnotise me and bring me back to a past life. I didn't know if she was just crazy or just joking around, but I agree to let her hypnotise me. Do you believe in reincarnation?"

"After all the shit that happened in ninety-seven, I believe in anything now."

"Well, she took me back to a time when Emma wasn't my mother, when I had another mother, a father and when I had an older sister." Lydia's eyes narrowed as she listened to her. "A sister I loved more than anything in the world, one who would protect me. Sadly, that life was cut short when I was hit by a lorry. Three lives were ruined that day. The driver of the lorry who was never able to forgive himself. He could not stop thinking of me until he hanged himself two years after my death. My father spent his life trying to find ways to see me again and my sister blamed herself even though she had no right to."

The tears slowly ran down Lydia's face, but still, she smiled and laughed. "So you're Vicky, is that what you are telling me?"

"No, I'm telling you I was Victoria Knightley once, but now I'm Elizabeth Holland but don't think that means I have lost my love for you. I may no longer be Vicky, but to me, you are still my big sister. Maybe no longer in blood but in my heart, you are," she told Lydia, who smiled and reached her hand over the table, gently touching Libby's. "The world is a stranger place than you would ever imagine. Isn't that right, Danny," Libby said, her head turned to her side. It was as if he was standing next to her. Lydia couldn't see him, but somehow, she believed that not only was Danny standing there but that Libby was once her sister. Libby was more than likely mad, but Lydia quickly concluded that if she was, she would very much like to be mad along with her.

THE END